CW01183058

VAMPIRE KING

Nightshade Vampires

ROWAN HART

Copyright © 2022 by The Lion and Raven Press, LLC

Cover by Covers by Combs

All rights reserved.

No part of this book may be reproduced in any form or by any electronic or mechanical means, including information storage and retrieval systems, without written permission from the author, except for the use of brief quotations in a book review.

*For myself.
Because this book and I went through a lot of shit
together. Pet cancer, covid, preschool graduation, and
a concussion but I finished it all the same.*

ALSO BY ROWAN HART

Matched With the Monster

Married to the Minotaur (Summer 2022)

Hell of a Husband (Kindle Vella)

Nightshade Vampires

Vampire King (Fall 2022)

Vampire Enforcer (Winter 2022)

Vampire Savage (Spring 2023)

As Marie Robinson

Blackfang Barons - Reverse Harem

Fawn

Fury

Fate

Chapter One
ELOISE

I'm about to leap over this desk and strangle the officer in front of me. I take a deep breath and remind myself why that is not a good idea. Getting myself thrown in jail for assaulting a police officer will not help me find Deidre. I give him my best smile, the one that's gotten me out of too much trouble to count. If this doesn't work, maybe I'll start to cry. I'm feeling stressed enough that it won't be hard.

"There really isn't anyone I can talk to? I know the first forty-eight hours is the most vital and it's already been almost twelve," I say, a quiver naturally making my voice wobble at the end. Shit, now my eyes are burning too. Whether or not I want to cry, it seems like it's happening.

He looks down at the form I already filled out and eyes me again. Officer Budd, according to his name patch, is clearly a man used to sitting behind a desk and not walking the streets, with the buttons of his uniform straining to keep it closed and his soft jaw and scraggly appearance. He's a man that puts in the minimum effort and he's who I have to convince to have the police start looking for my best friend.

His beady dull brown eyes turn lecherous and I repress a shudder, curling my toes as hard as I can since he'd see if I make a fist.

"You sure she isn't sleeping off a bender?" he asks, shaking the report. "People go missing in The Barrows all the time. Sometimes they come back, sometimes they don't. Up here we don't send officers there looking for every lost lamb who wanted a taste of Rapture. We wouldn't have enough officers left to defend the rest of the city." He eyes me again and I brace myself, knowing exactly where this is going. "But maybe I can interview you privately and you'll have new information that'll prioritize your friend's case. What do you say?"

I force a smile and I know he's not convinced just as much as I know he doesn't care. "I've written everything I know down on the report, Officer Budd," I say between gritted teeth.

He shrugs and turns, putting the missing person's report on the top of a stack in a "The Barrows" box. Officially, the city was named Oldgate but no one calls it that. There has to be at least fifty other forms in there. Jeez, when did they collect those? All the other boxes are empty, so clearly other officers or detectives come by and collect the reports from the city. Isn't there at least a division of officers meant to handle The Barrows?

Deidre's voice drifts to the front of my mind, one of the many times she paced back and forth in our tiny shared studio.

"The cops are all on his payroll down in The Barrows. They aren't dirty, not like a lot of us would think. But they know they aren't the real authority down there so they keep to the duties he's approved."

Right. That's what she said when I asked why she didn't ask the police for any public records in The Barrows. So there's no chance they'd be able to help me either, especially since Deidre has been investigating Rapture.

"Thank you for your time," I force out and Office Budd grunts, having dismissed me already when I turned down the so-called personal interview. I don't wait for the scripted "we'll call if we have further questions or find anything," speech, not that I think he'll give it.

I march out of the Newgate Police Department station, tugging my hood up over my head against the rain. It's October and the autumn warmth is slowly being replaced with the constant rains as we get closer to winter. Already the drops are colder than they were a week ago.

I hurry over to the bus stop and squeeze into the

small space between three other people and the weather shelter. The man closest to me, some sort of hoity-toity professional given his hat, long jacket, and briefcase, huffs at me and exaggerates stepping to the side, as if I'm shoved right up against him.

Asshole. I know I'm chubby but I'm not that big. I didn't even touch him. Whatever. Just another day in a so-called fat girl's life.

Deidre hates that I call myself fat, and if she wasn't tall and statuesque like one of those Amazon warriors who eat men for breakfast, I'd probably take it better. But she's been my best friend since middle school, sticking together through all the ups and downs life has thrown at us. We're each other's ride or die.

Which is why I'm going to do whatever it takes to find her.

A short bus ride later and I'm walking up the creaky stairs of our apartment building. Supposedly, it used to be a school for children—specifically children taken from supernaturals down in The Barrows. Kind of like how the colonizers took kids away from their indigenous families in an attempt to "civilize" them, only this happened only fifty years ago. The idea was that nurture could overcome nature and kids who could shift forms or weren't technically human could be taught to ignore their instincts and very nature.

It was a horrible practice that thankfully was

shut down within a year and the president lost the next election. Everyone who had participated in it, and the abuses that were performed, was charged and jailed. Some of the more powerful or wealthy politicians got off light, but it was better than nothing.

This building was remodeled into apartments and the kids were tossed back to The Barrows. Deidre and I can rant for hours at how terrible the injustice was, but people up top, as we call it, like to believe it's all better now. Turning this building into apartments was just another way to hide the atrocity in plain sight.

It makes for really cheap rent, at least.

Deidre and I only have each other. I bounced between foster homes until my eighteenth birthday and Deidre only had her dad and gran until her dad died our senior year of high school. Together we made it through those years; college, shitty boyfriends, and more. Now she's a junior investigative journalist for a national magazine and I've worked my ass off as a freelance graphic designer.

To say I have an issue with authority is kind of putting it lightly. It's best for everyone involved if I don't have a boss.

The bulky neighbor is coming out of his door, his hood pulled up so his face is in the shadows like always. We've never spoken, just did head bobs of acknowledgment as we move past each other in the hall. I'm pretty sure he's a half-breed. Orc or something. A lot of the bigger half-breeds have found their way up out of The Barrows through military service, but they still get treated pretty crappy.

Unlocking the door, I slip inside before quickly closing the door and turning the deadbolt and putting the chain on. Not like it'd stop anyone like my neighbor from getting in but there's comfort in lies we tell ourselves.

I shed my raincoat, my green tee and leggings dry enough to stay in as I start to pace. Pacing is Deidre's thing, but she's not here.

"Why the hell couldn't you wait for me?" I ask aloud as I turn my gaze out the window. It's just after three in the afternoon. The police are useless, and time is ticking. Deidre could already be dead, I'm not stupid. But I can't sit back and let the rusty cogs of justice attempt to turn.

Deidre was meeting a supposed informant about the spread of Rapture—the euphoric drug created and controlled by the powerful creatures in The Barrows. It let humans have a taste of magic and even though it was illegal, the city officials didn't touch it.

It's always been controlled by the leader of the Nightshades. A vampire so powerful that he's whispered about as if speaking his name will summon him. Even the council members avoid confronting him if they can. Topside, we may have technology to outfit our military, but most of us realize that if The

Barrows want to, they can overpower us. There have been a couple uprising attempts, but each time they were squashed with the help of *him*. He controls The Barrows, at least the vampires.

Rapture is supposed to stay confined to The Barrows; we all know that. Except it's starting to turn up topside, with a couple people having overdosed. It's been kept covered up and Deidre only happened to catch wind of it because she was at the hospital interviewing families who were in a complex fire and lost everything.

I stand in the middle of our small apartment, old worn bunk beds with desks under them on two sides of the apartment, the third wall taken up by the small kitchenette and bathroom, and the fourth holds the dresser we share and Deidre's books and my art supplies. We've got a small table and chairs, but decided against a couch since neither of us wanted to lug the thing up four flights of stairs.

Deidre asked me to go with her to meet a possible informant at Gato's Paw, a bar in The Barrows last night. I asked if she could wait until I wrapped up the project I was working on for a high-paying client. She seemed fine to wait, saying she'd go out and get us coffee since it was already dark. I should have known that she was going to be her rash self and head out on her own. Guilt weighs my stomach down as I remember how long it took me to realize she hadn't come back. When I get absorbed into a project, especially so close to the finish line, the rest of the world disappears.

I tried calling her phone, but she wouldn't answer. So I got my own ride down there, spam texting and calling her in the car. By the time the car stopped at the bar, my calls were going straight to voicemail. The driver wouldn't stick around, peeling out as soon as the door closed behind me.

It isn't just supernaturals who live in The Barrows, at least. So the only reason why I stuck out was how casually I was dressed: pants, oversized college sweatshirt, and slide-on sneakers with my black hair piled up in a really, really messy bun. Like an "I haven't showered in three days" messy bun. Still, I pushed through the crowd, pulling up Deidre's photo on my phone and asking people if they'd seen her.

I asked one of the bartenders, but the man with golden eyes refused to say anything until I bought a drink. Then he said he'd seen her heading out back with a vampire. I didn't wait for him to pour the vodka soda. By the time I made it out the back exit door, helpfully propped open by a large rock, there wasn't anyone there.

Only because of all of the crime movies I watch did I think to check the reeking dumpsters. Her purse and phone were in the second one I checked and my heart broke. I looked around, trying to see if anyone else was there in the dim light of the alley but my human eyes are nothing against the ink black of The Barrows. I pull her things out and dig through them, denying what I was seeing.

Her wallet and cards, even her cash, were still there. Meaning they wanted her, not just to rob her.

I wasn't stupid. I called the police right away, but I was connected with The Barrows station and now I know why they were dismissive.

I haven't slept since then as I made it back home and waited, praying I was wrong and that she'd walk through the door laughing about the crazy adventure she had and it would all blow over.

When I knew she wasn't coming back, I went to the police. I gave them her bag, but something about Deidre's work made me consider keeping her phone. In the end, I still gave it to them, hoping against hope it might help. Whoever took her is connected to Rapture and how it's leaking into the city. The police will be no help, either in Newgate or The Barrows.

A plan starts forming, and I head to Deidre's desk under her bunk. Her laptop is still there and I type in the passcode and pull up her emails.

"Yell at me when you come home," I mutter to wherever she is as I start skimming her inbox. When I don't find anything, I start searching through her documents and I find practically an entire research paper with links to references and all on what she's found while looking into Rapture. It's an insane amount of information, organized in a way that only she can understand. Bullet points, half-articulated thoughts, single words next to a link to an article to a charity foundation. The very last page has my blood turning to ice.

Bargain with Ambrose d'Vil?

Ambrose d'Vil. The devil of the Nightshade vampires and de facto ruler of the Barrows. Very little is actually known about him, or if people know things, they know to keep their mouths shut. He's called the devil, not just because of his dark reputation but his penchant for offering bargains. If you didn't hold up your end, you're already dead, his vampires just haven't struck yet.

Was Deidre really considering making a bargain with him for information about Rapture? Or did he have something to do with her disappearance?

I close the laptop and pull up my phone and open up the rideshare app. Holy cow, I spent a couple hours poring over her research?! I should have paid better attention to the time. Every minute counts if she's still alive. She has to be.

It's Thursday. The day anyone can request an audience with Ambrose d'Vil, according to Deidre's research.

So it's time to go meet a vampire.

Chapter Two
ELOISE

This is a bad idea, but bad ideas are all I have left.

The earlier promised rain is pouring down on Oldgate, but the city still pulses with life. Topsiders looking for a thrill make their way down Blood Street, laughing and drinking as they run through the rain and jump over puddles. The streets are full of taxis and rideshares, because the wealthy always seem to want to taste the thrill of darkness before returning home and sleeping, safe in the knowledge that they're protected in Newgate.

The rain can't drown out the fried food and heavy spices, but at least it's washed away the sour smell of piss and vomit between buildings.

A group of ladies, probably close enough to my age in their late twenties and definitely old enough to know better, laugh and flirt with a pair of pale men claiming to be vampires. There are always the blind skeptics who refuse to believe that Oldgate is populated by real supernatural creatures, but more often people like to come here to pretend for a night. Then there are others like me, who know the supernatural world isn't a gimmick to sell tourists expensive trinkets or too-strong booze.

One of the men looks up as I walk closer, the collar of my black jacket pulled up against the rain. A passing car's headlines reflect off his pupils, making them reflect the strange golden color of vampire eyes. Deidre calls them cat eyes as a joke. She isn't far off.

I look away, not wanting to keep his attention and turn into the narrow alley between two buildings lit up and promising to tell futures or craft love potions. A couple people are scattered in the narrow alley, sharing smokes or talking in hushed voices, and we all ignore each other. My goal is the end, where a narrow green awning is lit by a single gas lamp that barely fits between the awning and the brick building beside it. A door straight out of a medieval castle is sheltered under it with no bouncer waiting to check IDs.

People come to this place for many different reasons, but rarely what most would consider good ones. As my stomach twists, I remind myself that she'd do the same for me and grip the iron wrought door handle. Rumor says the door is spelled to read a person's intentions and if they are a danger to the owner or people inside, vampire guards would be on them before they can let go. I feel nothing other than a normal door handle as it swings inwards to reveal a similarly narrow hall bathed in red light.

"How appropriate," I mutter as I let the door swing closed behind me. I've never been to Noir before, but so far it's living up to my expectations.

Heavy bass vibrates through the floor as I move down the hallway. The walls are black with gold outlines of fleur-de-lis, adding to the old-world vampire atmosphere. Let it never be sad that Ambrose d'Vil doesn't provide what Topsiders expect.

I pull off my jacket, laying it over my arm and keeping it away from my dress as I finally reach the staircase that will take me into the depths of his kingdom. Most people, natural and supernatural alike, treat this place like a night club combined with a sex dungeon. What it really is, I remind myself as I descend below street level and into the catacombs, is a spider's web meant to trap the desperate.

Slow, sensual rock music fills the front room, the volume low enough to hold conversations without the need to shout. Black couches, chairs, and half-circular booths are filled with people, and the bar along one side is lined with others vying for the bartender's attention. No one looks up at my entrance, save the bored-looking woman sitting behind a podium that wouldn't be out of place in a high school auditorium.

"Cover is ten bucks or blood," she says, clearly used to the routine. "Coat check is another five."

I pull my wallet from the damp coat pocket and hand a twenty and my coat to her. She takes it, opening a gray tin box and shoving the bill in and returning a crinkled five for my change along with a numbered ticket for my coat. She goes back to her phone, dismissing me, and I clear my throat.

She raises an eyebrow. "Yeah?"

This is it. "I'd like to meet with Ambrose d'Vil."

Her bored expression turns to one of intrigue and she looks me up and down again. Is she a vampire too? Her eyes are golden but at places like these, humans like to wear color contacts. "Is he expecting you?"

I shake my head once. "No," I say. "But I was told he takes audiences on Thursdays?"

She studies me for a minute longer, as if attempting to discern why I want to see the so-called king of vampires. Then she shrugs and raises her hand above her head, snapping loudly. "Oi, Lion," she calls over her shoulder to someone out of my sight. "We got a humie wanting to see the king."

I jump when a tall man appears beside me, as if he'd melted from the shadows and taken corporeal form. The woman inclines her head towards me and the man—very clearly a vampire—studies me. I refuse to be intimidated even if the man is a monster capable of killing me in moments. Vampires, it turns out, aren't like the old black and white films humans made at the turn of the twentieth century. Some may have been humans at first, but the old ones, really old ones, were born as vampires. As monsters.

"He's busy," the vampire tells the woman before turning away. She shrugs again and jerks her head towards the bar.

"You're welcome to wait, but I can't say how long the wait will be."

I press my lips into a line but nod. "Is there any way someone can come get me when he's ready to see me?"

"Sit at the bar and someone will."

I thank her but she's already ignoring me, her attention on the latest people who've come down the stairs. Pulling down the dress I borrowed out of Deidre's closet, I make my way over to the bar, doing my best to ignore the looks sent my way. I don't know if it's because the dress isn't meant for someone with curves like mine or because I scream human to any vampires. I have to stay focused on my goal, and that's seeing the vampire who runs the Barrows.

I claim an empty bar stool at the end of the bar and try to keep my back to the wall with the club in front of me. Nerves pulse in my stomach in beat with the music and when the bartender finally makes his way to me, I rush out an order.

"A lemon drop, please." I hadn't planned on drinking tonight, but I need something to steel my nerves. Water isn't going to cut it. I slide my card over to him, mentally calculating how much I have in my account.

"Open or closed?" he asks, indifferent. His eyes are a dark hazel, revealing his humanity. What is it like working surrounded by creatures who could bleed you dry in minutes?

"Closed for now." I glance down the bar, my foot bouncing on the rail of the barstool. I hate being so exposed and I pull out my phone, desperate for any type of distraction.

My background photo has my resolve returning. It's Deidre and me at the waterfront, powdered sugar on our faces from gorging ourselves on beignets. Some even speckled the dark hair framing her face, where mine escaped such treatment, pulled back into my usual tight ponytail. Compared to her, I've always felt like a plain Jane—not that she'd ever let me talk about myself that way. She was the best...is the best, I correct myself.

I smile in thanks to the bartender when he drops off the martini glass and receipt. I sign it, ignoring the obscene price of the drink, and try it. It might be the price of a fifth of bottom-shelf vodka, but at least it tastes good.

Mollified at the quality of my chosen drink, I take in the bar again. It isn't much different than any other bar I've been to, so long as I ignore the fact that half of the patrons aren't drinking from glasses. Clubs in general aren't my scene, but Deidre has dragged me to enough of them that I have my standards.

Is anyone using Rapture? I can't tell just by looking, but I wouldn't be surprised if so. Rapture is a favorite drug in the Barrows, for humans and supernatural alike. For humans, it supposedly gives them a taste of power that some say is magic. For supernaturals, it's like pot, mellowing while cranking the dial to ten on their pleasure receptors.

Ambrose d'Vil controls the creation and distribution with an iron fist. The drug is the reason Deidre's missing, so her disappearance is on his hands.

"You look in need of company."

I jolt at the smooth voice beside me. How did I not notice his approach? When I meet the man's eyes, I know exactly why. He's a vampire, and a hungry one at that if the red ring around his golden iris is any indication. I take a sip of the sweet and sour drink to buy time.

"I'm waiting on someone," I answer at last, holding his gaze. In The Barrows, you're either a monster or you're prey, and I'm not looking to wind up as anyone's dinner.

I admit he's beautiful, but all vampires seem to be. He wears a vest over a white button-up and suit pants, but has foregone a tie and, overall, has a generally rumpled casual appearance. It would have made anyone else look slovenly, but with his sharp cheekbones and wicked mouth, he looks positively rakish.

I stiffen when he drags his fingertip down my shoulder to my wrist. His touch is cold against my warm skin.

"I'm more than happy to keep you company until then," he murmurs, somehow his voice reaching me over the sound of the music.

I don't jerk away from him, as much as I want to. It could offend him, or worse, make him want me more. I need to extricate myself from the situation without making it worse. The bartender's back is to me and there are several empty seats between me and the next group of people.

"Back off, Lan," a rough voice orders and the vampire, Lan clearly, rolls his eyes before turning towards my potential savior.

"Just having a bit of fun, Kasar," he says with a smirk. "You remember what fun is, right?"

Kasar, the lion made of shadows from earlier, gives Lan an unimpressed look before sliding his eyes to me. "Ambrose will see you now."

Lan's face whips around to look at me, his brows furrowed and he studies me as if actually seeing me. "Now what would Ambrose want with you?"

I throw him a smirk with false bravado before sliding off my stool and abandoning my drink. I don't say anything, my throat is too tight from nerves, and to my relief, Kasar doesn't wait.

"This way." His voice is a harsh timbre, as if he's smoked two packs of cigarettes a day for centuries. He might look to be in his early thirties, but I know enough of vampires to know that I'll never guess his real age with accuracy. Lion could be in his thirties, or more likely, in his third century.

I follow him as he crosses the bar, having to take two strides for his every one. My gut tells me not to ask him to slow down, though. Well, actually my gut is begging me to turn and run out of here and never look back.

If I do that, though, Deidre could die and I'll be alone in this world.

It's for her that I follow the vampire radiating danger through a black metal door situated between the quieter bar and a loud dance floor. A brief glance towards the other room shows a hedonistic party full of vampires and humans. My cheeks burn as a man's hands run over the curves of a woman as she grinds against him to the beat. Her head is tilted away from me and a flash of one of the lights reveals a slick trail of blood along her neck and the man licks a pointed tongue up her skin, his hands still gripping her body to his.

Every flash of the strobe lights reveals more frozen stills of people together, dark smears of blood on skin or clothing of the dancers and others licking and groping them.

Ambrose d'Vil sits on the throne above this kingdom of debauchery and savagery.

As I leave the dance floor behind, following Kasar up the steep stairs, I wonder if it would have been better to search out Satan himself. If I knew how to get a hold of the archdemon, I might have. Everyone knows the devil's price, but when it comes to the king of vampires, there is only one guarantee. Whatever he demands will be steep. But he always follows through with his end.

That's what I'm counting on.

I refuse to let Deidre be another statistic about humans going missing down here. Which is why, when Kasar opens one of the ornate double doors in front of us, I steel myself as the scent of fresh blood hits me. I look straight ahead, and rather than seeing the king of vampires, I'm shown the consequences of working with him.

A freshly decapitated head.

Chapter Three
AMBROSE

My kingdom is rotting and it disgusts me. So much has changed since I was first turned into the monster I am now. Technology became better, medical advances, entertainment, governing bodies. But humans?

Humans have become so much worse.

Humans and vampires fill the club below me, the music vibrating the thick windows of my office. My modern castle, so to speak. Humans flock to Noir, the nightclub where I rule from on high. Even half a century ago, a sight like this would have been laughable. Humans willingly writhing against vampires, begging to be fed from? The holy vanguard from churches would have stormed us with pitchforks and torches.

I'd seen the rot growing in humanity's soul and I'd profited from it. I created this when vampires first began to reveal themselves to the world, much to the disapproval of my elder peers.

But the hedonism of humanity has begun to affect all of us who live in the shadows, and once again vampires are giving into their monstrous nature.

I turn from the window and look at the shaking vampire on his knees. My guards have already roughed him up, the metallic bite of his blood filling the air.

"You, Jedidiah, are old enough to have known better," I say as I move before my desk, opening the ironwood box. Two daggers, the blades the length of my forearm, with hilts made of old-world elk antler are nestled inside. "For decades, the supply and trade of Rapture has been tightly regulated through my hand. Do you understand why?"

"Please, sire. I was foolish—" the vampire attempts to plead. The back of my hand shuts him up as I spin, stronger and faster than any vampire in the city, to deliver the blow. He falls sideways, clutching his jaw with a sob.

"My kingdom contains the chaos of our kind—of sniveling idiots such as yourself. If Rapture were to be sold openly on the human streets, we'd be hunted once more. Except now, we can never return to the dark." I crouch in front of him, gripping his jaw and digging my fingers into his cheeks. Fear radiates off of him. Centuries ago, it may have affected me. But now, I am as unforgiving and uncaring as the dark. I don't relish the power as I once did. "And you tried to sell it outside of our territory without my permission. You risked my wrath for a few hundred dollars."

I shove him away and stand, and select one of the blades.

"No, please, I have a family. They needed—" Jedidiah begins to plead as he sees the blade.

"You should have thought of them before selling Rapture to another organization," I say as cold as the ice encasing my blackened heart. He crawls backwards, hoping to escape as I step towards him. Even if he miraculously evades me, Ashe and Malachi stand at the door, watching with stone expressions.

Jedidiah howls as I fist his hair, and he lashes out in a vain struggle. His nails dig into the flesh of my arm, drawing blood and staining my white sleeve crimson. Snarling, I lift the man up from the floor and slash through his throat, nearly decapitating him with the sharp blade. A wave of hot blood splashes across me, the vampire's eyes bulging out with fright. With his spine intact, he'd eventually recover. I make sure that doesn't happen. Dropping the blade, I grip his shoulder and tear his head the rest of the way from his neck.

His body falls with a wet thump, blood soaking into the thick black carpet. Sighing, I toss his head to the floor and cross back to my desk. There I sink into my leather high-back chair, picking up the cloth napkin that accompanied the warmed bottle of blood delivered earlier with the intent on cleaning the blade when someone knocks at my door.

"For fuck's sake," I grit out and gesture with the blade to Ashe, who opens the door at once. To Malachi, I say, "Get someone to take care of the body and clean the carpets. His blood smells foul with rot."

Typically, I let the blood dry before ordering only the surface of the carpets cleaned. I enjoy fortifying the lingering scent of vampire blood in this room. It serves as a constant reminder to all who enter that I'm not one to be fucked with. That is, when the person entering can smell it.

Ashe steps aside, revealing a short woman with enticing curves standing in front of the shadowed figure of Kasar—better known as Lion, my oldest ally and most trusted enforcer.

The woman is clearly human and her nerves fill the room with her scent. Her fear tastes sweet and nutty, like baklava, and my nostrils flare as I breathe her in. Delicious. Would her blood taste the same?

She practically screams when she sees Jedidiah's headless corpse. Intriguing enough, she swallows it back and forces herself to look anywhere else. Which means her eyes land on me, and her fair skin grows paler.

No doubt I present the devilish appearance that human priests claim of me. Malachi grips the leg of the dead vampire and hauls him towards the door. The woman is forced to decide between hurrying through the door into the den of the beast or turning tail and running.

It'd be smarter for her if she runs.

She is either brave or foolhardy, however, and steps forward before Malachi can walk through the door with his macabre burden behind him.

"What is this?" I ask Ashe, who moves to stand behind the woman. She may be human, but my guards will never assume she is harmless. I begin to wipe the blade clean of the blood, not wanting to tarnish the relic of a past life with such an unworthy life.

"She seeks an audience, sire."

I look up at her, taking her in. It's true I accept audiences on Thursdays, but rarely does anyone —*especially* a human—take the opportunity. That alone has me intrigued. What also intrigues me are her curves, wrapped as they are in an improperly fitting dress. Her black hair and dark brown eyes hold a depth I'm not used to seeing in humans anymore. Are her lips naturally that color, or has she darkened them with just a hint of red?

"Well, then," I say, giving her my full attention after giving the blade one more wipe and settling it back in the box with its twin. I lean back in my chair, bracing my arms along the rests. "If you're looking for Rapture, to sell or use, you're wasting your time, sweetheart."

"I'm not."

I don't expect the bite in her tone and I cock my head. While she's dressed like any one of the humans seeking the company of a vampire, a subtle sniff reveals no scent of my kind lingering on her.

Has she learned of the dismissal of my former feeder? The term was created and adopted by humans for those who allow a vampire to regularly feed from them and it's stuck. Many of those who share their blood share their bodies as well, all in exchange for a price. It's easy money for the humans who enjoy it. Kimberly, the woman who I'd been feeding from for the last month, apparently enjoyed it too much seeing as she allowed another to feed from her.

The moment I tasted the trace of another vampire in her blood, I'd cast her out, banning her from Noir entirely.

I do not share.

"Then explain, miss...?" I trail off, waiting for her to answer.

"Eloise Morse," she answers, keeping her hands clasped in front of her and holding my gaze. The smell of trepidation rolls from her in waves, but... is that a faint note of attraction?

"How lovely to make your acquaintance," I purr, dropping my voice an octave, and am rewarded by her slight shiver. "Tell me, what can I do for such a lovely creature as yourself?"

She purses her lips as if taking offense at the compliment. In less than five minutes, Eloise has intrigued me so thoroughly that no matter what she requests, I'll hear her out.

"My friend is missing and the police are useless. She was looking into Rapture when she disappeared."

How disappointing.

"Sweetheart, so many people disappear when looking for their next hit. Unfortunately, it is most likely she is dead in a den somewhere or at the bottom of the river."

"Deidre wasn't using it," Eloise bites out with enough defiance I sit upright at the disrespect. At my movement, the woman takes a deep breath with her eyes closed before beginning again. "Deidre is an investigative reporter. There's been a lot of talk of Rapture being sold outside of the d'Vil supply. To Topsiders."

I narrow my eyes, absorbing every word coming from Eloise's pink-coated lips. If she finds my renewed focus intimidating, she doesn't let it stop her.

"She found evidence that suggested a connection between the new supplier and high-powered businessmen. Last night, she asked me to go with her to

Gato's Paw to meet an informant. I couldn't go and told her to wait."

I run a thumb across my chin. The Gato's Paw. It's run by vampires under my control, but I'd granted them self-autonomy. Perhaps that had been a mistake. "I surmise she didn't."

"No, she didn't," Eloise says, sorrow entering her voice. The change tugs at me and I frown. Why should I care about this woman's emotional state? "By the time I realized she hadn't listened and I got there, she was gone. Her phone and purse were in a dumpster, so she had to have been captured by force. The police took the information, along with her phone and purse as evidence, and told me they'd call me with any news."

I snort. "Let me guess. The officer taking your statement then dropped the file on the top of an already large stack and no one looked at it before you left."

"That about sums it up," she agrees bitterly. "So I came here. To the source of Rapture and the king said to make deals."

Has Eloise been foolish enough to ask around the Barrows for her friend? If the woman has been captured by those in defiance of me, Eloise is fortunate she hasn't met the same fate. A missing human means nothing to me; however, if the woman has information about the leak in my Rapture supply, I must know. Jedidiah was too much of an idiot to be a large player in the supply of the drug.

He'd been an ant among cockroaches.

"I've been known to make deals, that is true." I tilt my head, curious to hear what she may offer. "Tell me your proposal." Does she know that words have power in my world, and words in a certain order could mean something different in another.

"I want help in finding and bringing Deidre home, safely if possible," she says. "In exchange, I can promise the information Deidre has collected on the new supplier of Rapture."

I cross my arms, smirking as Eloise eyes the dried blood on my shirt with distaste. "No."

"What?" She takes a step forward with balled fists. Ashe goes to grab her shoulder but a sharp glance from me has him retreating. "What do you mean *no*?"

"Exactly what you think," I answer cavalierly. "Now that I know of her name and last known location, there's no reason why I can't simply send my men to find her and extract the information she has. Kasar is very skilled at just that."

She blinks, her shoulders lowering along with her brows. "So, you'll look for her?"

I snort. "I may tell my men to pick her up if they come across her. But it isn't as if this friend of yours is the only source of information in this city. No. I will not make the deal because what you're offering isn't worth it."

I don't lie exactly. No matter what happens with Eloise, I will be releasing my Lion on a hunt. If this woman does have valid information on the leak from my clan as well as those Topside supporters of my rival, I need her. What Eloise doesn't realize is she's bargaining for her friend's life *after* I have the information I want.

"What do you want, then?" She's right to sound wary.

I make a point to drink her in. She really is a beautiful specimen.

Eloise is short, not even rising to my shoulders with her three-inch heels; and everything about her is thick and soft. Her wide brown eyes watch me with suspicion, but her pretty pink tongue darts out to wet her plump lips. My cock twitches as I wonder if her other lips are just as ripe.

A juicy lamb oblivious to the salivating beast in front of her.

"Your blood."

My answer surprises her but then she shrugs. "Fine. I'll trade some blood in exchange for my friend."

I hold up a hand. "You misunderstand, Ms. Morse." I look to Ashe, who moves to her side in a flash and grips her arm, twisting until the inside of her wrist is facing me.

Eloise struggles against him, but her strength is no match. A beautiful scream slips from her lips as he digs his nail into the meat of her wrist, her vibrant crimson blood welling up and dripping down her arm. I stand and take my time moving around my desk to them.

"What the hell are you doing?" she demands, still struggling against Ashe's hold but glaring up at me. The fight's leaving her as recognition enters her eyes—Ashe isn't who she should be afraid of. I take possession of her arm, my guard slipping away as quickly as he'd appeared, and hold her eyes.

"I don't want a few mere pints of blood, little lamb," I say, breathing in the sweet tangy smell coming from her wrist. It's so different, so much better, purer than Jedidiah's rotten stench. This close, her scent alone assures me she has no toxins in her blood meant to poison me. "You see, I had to dispose of my former feeder. She had problems remaining exclusive."

I make a show of running my nose along the line of her arm, barely avoiding the tempting red rivulets of blood. My fangs extend, need coiling tight around my spine as I fill my lungs with Eloise. I want to sink my teeth into her flesh and drink her dry. The nature of me, the monster I keep controlled, demands something more though.

I want Eloise. She's mine, no matter if she agrees to the bargain. After scenting her, I can't let her go. I refuse to consider what this sudden possessiveness could mean. It's impossible after so many centuries.

I breathe out in satisfaction, eyes following one of the red drops sliding down her arm. "Already I know you're going to taste so much sweeter than she ever did."

Her blood flows faster as her heartbeat increases, belying the stoic response Eloise is trying to present. I grin, the tips of my fangs revealed now that they're almost fully extended.

"I have a life," she snarls, yanking against my marble grip. She's a butterfly trying to push over an ancient tree with the flutter of delicate wings. "I won't spend the rest of it letting you suck me dry."

A dark laugh escapes me and she freezes. I look into her dark eyes, smirking wide enough to reveal all four of my fangs. Two longer ones the humans got right, and the smaller ones on either side that they always seem to miss. "I would never expect that, sweetheart. I found I much prefer lionesses over cattle."

Keeping her gaze, I lick along her wrist, collecting the liquid gold on my tongue. She's bursting with iron and sin and decadence. Eloise is gourmet, meant to be savored and enjoyed, not just consumed for survival.

Her lips part as she watches me taste her, the hand of the wrist I grip relaxing as she fights against the desire creeping into her eyes. I could seduce her further, enthrall her until she can only think of my cock and letting me feast on her. I wouldn't hesitate with any other human but I do with her for some reason.

I want her to accept the bargain of her free will.

"Six months at my side, letting me feed from you when I wish or require," I say before pressing my lips to the cut Ashe made and sucking gently. I want to bury my fangs in her, but I won't—not until she agrees to be only mine. I could get drunk on her blood, higher than any drug has ever taken me.

Eloise has never been fed from before, not even the faintest, oldest trace of a vampire lingers in her blood. My cock swells at that. I will claim her in all ways, her body and soul.

She swallows audibly. "One month in exchange for the safe return of Deidre."

I pulled back, licking the taste of her from my lips as I fight back a smile. Rarely do people attempt to counteroffer with me.

"Three months and Deidre is returned to you in good physical health or, in the likelihood of her already being dead, her body returned to you."

Her eyes harden at the suggestion that her friend may already be dead, the coals of desire being replaced with flames of anger. "Three months if she is returned whole, and if she is found and returned dead, I'm free to leave."

Raising an eyebrow, I let her go. Her terms

are fair, and I don't find myself annoyed at her audacity. If I want the full three months, my lion would have to find her very quickly. I have the feeling I'll need them to convince her to stay. If Kasar brings Deidre back dead, this juicy lamb will walk free, if short one dear friend. Then I'll have to hunt her, and something tells me she'll fight as fiercely as I would against such a thing.

"Three months with you living in my home. In addition to providing your blood, you will be at my side when I request and sleep in my bed."

"I'm not a fucking whore."

"No, but you will be *mine* for those three months if I cannot have your blood for six."

Eloise brings her wrist to her chest, holding it as she studies me. Her skin will be healing already, thanks to the enzymes in my saliva. Her shoulders curl inwards and there is a different sort of fear in her now.

"Will you force me to have sex with you?" Her voice is practically meek compared to the snark she'd used when she first addressed me. She's dropped her stare to the floor between us, the carpet matted with dried blood.

I have the overwhelming urge to hunt down whoever had hurt her and tear them apart, piece by slow piece. The response is unnatural and I push it away as a fluke of biology. She's simply the adorable runt of a dog litter, only surviving because someone felt the need to protect her.

"No," I say before the silence could drag on. Her eyes snap up to meet mine. My voice is gentle and I ignore the stare of Ashe. He's probably wondering what the fuck is going on with me and I'm wondering the same. I harden my tone. "If I fuck you, it will be when you're begging me. So, Ms. Morse. Do we have a bargain?"

To her credit, Eloise only hesitates for a single heartbeat before offering her hand—the same arm I'd tasted her from. I grip her hand, my own nearly wrapping entirely around hers, and shake once.

"We do," she says, her voice barely shaking.

When she tries to release my hand, I tug her forward instead. She lands hard against my chest, her other hand flat just above my cold heart. I wrap my other arm around her, my hand gripping her hair to hold her firmly in place. Eloise struggles against me, and I bite back a groan at the delicious feeling.

Ignoring her useless efforts, I speak to Ashe. "Tell Kasar he is to find this Deidre, last seen at the Gato's Paw before disappearing. I want her found quickly, and her safety is paramount."

"Yes, sire," Ashe says and slips from the room. I turn my attention back to the woman in my arms.

The scent of her fear is heady, and her heart slams against her ribs. This close I can hear it; a faint seductive thrum begging for my fangs. "I've made good on my part of the bargain," I say and pull her head back, forcing her to bare the unblemished column of her neck to me. "Now it is your turn."

I strike quickly, sinking my fangs into Eloise's neck.

Chapter Four
ELOISE

Primitive fear comes as Ambrose's fangs sink into my neck. There is pain too, but a small part of me notes it's no worse than getting blood drawn at the doctor's office.

Lightning scatters across my skin as his fangs withdraw and his lips—his sinfully soft lips—close around the punctures and suck greedily. Ambrose has captured me, his unnatural strength never giving up against my struggle. This is for Deidre, I remind myself as the fear fades. I close my eyes and sink into the vampire's embrace.

He growls with approval, and the sound goes straight to my core.

God, his feeding is doing something to me. I'm grateful we're alone; I don't want the other vampire to see my defenses crumbling. I grip the front of his pressed shirt with both hands, trying in vain to anchor myself to reality while ignoring the feel of him. With his mouth on my neck, his tongue against my skin, the idea of Ambrose using me for sex isn't so terrible. Especially when his hand in my hair slides down under my jaw, his strong fingers wrapping around my neck in a way that screams possession. It doesn't hurt that he smells amazing; of rich leather and frankincense.

I whimper as he licks my neck and then his mouth is gone, and so is he. I stagger, no longer held up by Ambrose, who has moved to the other side of the desk. My head spins and my heart beats so loud I'm convinced he can hear it.

"Ashe will take you to my home," he says, lowering onto the leather chair as if it were a throne. I look at him, unmoored, and blink. Ambrose looks up, as if annoyed to see me still standing there. He appears completely unaffected from his feeding, save for his lips having a flush of color. "Do you require assistance?"

Stark reality crashes into the strange haze that'd taken me when Ambrose fed and I jerk backwards away from him. He smirks and I'm like a small rabbit breaking out of the freeze response in front of a wolf who is no longer quite as hungry as before.

"No," I bite out and tug the damn dress down where it's ridden up higher on my thighs. Ambrose's pupils are dilated, and he watches my movements with a heat-inducing assessment. I harden my gaze and lift my chin. He'd surprised me once with the sensation of feeding from me and I refuse to be taken by surprise again. "I will need to get my things from my place. If that's all right, *your majesty.*"

Ambrose's brows narrow at the sarcasm in my voice and a warning flashes in his eyes. I should heed it and step back, but I haven't ever let a man with power send me running with my tail between my legs and Ambrose won't be the first. He may be a vampire, but he's just the same as any human man with power. They take and take and take, because powerful men believe it's their due and when they're challenged, they do whatever it takes to crush their opponents.

Greater men than Ambrose d'Vil have tried to crush me only to discover my spine is wrought of steel.

"Don't bother with clothing," he says, studying me with renewed detachment. "I will provide a wardrobe befitting someone in your place. The clothing will be delivered tomorrow. Ashe."

At his name, the second vampire steps beside me. I never noticed his return. He has a polite expression as he extends an arm to herd me towards the door. I bite back a sharp retort. I have no doubt that the clothing Ambrose will provide will be nothing like the style I prefer. I have to deal with Ambrose for three months and I do, in fact, have a survival instinct. So I let Ashe guide me out of the office, doing my best to leave as if Ambrose hasn't affected me in the slightest.

Leaving his office, I'm met with the music of the club below, practically deafening after the quiet of the previous room.

"This way," Ashe says, turning me towards a door hidden in the dark. It opens to a short hall which ends in stairs leading upwards. This hallway isn't like the entrance to Noir. There are no sensual color schemes promising a chamber of sin below, no dim lighting to prepare your eyes for the darkness found under the street. The walls are the boring white of office buildings filled with cubicles, and fluorescent lights shine without the flicker of gilded wall sconces.

I hesitate before the stairway, turning to look up at the vampire over my shoulder. Like Ambrose, Ashe looks like an angel carved of marble who wouldn't be out of place in a grand cathedral. He isn't as tall as the vampire king, but I still barely manage to come up to his shoulder in my heels. He raises a thick brow in question, and I decide if it was possible to be both supernaturally beautiful *and* homely, Ashe would fit the description.

"I left my coat at the front," I whisper, the quiet of the short hall not letting me speak any louder.

Ashe nods once and holds out a hand. "If you give me your ticket, Ms. Morse, I'll see that it's returned to you."

His voice is like warm silk and yet, it doesn't affect me like Ambrose's. I duck my head and struggle with my clutch. Ashe waits patiently as I manage to get it open and find the ticket the lady gave me. I make sure to place it in the center of his palm without touching his skin. Physical contact with one vampire was more than enough for my night.

If I offend Ashe, he makes no show of it as he slips the ticket into the front pocket of his black slacks. Like Kasar and Lan, Ashe wears a well-tailored black suit with a crisp white shirt underneath. Is it a uniform Ambrose insists on? Unlike Kasar, Ashe has opted to wear a narrow black tie. He inclines his head towards the stairs in a silent command, and I turn back towards them, climbing carefully in my tall heels. I refuse to make an idiot of myself in front of the first vampire who seems to treat me with civil respect.

When I reach the landing, Ashe reaches from behind me to open the door that reveals a moderate-sized garage bay. Two massive gray Mercedes SUVs, each one costing more that I'd make in ten years, are parked one in front of the other on one side and a gunmetal silver Subaru WRX with a vanity plate dominates the other side. I roll my eyes when I read the plate. *King*

"I would have expected something more like a Bugatti or Ferrari," I comment as Ashe moves towards the SUV closest to the garage bay door. He opens the back passenger door and looks over at the WRX before back at me.

"Ambrose prefers to blend performance with practicality," he explains as he offers a hand to help me step into the high backseat, dropping it gracefully when I don't take it.

"I guess Ferraris wouldn't do well on gravel roads into the woods," I say, thinking of the landscape around Newgate and Oldgate, and the coastal swamplands.

Ashe closes the door as I buckle up, moving around to the driver's seat. I stare at the WRX, trying to imagine Ambrose sliding into the black seats. I peer closer, my nose bumping the window.

"Are those racing harnesses?" I whip around to find Ashe meeting my gaze in the rearview mirror, his amusement plain.

"They are," he confirms and turns the key, the Mercedes humming to life with a sweet growl. I pinch my lips together, trying to ignore the thought of beautiful, ice sculpted Ambrose d'Vil strapped into the performance car and racing around tight curves on gravel roads, a hair's breadth away from disaster. My aunt always shook her head at my choice in boys, but she never got it. It wasn't the boys I was interested in, before everything went to shit. It was their cars and the thrill they offered.

Fortunately, Ashe pulls from the garage after the

door is raised and onto the dimly lit streets. The rain has let up, but everything still reflects the headlights as if the storm has polished the city. At the first stoplight, Ashe asks for my address and I give it to him, only hesitating slightly. I have to remember that "stranger danger" isn't really available for me right now, not after agreeing to be Ambrose's feeder for the next three months. I refuse to believe that Deidre is dead, even if it would mean I'd escape Ambrose's deal earlier.

I press the heels of my palms into my eyes, not giving a crap about ruining my makeup. I've gotten the help for Deidre I'd wanted, so what does it matter if my makeup turns into raccoon eyes?

"We're here." Ashe's calm voice pulls me from the rising anxiety and I take a deep breath before looking up at my building.

"I'll be right back down." I open the door and slide out of the car. Before I can shut it, Ashe is in front of me, his massive hand gripping the top of the door. "Holy shit," I practically shriek, my hand going to my chest as if I can keep my heart from beating straight out of my ribs. "Don't do that!"

Ashe doesn't look apologetic as he closes the door. "I'll be escorting you, Ms. Morse."

I cross my arms and glare. "I don't need a babysitter. I'm not going to run off and flake on my side of the bargain."

Ashe's dark eyes hold mine, his expression placid.

The wind picks up, ruffling my hair and filling my nose with the promise of more rain. I roll my eyes and give in. I'm not so full of pride that I'll let myself get drenched just to prove a point.

"Well, come on then," I throw over my shoulder as I pull my lone key from the clutch pocket I'd secured it in. At least I hadn't left it in my coat pocket.

Ashe is my silent sentinel as I slip off my heels before walking up the flights of stairs. He can judge me all he wants for walking barefoot in what is technically a common stairwell, but he wasn't the one wearing three-inch heels. But he's quiet and leaves me to my thoughts as I step up each riser.

I really bartered myself to Ambrose to save Deidre. When I'd made the decision to seek him out, I hadn't expected such a personal demand. I'd been prepared to offer to work at Noir, or, well, I don't know what. But I certainly hadn't thought I'd have a vampire feeding on me by the end of the night. A chill rushes down my spine as we make it to my floor and I walk the short distance from the landing. Out of habit, I straighten the loose unit number, 22B, screwed into the center of the door before unlocking it.

Deidre loves it, and often jokes about drawing a 1 between the last two and B. She's an investigative journalist, so of course she has a thing for Sherlock Holmes.

I don't want to look at Ashe as he studies the cramped studio. No doubt it's nothing as grand as someone working under Ambrose d'Vil is accustomed to. Three months, I remind myself and grab the duffle bag I'd had since I was sixteen and debate what to take.

I hate the familiar sense of dread and anxiety and trauma wrapped up in having to suddenly pack my bag and leave a home. I push it away, telling myself I've made my own place in this world and I'm not leaving it for good. I *am* coming back.

Ambrose said he'd provide clothing but I have no idea if I'll even like what he picks. So my favorite leggings and yoga pants go in first, along with my favorite pajamas. Bras and underwear quickly follow along with my trusty running shoes. I make a face when my bag is already half-filled. I really need a big suitcase, but I never travel anywhere for long enough to justify something larger than a carry-on.

Heading into the small bathroom, I change into jeans and a baby blue t-shirt that has a head of lettuce on it along with the text, *Lettuce be friends*.

So I like cute things, I think as I zip up my hoodie. Ambrose can suck it if he doesn't like it. I opt to wear my reliable, go-to brown boots to save space in my bag. Space that I quickly grow conflicted over how to fill. I need my laptop to keep up with my client work, but it has its own bag. I reach for a few of my favorite books before hesitating. I'd reread them all, but if I take each one, I'll run out of bag space, and I still need my toothbrush and stuff. I hadn't even begun to consider my house plants. As for Deidre's research and laptop, it's going into its own bag.

I lower my bag and wrench around, frantic anxiety twisting my stomach and taking control.

Ashe is leaning against the wall by the door, one ankle crossed over the other and hands in his front pockets, looking as if he has all the time in the world. In a way, I guess he does.

"Is something the matter?" he asks, completely unaware of the storm brewing inside of me. I need to get myself together. This isn't the time to go into one of my typical Eloise Panic Over Small Things situations.

"What about my house plants?" The words rush out of me as I grip the strap of my bag tight enough that my knuckles are white. "Even if Deidre comes home, she sucks at watering them. If I leave them here, they'll die. And I've had some of these for years! I can't—" I snap my mouth shut and squeeze my eyes closed, taking deep breaths in through my nose and letting them out my mouth. When I open them again, Ashe is inspecting my Monstera that dominates the one window.

"Leave me your key and I'll see it addressed," Ashe says in an easy tone, but my cheeks still heat with embarrassment at how silly I must seem. He looks up at me and then pointedly at the bag hanging against my shins. "Are you finished packing? Ambrose will expect you to be installed in your room soon."

"Installed?" I huff but turn back to my desk and grab some of my books to shove in while muttering. "I'm not a damn new kitchen appliance."

From the look Ashe gives me as I pull the strap over my head and head towards the bathroom, the vampire heard my commentary. I ignore it and go back into the bathroom. It takes all of a minute to dump my toothbrush, facewash, hairbrush, and makeup into the remaining space in my duffle. I debate for a heartbeat over whether to take my shower supplies before deciding I don't want to know what vampires think smell good. Knowing my luck, it'd be raw meat. So in goes my apricot body wash and lavender shampoo.

"Okay." I try to say the word with confidence, but the quick pack with limited options is still dredging up old memories no matter how hard I tell myself this isn't the same. I grip the strap where it rests on my shoulder like a lifeline as I take in my home. I'm not leaving for good. I'll be back here in a few months, with Deidre safe and happy.

"I'll take your bag," Ashe offers and opens my front door, but I shake my head and grip it tighter, as if he'll take it from me.

"I got it," I insist and I expect him to argue, but

he steps out into the hall. My feet drag as I follow him and I drink in a last look at my small slice of safety in this world. Then I close the door and lock it before slipping the key into my front pocket. "Let's go."

I march down those stairs and slide into the backseat as if I'm in control of the situation. I was the one to make the choice to spend the next three months with Ambrose. It was a terrible choice, but I'll be damned sure it isn't my last.

Ambrose d'Vil may be the king of vampires, but I am nobody's servant.

Chapter Five
AMBROSE

The pen practically snaps in my grip as Ashe leads Eloise out of the office. Fuck, her blood buzzes through my veins like honeyed lightning. I had to force myself away from her the moment I realized she was different from any other human I've fed on. It didn't affect me like that when I sampled her blood from the cut and the only reason I can think of is because it hadn't been me who'd brought her blood to the surface.

Eloise had resisted for several rapid heartbeats before submitting to me, and even now when she's no longer in the room, my cock is hard and demanding. Her rich blood is like the smoothest whiskey, her taste still lingering on my tongue.

I snarl and throw the hapless pen across the room, embedding the point in the bulletproof windows overlooking the dance floor below me. I don't have time to let a human woman affect me like this, but I've made a bargain with her and I never go back on my word. I run my kingdom on my honor, and everyone in my world—humans, vampires and shifters alike—knows my word is as good as a sworn oath.

For a moment, I consider ordering Kasar to kill this Deidre after learning everything she knows. Eloise would leave on her friend's death, and I could be rid of her. My lip curls again.

I will never be satisfied with that brief taste of Eloise's blood. It's as if Idunn has descended from Asgard to turn Eloise's blood into my own personal nectar of life. I could easily become addicted to her blood, and I fucking loathe the idea of anyone, especially a human, having such power over me.

No, I can't have Deidre killed. Not when the bargain I'd made said I'd return Eloise's friend alive if she isn't already dead. Three months of glorious hell awaits me, then. I'm Ambrose d'Vil, king of the Nightshade empire, and centuries old. Three months is a blink in time for someone as old as me, and I can endure the siren song of Eloise's blood.

She's the least of my issues, which I'm promptly reminded of when Malachi returns.

"His family?" I ask as I rise from my seat, moving towards the credenza that is now considered an antique. I'd brought it with me, along with many other pieces, when I left the Old World and crossed the ocean. It and four other pieces at my current residence are all I kept from that life. Well, those and my daggers. But those knives are as ancient as me, making the credenza practically modern in comparison.

As I pour three fingers of whiskey, the color so dark to almost be black, Malachi answers, standing at ease with his hands behind his back like the soldier he'd once been.

"I've sent Lan to deliver the news, sire, along with reparations and the standard choices."

"Good." I take a long sip of the whiskey, enjoying the rich peat heat, but it isn't enough to wash the taste of Eloise away. Jedidiah's execution was warranted but I hadn't maintained my position as king for this long by bloodshed alone. His family, the supposed reason he'd sold Rapture outside of my regulations, will be taken care of until they are able to do so themselves. If they do not wish to accept my judgment, then they will be given one week's time to leave the Nightshade's territory.

Considering how it spans multiple states in this country, they'll need every day of that time.

And if any of his family tries to take revenge for the vampire's death, I'll have each one of them slaughtered, no matter their age.

"This fucking Rapture leak is becoming troublesome," I say before taking another sip of whiskey then abandoning it on my desk. I go to the window where my pen is embedded in the glass and rip it out. It's ruined, of course, but it isn't what holds my attention. My gaze travels along the narrow spiderweb of cracks left in the window and invisible to the human eye. Jedidiah was one of those cracks, but who is the damn center, the one who was digging into my kingdom? And how has a human found information when my spies haven't?

"Do you think the human found a lead we haven't?"

"Perhaps. If so, Kasar knows what to do."

If Deidre is alive, Kasar will find her. The vampire is nearly as old as me, though he's never cared for leadership. I'm the judge and jury, and Kasar is my executioner. I slide my hands into my pockets, my right hand curling around the coin there, its surface worn away after so many years. The crowd below moves like a living creature, unaware of the watchful gaze of a vicious predator. I know the legal maximum capacity of Noir is just over three hundred, and the crowd's approaching that number.

I can slaughter them all in minutes, humans and vampires alike. I'd fill that room with blood, inches deep. I'd slaughtered hundreds before, and I will again. I'm too experienced with the ways of the world to think otherwise.

With Eloise's blood burning inside me, I'd be faster and stronger than before. I wouldn't need to go into a blood frenzy to tear limbs apart and rip throats out.

I squeeze the coin harder, the edge digging into my palm in silent reprimand.

"Rapture sales are steady on the street. Lush is at half capacity tonight, so sales are down but that's to be expected."

I hum in agreement. Lush is another of my clubs, another location where the supernatural come to play under my protection. Despite its name, it has a fiercer reputation and only the most brash or daring humans venture within. If Noir is whispered temptation and teasing touches, Lush is metal handcuffs and riding crops. I listen to Malachi as he continues, only sparing him a fraction of my attention.

Rapture is highly sought after; a drug that offers those without magic a taste of it. A taste of the supernatural life. If left unregulated, it can destroy my territory and the humans within it. We vampires do not hide our existence from the humans in power anymore. Fuck, I have the elected officials in my pockets to ensure their cooperation. It's astounding, though, what mental justifications and explanations the human mind can conjure when faced with my kind.

I do not hide, and yet, so much of the human population still clings to the belief that we only exist in legends and stories. That vampires are like Count Dracula, a legend evolved from a very mortal, very brutal dictator. Demons only exist in television shows or the delicate paper of their bibles. Animals are only ever animals and never able to shift into human form.

Stories don't sink their fangs into a human's neck and feast.

If the distribution of Rapture becomes uncontrolled, those humans in Topside will be forced to confront their nightmares. I've lived through that too many times to allow it to happen again. Humans respond to their fears with violence. They turn on each other as easily as they turn on us.

It's why I control the drug with an iron fist. When I'd first discovered its creation, I knew there was no way of stopping its spread. So I brought the demon into the Nightshades and controlled the flow instead.

And now there is someone out there fucking with my years of carefully laid plans. Someone is trying to take away my control.

Once I'd consider it was Markus and those who followed him—a descendent of Queen Mishena— who'd been obsessed with bringing all shifters under his control through his daughter. I appreciated the bloody poetry of Jemma killing Markus with her mates at her side. While vampires and wolf shifters seldom get along, the Blackfang Barons are now staunch allies with my Nightshade vampires.

His death, and the dissolution of his followers, had no impact on the Rapture leaks, making it clear he had no hand in it.

Malachi falls silent and I raise a hand to dismiss him but pause halfway through the movement.

"I'm done here for the night," I say, turning on my heel. "Keep watch and deal with any issues."

It's a matter of moments, my thoughts struggling for clarity against the thrum of Eloise's blood in my veins, before I'm pulling on my double-breasted peacoat as I exit the club through my private hatch on the roof. The rain has lessened to a drizzle, but the clouds block out the light of the moon, leaving the Barrows to glow neon from the streets below.

I need to hunt. To give in to the monster within and let it prowl the streets and search out the hidden threat buried underneath the cobblestone streets of Oldgate. I close my eyes, rolling my neck, as I inhale deeply. I'm assaulted by a maelstrom of scents. Sex, death, pain, fear, alcohol, blood, piss, vomit, trash and rotting food and flesh—all the scents of a city under a siege of its own desires.

I focus on one scent. It shouldn't be strong enough to cut through the sewage of the city and yet it's the only one I can focus on. Baring my fangs, I bellow rage and defiance across the uneven rooftops.

I have my target, even if it's not the one I should be hunting.

Eloise's scent taunts me, a whisper growing fainter the further she travels away from me.

Fine. I will hunt this human and discover why she has such a strong hold over me. I could simply return to my home and wait for her there, but no... that will not do at all, I think as I step onto the edge of the building. The drop is over four stories, practically a promise of death if a mortal fell from this height.

I take a step, the wind screaming in my ears as gravity asserts its dominance over my form. Like my foes, I deny it my death, landing on my feet without fear. A few high-pitched screams from the women at the front of alley have me snarling in distaste. They stumble back into the better lit streets, their outfits leaving very little to the imagination, and each one of them smells of Rapture. Not even the drug can overcome their primal instincts warning them of the danger I present.

Good. Maybe they'll get into a car and go back to their homes to hide under their blankets and do their best to forget about the Barrows.

I breathe in again, sorting through the scents of my kingdom, and once I locate Eloise, I'm running. I melt into the shadows, slipping through the black between neon glows, as the city streets turn into a blur around me. Humans don't sense my passing, though a few shifters and vampires do. They know better than to let their attention linger on me, though.

It takes moments to arrive at Eloise's building, and I wait at the edge of darkness as I see Ashe escort her from the front door to the car. His gaze finds mine, the golden hue reflecting the dim streetlights. He doesn't acknowledge me beyond a slow blink, and I nod once before letting my gaze settle on Eloise.

She's changed clothing, and yet somehow she's even more tempting now that I've had a taste of her. She looks better like this, in clothing that she clearly prefers, as much as I enjoyed the displays of creamy skin of the earlier dress. Ashe tries to take her bag as he opens the door but she clings to it tighter as she slides in. His eyes find mine again, a silent message of irritation and I can't help the small smirk that tilts my lips.

Eloise is stubborn and defiant. I will enjoy breaking her.

When Ashe closes the door and takes his place as the driver, I step out of the darkness and stalk towards the front door. It's a simple tug to break the door free of the lock, and then I'm in. Following her scent, I climb the stairs, tracking it until I'm in front of the plain wooden door with a crooked apartment number.

I hesitate as I wrap my hand around the doorknob. If I break the latch, then even a simple human could get in. Snorting at my concern, I grip the handle and twist, the metal and wood splintering as it opens.

I'll have someone come fix the door. Her home needs to be safe. I need to protect her, even if I don't want to think about why.

Standing in the small apartment, my senses are flooded by Eloise's scent and another woman's—no doubt Deidre's. I stalk through the apartment, inspecting the contents of the bookshelves, the kitchen, the numerous house plants. Sliding my phone out, I dial Kasar while stepping into Eloise's room.

The phone connects, though Kasar says nothing.

"I'm sending you the location of the girl's apartment," I say, approaching the bed. "Have you found her trail?"

"Yes," Kasar answered. The lack of sound in the background makes me believe he's in a car. "She was taken by vampires. None of whom I recognize the scent of."

I snarl and sink onto the edge of Eloise's bed. "Find out everything."

"Of course," he says. "The woman?"

I grit my teeth. "Keep her alive as best you can. But if it comes to choosing her or the Nightshades..."

"Understood, sire."

I hang up and ping him the address. He'll find

the apartment here if necessary in his hunt. Other messages command Lan to ensure tighter security measures for their front door and posting someone outside to watch who may try to enter their location. If this Deidre has truly discovered something of value about the Rapture leak and Kasar extracts her, they will look for her here.

Duties done, I lie down on Eloise's bed, surrounded and drowning in her scent. My heart beats faster than it ever did as a mortal, and my mind fills with trace memories of her in this very room. The small sampling of her blood only gives me the faintest images to call on, but it's enough for my cock to fill as I lie where she has slept for years. Her scents have permeated the walls, the fabrics of her blankets, her pillow, everything. Even the scent of arousal and pleasure from her past has sunk into the fabric cradling me and my body responds to its call.

Another part of me wants to hunt down those males who had experienced that pleasure and gut them.

Forcing myself up off the bed, agitated and pacing, I refuse to acknowledge my desire, and I leave the apartment before I do something stupid and rash. Like search her drawers for a scrap of lace that's cradled her sex over time and stroke myself.

Even out of the building and into the renewed storm, I can't get my head to focus on anything other than Eloise.

I let my feet carry me towards my home, tailing the car in which Ashe drives Eloise. He senses me—I sired him over a century ago, our connection linking us like I'm linked to so many others in my clan. I'm a silent guardian over the car until it turns into the underground gated garage that I installed under my home in this city.

Instead of following, I climb the side of my building with ease despite the rain, and slip in through the window that only opens at my touch. Mortals believe it magic, and perhaps to a degree it is. But runes and blood rituals had been around for thousands of years before mortals began to swarm this earth and sought to control things they didn't understand.

In the relative safety of my home, I let my senses fan out—searching the house for any sign of abnormalities.

Only the sound of my staff and the vampires of my empire reach me. Good. I let out a low growl, too low for humans to hear—only sense it. But the vampires who room here occasionally would head the order. In seconds, I sense them fleeing the home with supernatural speed.

To the staff, I use the intercom in the wall to dismiss them for the night with clear instructions to not return until I call. Ashe gets a text message with instructions on what to do with the human woman.

Satisfied my orders would be followed, I change

out of the wet clothes and into a fresh suit, though I leave off the vest and coat. Only when I hear the door from the garage open into the house, two floors below, do I let myself leave the room.

It's time to see what Eloise makes of her new surroundings.

Chapter Six
ELOISE

The first impression I have when walking into the place I'll be living for the next three months is that there aren't any coffins. The next impression immediately on the heels of that one is that it's rather light and airy compared to Noir, and I'm kind of in disbelief that the king of vampires calls this his palace.

"Where am I staying?" I ask, turning back towards the garage door to Ashe. Except the door is closed and I'm all alone.

"Okay," I drag out, turning back around to the rest of the house, a bit creeped out. I clutch the strap of my duffle bag tighter and head deeper into the house.

The garage door opened to a pristine space of pale hardwood floors and cream-colored walls. Plush runners with geometric patterns keep the floors from being bare while the walls have art prints of evergreen forests and mountains backed with blue skies. Light comes from wall sconces, making the space inviting rather than intimidating.

The entryway passes through an arched doorway into a living space crowded with life. Plants seem to take up every surface, turning the room into one of those urban jungles. I close my eyes, breathing in the rich scent of healthy soil and thriving plants. My fear for my own plants is immediately lessened. If these plants are any indication, I can trust Ashe to see to my own babies. Or maybe I can request they be brought to me, since they'll be in good company.

In the center of the indoor garden is a low round table surrounded by a pair of wingback armchairs in green velvet and a matching couch. Ashe's words of how Ambrose balances performance and practicality come back to me and it seems applicable to his home as well.

I want to linger in the room and introduce myself to each plant, most I recognize and others I've never seen before. I force myself to move on, my curiosity about the rest of the house too strong. From the car, I'd glimpsed the southern manor exterior and three stories of windows before we'd disappeared down underground into the garage.

On the lower level, there are no hallways as one room opens into the next. Each one has quite a few indoor plants, especially near the large windows, but none have as many as that first room. There are at least two different living rooms and a large dining room with a long table that my last foster mother would be envious of. It has at least a dozen chairs pushed in, and the cherry oak gleams in the white light from the wall lights. Even the table has two golden pothos plants sprawling its yellow and green leaves across the tabletop.

I only poke my head into the kitchen, the first room I've seen behind a closed door. My eyebrows rise at the pure functionality of the place. For a vampire's residence, I didn't expect a full kitchen, considering they drank blood. Or maybe the massive stainless-steel fridge across the kitchen isn't full of freezer meals, fruits, and veggies. For all I know, it could be filled with bags of blood, like the ones at blood drives.

Deciding against finding out, I make my way towards a set of stairs in a room lined with bookshelves. Not all the shelves held books. Things that looked better suited to a museum are scattered across the shelves as if set there years ago and long forgotten. They look expensive enough I'm too nervous to even get close.

Climbing the stairs, I'm struck by how big this house actually is as I look upwards. The stairs continue up to a third floor as I'd expected and there is no ornate chandelier as I half-expected. Isn't that what the obscenely wealthy do with spaces like this?

When I make it to the second landing, a chill goes down my spine and the hair on my arms rise. I stop and spin slowly, searching for what—or more likely, who has made me feel like this.

"Hello?"

I'm pretty proud of myself that it didn't come out as a squeak. Of course, there's no response, which only creeps me out even more.

This floor surrounds the staircase, with doors leading off of the U-shaped landing. There's a hallway to my right, dark with none of the lights on. But whoever is watching me isn't there; I'm not sure how I know, but I'm certain.

Swallowing, I consider continuing on my exploration but I've used up all of my courage for the night. Not caring if someone is watching me, I turn and hurry back down the stairs, barely managing not to break into a run.

Clutching my bag, I hurry back to the first room filled with plants. I sit on the couch, and set my duffle beside me, my thighs pressed together and hands clutching my knees. I'm too aware of my heart racing, the sound pounding in my ears as I strain for any sign of movement in the house.

I've always hated haunted houses, but knowing a vampire—one who's already bitten me, at that—lives here is setting my teeth on edge. The sensation of no longer being alone only intensifies the longer I sit. My hands are clammy and a scream is building up in my chest. I have no idea if it's from fear or irritation. Grabbing hold of the anger, I take a deep breath and try to calm myself down.

Once I feel like I can talk normally, I shoot a glare towards the archway which leads to the stairs.

"Are you too scared to show yourself, Ambrose?" I say, almost achieving a nonchalant tone. It's just a guess that my silent watcher is the vampire king, even knowing I'd left him at Noir. If I don't get a handle on our interactions now, I won't retain any semblance of control and I need that if I'm going to make it here for three months.

Deidre has to be alive; even if it means I get out of the deal earlier, she can't be dead.

There's no immediate answer but the air around me thins, as if I'm no longer being studied quite so intently. I'm about to say something else, maybe a goad to challenge the man, when a streak of movement ripples past me and makes the massive leaves of the Monsteras, Devil's Ivy, and spider plants rustle. A yelp ekes out between my lips as one of the wingback chairs across the low table from me is suddenly occupied.

Ambrose d'Vil is a bastard.

I glare at the vampire, unamused even as my heart tries to make its way back into my chest from the afterlife. He's sitting there, ankle across his knee, and golden honey hair in perfect place. He's clearly changed clothes, since there's no more blood speckled on his white shirt, and in place of a narrow black tie, he's left the first few buttons undone. The tease of pale skin draws my attention no matter how much I fight it. There's the smallest black curve, half-hidden in the shadow of his shirt collar. Does Ambrose have tattoos?

My mind goes crazy with thoughts of unbuttoning the rest of his shirt and sliding my hands over his chest to discover what secrets lie underneath. My core tightens as my body remembers exactly how it felt to be held up against his strong body.

No, nope. We aren't going there. I will not be another human who falls at the feet of the sexy vampire. The really, really sexy vampire.

"Kasar has a lead on Deidre."

I jump, my shoulders practically slamming into my ears, as Ambrose breaks the silence. He's watching me with impassivity, but I swear I get the sense I amuse him.

"That's good, right?" I ask after swallowing. I hesitate, but force myself to ask the next question. "Does he think she's still…" My eyes fall closed as my throat tightens.

"Alive?" Ambrose's voice is even, and when I open my eyes, his are trained on me as he shifts to rest his elbows casually on the rests of the chair. He waits until I get a jerky nod. "He believes that she is still alive, yes. As for if she will still be so when he catches up to her abductors, I cannot say."

Pain knots my stomach as his words hit me. A breath shudders from me and I bring my fingers to my mouth, trying to keep back a moan of grief. I should be grateful that Ambrose speaks so clinically about Deidre's life, that he isn't trying to give me false hope or sympathy, but it still hurts.

"Eloise."

I refocus my gaze, and he's crouched beside me, a strained look on his face. This close, I can see the gold patterns in his irises, and they remind me of those stars with a dozen points bursting from the pitch black of his pupils. There's not a single hint of red in those depths. Had the little blood he'd taken from me satisfied his hunger so easily?

"Kasar is the best at what he does," Ambrose says, his voice stiff and awkward. I realize he's trying to reassure me and I don't think he has much experience in it. "He will find your friend, and bring her back alive. If he cannot, he will see to it that every person who laid a hand on her no longer walks this earth."

His voice is low and full of gravitas as he promises his wrath and something in his tone makes me believe in him. I hold his amber gaze, a part of me reaching out to this vampire, this monster, and finding a connection. Why is that part of me urging me to trust this creature, this man that when I first walked into his office, I saw the evidence of his wrath and darkness in the form of a decapitated head and its bloody corpse being dragged away?

As if on its own, my hand lifts from my lap and reaches towards Ambrose's face. He stays unnaturally still, his eyes trained on me as I touch his sharp cheekbone, no firmer than the brush of a butterfly's wing. Emboldened by this, I drag my fingertips out towards his temple and further until I'm brushing the short dark hair along the side of his head and then down around the back of his ear, my eyes stuck on the path my hand travels. When I reach his neck, Ambrose lets out a slow breath and I look at his face only to see his eyes are closed, a furrow between his eyebrows as if my touch is causing him pain.

The moment I pull my hand from him, his eyes open, his pupils dilating and his nostrils flaring as he looks at me with unabashed desire. My own body responds, heat flooding my sex and the place he bit me tingling. His eyes drop to my neck and the air grows thick between us. I tilt my head, feeling as if I'm under a spell, wanting to affect Ambrose as much as he is affecting me.

He responds, a predator responding to the prey; leaning in, his hands land on either side of me on the couch, surrounding me with his presence as he lowers his face to my neck.

I gasp, my eyes fluttering as they try to close, as Ambrose's nose ghosts over his bite mark. Lightning bolts of pleasure shoot from the spot down my spine, curl around my nipples, and combust in my core. I can feel him breathe me in, the air moving between the infinitesimal distance between us.

Then he's gone, moved back to stand beside the chair he'd sat in, all signs of desire and hunger replaced by a marble exterior. I sway towards him, that small part of me being pulled towards him, craving him to come back and give me the pleasure his bite promised.

"Let me show you where you will be sleeping," he says, his voice once more the even keel of an unaffected king sure of his power.

I rapidly blink away the haze in my mind, forcibly reminding myself of who I face and what our bargain entails and what it does not. I grab the duffle bag beside me and stand, my legs not as weak as my racing heart might suggest. Still, I don't say anything, not trusting my voice to be as steady as his, so I nod instead.

I follow him up the stairs that I'd tentatively ventured up before retreating, this time the sense of being watched is missing. It only confirms that it was Ambrose watching me from somewhere in the shadows. When we turn to climb the next flight of stairs, I'm able to find my voice, even if I'm quiet.

"How many people live here?"

"Several of my inner circle have rooms here," Ambrose says without looking back as he climbs the risers, his hands in his pockets. "You will meet more of them in time."

I press my lips into a flat line. "Will I be serving them, as well?"

Ambrose halts, one foot on the third landing, and turns to look down at me, a quiet ferocity in his gaze that stops my heart. "No. And if any of them make the mistake of thinking so, they will be dealt with swiftly."

Well, I think as Ambrose turns forward again and resumes walking, I won't have to clean all of the rooms in the house. Thank goodness, seeing as I hate cleaning my own room, let alone others.

"This is my bedroom," he says, opening a broad door with a large brass handle. I'd noticed it was only one of three doors on this floor surrounding the staircase, and in the middle of the other two. He walks in before me, a reminder that this may be my room, but this house and even myself are his.

I stutter to a stop only a few steps in, my eyes wide as I take everything in. The room is warmly lit by the same wall lights that dominate the rest of the house, no harsh overhead lighting to be found, apparently. Everything is the color of fresh cream, pale lavender, or tea greens. While there aren't enough plants to turn the bedroom into a conservatory, trailing pothos hang from one corner and a vase filled with calla lilies sits in the center of the antique dresser along the closest wall.

It's as if I've been transported to the French countryside, with the Provencal style dresser, chaise lounge below the two tall windows curtained by transparent ivory, and thicker lavender drapery. The bed dominates the room, easily three times the size of my bed and would never fit in my small bedroom. Both the headboard and footboard are upholstered in the same fresh cream fabric that matches the plush carpet underfoot, and are framed with carved wood that screams wealth and luxury. Piles of pillows in the pale lavender and white promise mornings of sleeping in and sweet dreams, and the white coverlet is thick and fluffy, the top folded back to reveal the narrow strip of tea green sheets underneath.

It doesn't seem to match the brutality I've already experienced from the vampire.

"The en-suite is through there." Ambrose pulls me from my staring and I look to where he's pointing to another broad door in the wall opposite the windows. "You will find the wardrobe there as well. Tomorrow morning, my tailor will take your measurements as well as bring a selection of garments I've deemed appropriate."

I snort, unable to help the derisive noise. He raises a brow and I'm glad of the timely reminder of the truth of my situation. I walk forward and drop my bag on the too-fancy bed, reminding myself to keep my feet firmly on the ground and head out of the clouds. I ignore how this room seems to soften the man, how the severity of his poise has lessened as if he'd set the mantle of king at the door before stepping inside.

"Do you usually spend so much money on your servants, or are you just so rich that outfitting me in a custom uniform is something you don't even count as an expense?"

Ambrose doesn't reply right away and I busy myself with unzipping my bag and pulling out the contents. His gaze is heavy, but I refuse to stop what I'm doing and wait him out.

"Why would I have you as a servant when I have a paid staff of twenty to maintain my house, Eloise?"

I stiffen when his voice comes from directly behind me, soft and full of decadent promises. I do not move as I feel his fingers brush through my hair, the movement radiating curiosity. It's as if I'm a possession and he's learning all that he can before delving deeper to take me apart.

"So," I swallow hard before continuing, my voice more breathless than I want, "I'm simply a well-kept prized livestock? Since I'm to feed you whenever you wish and sleep in your bed." I gesture to the bed in front of me, the same bed Ambrose is trapping me against by merely standing behind me.

His touch disappears, yet I can still feel him behind me, close enough I could lean back and we'd be pressed against one another. The air shifts and his head is lowered towards my shoulder, the opposite side of my bite at least, and the deep timbre of his voice caresses my ear.

"You are *mine*, Eloise," Ambrose says, the possession in his words intoxicating. "I forbid you to think of yourself as livestock. If I thought of you as such, there would be no mistaking it. For now, you should rest."

Ambrose drops his lips to my neck, just before it meets my shoulder and I hold my breath, waiting for the sharp pain of his fangs. I don't know if I'm afraid he'll bite me, or afraid that he won't.

The room grows cooler and I know I'm alone, even if Ambrose didn't say anything. I turn, just to be sure, and then I keep turning until I can sink onto the bed and bury my face in my hands.

With a heavy groan, I flop onto my back, ignoring the pile of clothes I'd laid out, and stare up at the ceiling. The mind games have begun, and I have to survive three more months of Ambrose and the temptations he promises.

A part of me wonders if it would be easier to just give in to these new cravings.

Chapter Seven
ELOISE

When I wake, the other side of the bed is still as neat as it was the night before. When Ambrose said I'd be sleeping in his bed, I thought he'd be sleeping in it too. My phone buzzes again and I flop my hand out for it, turning the alarm off by memory alone. In spite of my late night, I'm well rested and I give full credit to the glorious bed and buttery soft sheets spoiling me. If I can convince myself to think of this as a working vacation, I can go back to my tiny apartment and cheap twin mattress without too much heartache.

A chirp has me picking up the phone with one hand and rubbing the sleep out of my right eye with the other. Opening it, I pull up my task list for the day, calculating how much time I'll need to wrap up the project for the boutique in Newgate. They are one of my biggest clients, and I hadn't finished the project because I realized Deidre was gone. The deadline is tomorrow, so at least I can wrap it up today. Rolling out of the bed, I trudge into the bathroom, eyes still bleary with sleep. I need caffeine, whether it be tea or soda or maybe even a drink that's more sugar than liquid.

Ambrose's bathroom is as simple yet ostentatious as the bedroom, but in my current state, I don't frankly care about the marble counters and massive freestanding claw-foot tub. All I care about is the toilet, hidden behind a half wall, and then the shower stall dominating the corner. Before sleeping, I'd set all of my toiletries in the shower and put away my clothes in the empty drawers of the dresser. Half of the drawers were filled with neatly folded t-shirts, something I have trouble picturing the clean-cut Ambrose wearing.

Shucking my clothes, I leave them in a pile before stepping into the gratuitously large marble shower. It has one of those rainfall shower heads in the ceiling as well as three shower heads in a straight line on one wall, making sure whoever is in here has to make an effort to avoid the water.

Thoroughly soaked in warm water, I bend down to grab my shampoo only to see a different bottle in its place. Frowning, I open the glass door, looking for any sign of my stuff. Rolling my eyes at Ambrose, who no doubt must think my ten-dollar shampoo is too plebeian, I pop the lid of the shampoo that I'm pretty sure is Swedish. Okay, I have to give him credit. It's at least the same scent as mine, just a more natural and less chemical smelling version of lavender.

He *is* a vampire, after all, I muse as I lather my hair. My shampoo probably smells different to him. Satisfied with the mental justifications instead of just thinking he's a controlling asshole, I finish my shower with my habitual efficiency. I towel off my hair before putting it up in a still-damp bun and peek into the bedroom to make sure I'm still alone. A few minutes later and I'm dressed in my most professional freelancer-who-works-from-home style: black leggings, comfy socks, and a white and pink striped tee shirt. Setting my glasses on my nose, I give myself a smirk in the mirror above the dresser.

If Ambrose thinks I spend my days dressed up and ready to club, he's in for a real treat. The only reason why I'm wearing a bra right now is because I'm not at home. Hell, knowing me, I'll be abandoning the boob prison in less than a month. Who am I kidding, I'll be amazed if I make it two weeks before saying screw it and freeing my tatas. Snagging my laptop and Deidre's from the drawer I'd tucked it into, I metaphorically pull up my big-girl panties and head downstairs.

This morning the house doesn't feel nearly as empty, though I don't see anyone yet. I do, however, smell something delicious and I set the laptops on the massive dining table and head into the kitchen. To my surprise, there are three different people in there, all of them looking at me when I walk in. Face burning, I come to a stop and raise a hand in an awkward wave.

"Hi. I'm Eloise?" I sound like I don't even know if that's my name or not. Superb. "I'm staying here for a while. Total human, by the way."

Shit, do they know Ambrose is a vampire?

A woman who looks old enough to be my mother gives me a welcoming grin, and I want to swipe my hand across my forehead as I see the golden gleam of her eyes.

"Welcome, Ms. Morse," she says, her voice heavily French accented. "Sire Ambrose has informed us of your stay. I am Joséphine. Do you want breakfast? We have beignets, fresh eggs, and bacon or sausage if you prefer? If you want something else, do not hesitate to ask."

"Uh. You can just call me Eloise," I mumble, feeling awkward as hell.

The matronly vampire walks towards me, waving a dismissive hand. "Nonsense. You are the sire's guest and will be addressed with respect."

She's nothing like the vampires I've met before. They are all lean lines, sharp edges, their youth preserved for eternity. This woman has the curves of a mother of many, and like me, enjoys food, let alone her slightly wrinkled face and neatly braided silver hair. I find myself ushered out of the kitchen and suddenly sitting in front of my laptops near the end of the dining table.

"Do you prefer tea or coffee?" she asks briskly and I'm hapless except to go along with her.

"Uh, tea, please, black," I answer, then rush out, "You don't need to get it for me. I can."

"Nonsense," she replies tartly, giving me a sharp look. "You are the sire's guest. Now, here is the tea. Have you thought of what you would like to eat?"

The teacup she hands me is delicate porcelain that I'm terrified of drinking out of. They don't make this style anymore, and it screams antique. I realize Joséphine is still waiting for an answer and I carefully set the teacup down, waiting for it to shatter as it touches the table.

"Toast is fine?" I answer sheepishly. I'm not a big breakfast person, really. Deidre is, but budgets being tight as they are, we both prioritized caffeine over real food in the morning.

The woman hums, her thin eyebrows narrowing in what I suspect is disapproval, but she returns to the kitchen and I brave the porcelain teacup to take a sip of the much-needed hot caffeine. If I'm to make it through the next three months, I can't be sleepyheaded.

It's pretty damn good and I quickly drink it down, relishing the warm burn filling my stomach. I get up to bring the matching teapot over to my spot and top myself off before setting up my laptop. Tucking a foot under my butt and tea in one hand, I let myself fall into my normal routine of checking emails and social media sites.

"Oh, no, Ms. Morse, this will not do."

It takes a few seconds for me to drag my eyes from the prospective client's email to look at the vampire in confusion. One of the people from the kitchen, a young man close to my age that doesn't have a hint of gold in his eyes, is carrying a tray with more than just my requested toast. In fact, I don't even see any toast.

"Huh?" I ask and then Joséphine reaches over and closes my laptop before collecting both and setting them beside the tea set on the sideboard. The young man sets the tray down before unloading it in front of me.

"If I do not allow Sire Ambrose to work while he eats, then I will not allow you either," Joséphine says in a tone that brooks no argument. "Work is not good for the digestion. When I am satisfied you have eaten enough, you may have your laptops back and not a moment sooner."

"I'd think it's kind of hard to work and suck blood at the same time," I mutter, looking at the food in front of me. The young man snorts, and we share a grin while Joséphine sighs like an irritated schoolmistress.

"Vampires require sustenance beyond blood, Ms.

Morse. You clearly have much to learn. Now eat; you're like a little kit and need to put more meat on those bones."

I stare at the retreating woman's back. I don't think I've ever heard anyone say I need to gain weight, and I don't know how I feel about it. Is she like the evil witch in the gingerbread house, fattening up the kids on sweets so they taste better when she finally cooks them? Is she fattening me up for Ambrose?

When I went to Noir last night, I could never have predicted how quickly my life would change.

Rather than the requested toast, I'd been served poached eggs, grilled butternut squash, fruit, bacon and sausage, as well as a golden fluffy croissant and bright red raspberry jam. There's no way I'm finishing all of this, but the snide voice of one of my foster parents scolding me for wasting their food has me picking up a fork. The food is simple, but I close my eyes in enjoyment. The spices must have worked a miracle on my appetite, as it's not long before I find myself soaking up the little bit of yolk left on the empty plate with the last bite of the croissant.

"Good, you're finished eating."

I whip around, eyes wide as Ambrose strolls in and selects his own teacup before taking a seat beside me at the head of the table. I grab the cloth napkin, hastily wiping my mouth free of any jam or yolk, scowling down at the red drop on my shirt. It's impossible for me to not spill anything when I'm eating, and compared to how pristine Ambrose's white button-down is, I feel like an utter slob.

He fills his teacup, and looks at me as he takes a sip.

"Can I help you?" I ask when the silence stretches out between us. I refill my tea, waiting for his answer.

"My tailor is on his way," he answers, keeping his fingers loosely around the teacup after he sets it down in front of him. "After that, your time is your own until this evening."

From his tone, Ambrose isn't going to explain any further. He doesn't get back up, but he does seem to settle in like he's waiting for his own breakfast to be served. His blasé attitude has me bristling.

"Are you going to bother telling me what you expect me to do this evening?" I perfected my saccharine sweet fuck-you voice at my first customer service job in high school. If Ambrose expects me to be at his beck and call without any explanations, I've got to correct him right now.

Ambrose gives me a bland look that makes him look like a statue and it only makes me glare at him. "Our bargain does not include explanations, Eloise. And I have not had to explain myself or my demands for centuries. I see no reason to start now."

I swear he's being an ass on purpose. My skin heats with irritation at his unquestioned authority. It makes me want to pour my tea on his lap and stain that crisp white shirt. I grew up with too many people trying to control me. The look he's giving me now has me grinding my teeth and refusing out of sheer obstinance.

Pressing my hands flat on the table to keep myself from acting on that desire, I meet his gaze. "We're going to have a really unpleasant three months if you expect me to just do whatever you say, whenever you say it, without being told beforehand."

Ambrose holds my gaze, unblinking, and I don't break eye contact. Last night I was the terrified rabbit in front of the beast, but now in the light of day, I won't bend. I've got my own claws, and the sooner he accepts it, the better.

"We are having dinner with someone."

I'm sort of surprised he actually told me. I cock my head, interested. "Who?"

Ambrose finishes his tea and stands, holding out a hand as if to help me up. "No one of importance to you. Come, the tailor has arrived."

I ignore his hand and don't miss the flash of irritation in his eyes. Smirking, I step around him and collect the laptops, holding them against my chest with one arm as I sweep the other hand out in an after-you gesture. Ambrose's eyebrows pinch, but he says nothing as he strides out of the room, his regal nonchalance cloaking his shoulders once more.

Irritating Ambrose d'Vil might just become my new favorite hobby.

I follow the vampire through the maze of rooms on the lower level until we're in an open room sparsely decorated. In fact, I think this room had couches in it last night. Now it's been redecorated to look like one of those fancy fitting rooms with a pedestal in the middle of three full-length gilded mirrors. The curtains are closed, but they're white and thin enough that late morning light makes them glow and fills the room with the soft natural light.

Two people are waiting for us, and they bow when Ambrose enters the room. I roll my eyes at the display, but make sure no one sees it. Ambrose turns back, gesturing towards me with his hand.

"Mr. Carter, this is Eloise Morse, whom you will be outfitting," Ambrose introduces me before plucking the laptops from my grasp despite my protests.

"A pleasure, Ms. Morse," the man says politely, who by his eyes isn't a vampire but he doesn't feel human. Wary, I give a forced smile, which seems to be good enough for the tailor. He gestures to the woman at his side. "My assistant, Tara. She will be taking your measurements today. If you would?" Another gesture has him pointing to the stand.

Unable to avoid it, I step onto it, keeping my arms at my side and feeling incredibly awkward. It's impossible to avoid my reflection, seeing as there are three mirrors in front of me. There's no way I can escape how much of a couch potato I look like compared to the other three people in the room.

Tara, a willowy young woman with pale blonde hair and fair skin, steps up beside me, offering a genuine smile as she unrolls a tape measure.

"First time?" she asks, before instructing me to lift my arms.

I huff out a laugh as I stare up at the ceiling while she measures my bust and then waist. "Had to get measured once for a bridesmaid dress years ago. It was just as awkward then."

Tara hums with sympathy. "At least you won't have to wear a dress that isn't to your taste," she offers. She isn't writing down my measurements, so she must have an amazing memory.

"I don't know about that," I say, shooting a glare at Ambrose in the mirror. "He's the one picking everything out."

She doesn't even glance in Ambrose's direction as she shrugs. "He may pick it out, but he won't force you to wear it if you hate it."

The corner of Ambrose's mouth lifts in a sly smirk as his eyes heat. "You are more than welcome to spend your time naked, little lamb," he purrs and my face burns as I look anywhere but him. A low, dark laugh rolls from him and I can't hold back the shiver that trickles down my spine. "But I think you'll enjoy your new trousseau. It is time you stop hiding your beauty."

I can't help it. I meet his gaze in the mirror again, tentative like I'm the little lamb he calls me. The sarcastic retort dies before it can even form, struck down by the adamant declaration of Ambrose's voice. It's impossible to call his bluff when he's looking at me like that.

"I've never seen a reason to bother," I mutter, focusing on Tara moving around me and measuring my instep.

The assistant looks up at me, giving me another one of her encouraging smiles. "Well, you should want to show yourself off for your own sake." She stands up, graceful enough I wonder if she's some sort of fae despite her perfectly round ears, and holds my gaze. Her eyes are a pale blue, and it's as if something has stolen the color from her body and left her with the faded remains. "Embrace yourself, Ms. Morse. There's no need to be cruel to yourself when the world is cruel enough."

Well, damn.

"If you would please take a seat?" Mr. Carter gestures to the couch and the pile of shoeboxes beside it. I do as instructed, relieved to be off of the stand even if it means sitting next to Ambrose. He is the picture of relaxation as he reclines into the corner of the seat, one of his long legs crossed at his knee, one arm stretched along the back of the couch while the other frames his face as he watches me with frank interest.

Tara leaves out of the opposite doorway that we entered and Mr. Carter distracts me by opening the first shoebox. To my relief, they're black flats. Sure, they're a much higher quality than my cheap big box store ones, but I was worried I'd be trying on tall heels better suited to A-list celebrities.

The man opens the second box after I give the flats a thumbs-up and my eyes widen. Here are the heels I was expecting, but damn if the black stilettos with narrow straps aren't sexy as hell. I wanted to put them on even if I can't walk in them because they're so tall. I can just perch myself in a window seat surrounded by plants and work on my laptop, every now and then kicking my leg out to admire the "fuck-me" heels.

"So you do have a taste for the decadent," Ambrose crooned in my ear, my cheeks flaming as I turned my head just enough to look at him. Any closer and our lips would be touching. I can hardly breathe, warring between two instincts. One is telling me to run away and never look back; the other is telling me to press my lips to his and take everything his kingdom and power promises.

Ambrose's golden eyes drop to my lips, pupils dilating when I wet them quickly in my nervousness. There's no one else in the room, not when my world narrows down to this couch, this space between our bodies, the air we share as we breathe.

The conflict inside me grows tighter and tight, like a violin string being tuned too tight. Each heartbeat is another twist of the peg, bringing me closer to snapping. I have no idea what I'll do when it snaps.

The sound of a clothes rack being wheeled in cuts through the spell, yanking me out like a lifeguard from a raging whirlpool. I whip my head away from Ambrose, panting and unable to hide it. Mr. Carter and Tara give me the courtesy of looking at the clothes and giving me their opinions on each piece, giving me the space to regain composure.

Ambrose rises, and I brave a glance upwards. The vampire is as cool and collected as he always seems to be. Was I the only one who felt the pull between us? Is his interest purely in feeding and ensuring I don't embarrass him when we're in public together?

"Excuse me, there are matters I must attend to," he says, and if he wasn't so poised, I'd swear it's Ambrose's way of saying "oh, did I leave the stove on?" He doesn't even look at me as he walks out, only calling over his shoulder. "I will collect you at seven. Do be presentable, Eloise."

Asshole.

Chapter Eight
AMBROSE

I stare at the computer monitor, reading the same email over and over again yet not comprehending it. It's not that I don't understand the contents. The reason for my lack of focus sits cross-legged in the high-backed leather armchair opposite of my desk.

After her fittings, Eloise wandered into my office and planted herself there, the chair set in a nook created by the hutches I kept my records in. A matching narrow table had just enough room for a pen and paper, or as she's using it—a cup of tea and small plate of crackers, fruit, and cured meats that Joséphine brought in about ten minutes after Eloise had sat down.

It's impossible to not study her as she works, her laptop perched on her lap. Some of her black hair drifted loose from the haphazard bun on the crown of her head to float around her face, her feet bare and ridiculously distracting. She shifts too frequently, reaching for the tea or a snack blindly, but her eyes never leave the screen in front of her. Does she know how many expressions she has while working? Her eyes narrow, a line between her brows as her focus intensifies; her lips purse and shift to the side as she's debating a decision; the smallest smile graces her lips and her eyes crinkle when she's pleased with her work.

It's infuriating how much I want to do nothing but watch her work.

She only looks towards me a handful of times, seeming to study me, and her gaze burns every second I'm her focus.

It's equally infuriating how my cock twitches each time I become her focus. Instead of addressing the issues of The Barrows, increasingly imaginative plans of every way to explore Eloise's body fill my thoughts.

My cock is at half-mast as I picture striding over to the unassuming human, taking her laptop from her flying fingertips and setting it aside as I grip her chin with one hand and force her eyes to meet mine. She'll glare at me for daring to interrupt her, but I'll silence her fury by holding her in place as I taste her lips before delving between them.

Eloise won't melt against me right away, not with the fire of independence burning inside of her. She'll resist, just enough to make sure I know she isn't like all the other humans who fall at my feet. Then she'll give in. To a degree.

Will she try to take control? Or will she submit like a little lamb and bare her neck and body to me? How far will she let me explore under the guise of letting me feed from her?

My cell phone vibrates in my pocket, yanking me from my indiscretions and back to the present. It's Kasar. I look at Eloise as I bring the phone to my ear, swiping it as I do. Her wide eyes are boring into mine, her lower lip trapped between her teeth.

"Kasar." With his name, her back straightens and she closes her laptop.

"I've got the girl," he replies, straight to the point. "There was no way to avoid casualties. I've sent Lan and Malachi the coordinates to deal with the mess."

Damn. I'd hoped to have two vampires alive for questioning. I clear my expression as I hold Eloise's gaze.

"And Deidre?" I ask, more for Eloise than my own care. Eloise stands, her laptop almost tumbling to the floor before she catches it. I hold up a finger, silently ordering her to wait, but the woman moves until she's at the side of my desk. She's close enough I could reach out and pull her onto my lap.

Kasar hesitates, which is telling. I wait him out, not breaking eye contact with the woman beside me.

"Has Deidre ever used Rapture?" my most trusted vampire asks at last.

Only Eloise can answer that question.

I gentle my voice, in spite of Kasar being able to hear. At least, I lower my voice enough to prevent others from hearing our conversation, my inner circle still vacated from the house.

"You said Deidre isn't using Rapture," I begin, taking in every slight change in Eloise at my words. "How certain are you of that, and has she ever used it before?"

Eloise shakes her head, her eyes hard. "No." Her voice is full of conviction. "Deidre and I have tried weed, but she doesn't like not being in control. She doesn't even have more than two cocktails unless she's at home."

I nod once sharply. "You heard her," I say into the phone.

"Why—what's going on?" Eloise pushes, taking a step closer and I shoot a warning look, making her freeze in place but now without a scowl.

"They drugged her then," Kasar replies. "I'm taking her to a safe house now, but I've had to bind her for her own safety. She's fucked-up high."

"Do what you must to keep her safe and alive," I order. I refuse to accept that Eloise may walk away from me in the next forty-eight hours because she dies from an overdose of the drug I'm supposed to control.

"Noted—fuck!" Kasar bites out the curse, snarling viciously.

"Kasar?" His name is a command.

"I'm being pursued. I'll call later."

The line goes dead and I toss the phone to the desk with a scowl.

"What's going on?" Eloise demands and I hold up a finger again as I reach for the phone. As I do, it lights up with a notification—a message from Malachi. Unlocking it, it takes less than a glance to note the confirmation of Kasar's assignment. I respond with the information that Kasar's being pursued but didn't request backup, though he and Lan should be ready to do so.

Lan, no doubt, will be hoping to be let off his leash and wet his teeth.

Turning the screen off, I return my attention to the increasingly irritated Eloise. Her arms are now crossed, and I can't help appreciating how the pose pushes her breasts up as if offering them to me to worship.

"Well?"

I steeple my fingers before I reply. "Kasar has Deidre. Her captors are dead, though others are now in pursuit. He is taking her to a safe location."

Her face pales when I tell her of the pursuit, then frowns at the last. "He isn't coming here?"

I raise an eyebrow, giving her a sardonic look.

"And have the fight brought here? That is not how war works, little lamb."

She rolls her eyes. "This isn't war—"

I stand up, pressing a finger to her lips to silence her. "It is, in fact, war, Eloise. It is a war that started months ago, before your friend ever stumbled into it. Kasar will keep her safe. If not, you will be free to leave as I agreed."

I move the finger from her lips over her cheek and then along her jaw, taking in every inch of her face. She's beautiful; soft, filled with life and fire, a spine of steel wrought from a life of hardship. Something in me screams to protect her, to spoil her, to take care of the lioness before me who should never have needed to grow claws.

"I want to talk to her," Eloise says, her tone nowhere as demanding as her words. My finger traces a line down the column of her neck to where her pulse flutters.

"When it is safe to do so," I say, my fangs elongating as I breathe her in. She gasps when my hand moves from a brushing tease to gripping the back of her neck, my thumb firmly pressed into her cheek just below her ear. She moves as if to push me away, her hands pausing just before they press against my chest.

I turn, forcing her to turn with me until her ass is pressed against my desk. With a bend of my knees, I grab the back of her thigh just under her ass and lift her until she's seated where I want her. She lets her legs widen as she stares at me with wide dark eyes, her chest rising and falling. I can smell the fear and anticipation coming from her as her pulse speeds up.

"Good girl," I murmur, my cock twitching as Eloise inhales at the praise, the faintest notes of arousal reaching my nose.

It would be so easy to pull her core against me, to let her feel how hard I am against her heat. I won't, though, not yet.

"What—what are you doing?" she asks in a whisper, as if she hadn't expected me to feed so soon after last night.

My hunger for Eloise will never be satisfied.

I tilt her head to the side, trailing my hand up to the top of her thigh, along her side, until I'm gripping her with my thumb just under her breast. I lower my head until I can scent her hair, her temple, her neck; relishing her as I would a priceless bottle of wine.

"I'm hungry," I whisper against her earlobe, my cock straining as she shudders in response.

"Do you have to draw it out?" she grits out, struggling to take control of the situation and I smile as I tilt her head far enough to force a slight strain. I will always remind her who is really in control here.

I scrape my fangs over the practically invisible silver scar tissue from last night. To the human eye, they're undetectable, but my eyes find them unfailingly, just as I can smell myself on her neck. A possessive growl rumbles in my chest as I grip her head and neck tighter, and my fangs elongate with anticipation.

"Your blood is like fine wine," I murmur, enjoying how my lips brush against her neck. This close, I can hear the seductive beat of her heart, the blood pumping underneath my touch. "I wish to savor you."

Pheromones roll off of Eloise; an intoxicating perfume that has the primal beast in me salivating for more than her blood.

Without waiting for her response, I sink my fangs into her neck with perfect accuracy over my previous marks. Her hands land on my chest, fisting my shirt and wrinkling the expensive pressed fabric. Rich, coppery ambrosia teases my tongue and I retract the fangs, keeping my lips sealed over the bite. I drink deeply, unable to stop the satisfied groan as I swallow her down.

Eloise's head goes limp, leaning back and relying on my grip to keep her upright even as she clings to my shirt. Her legs close against me, and I drop my hand at her side to grip her thigh, not interested in resisting my desire for the human. The moan that escapes her when I pull her against my waist makes me smile against her neck. I relax my grip on her neck and slide my hand down until it's splayed between her shoulder blades.

Learning forward, I tip her back and one of her

hands slams backwards to prop herself up even as her head drops back, keeping her throat open to me. She gasps and jolts when my arousal presses against her hot core, and I grind down harder against her, eager for the day when she begs me to take her with my cock as well my fangs.

Her nipples are hard against my chest, and her other hand has slid up my shoulder to my neck, as if she can control me as I had her.

A sharp scent breaks through the haze of feeding, along with purposefully loud footsteps. I growl again, and the footsteps hesitate before continuing. Dammit.

I ease Eloise upright, no longer suckling at her neck and instead lapping the punctures with my tongue to promote quick healing, as well as clean her neck of any blood to tempt my visitor.

I will be the only vampire to taste her sweetness.

I pull away, sated and yet not nearly enough. Especially as she looks at me with eyes glazed with pleasure, the scent of her arousal drowning out every other emotion. Her brown eyes go to my lips, her hand sliding from my neck to my chest as I straighten, and damn, I'm tempted to give in to that silent plea.

But no, I won't kiss her until she asks. And after I pull my hips back from hers, the haze of desire fades quickly, her brows narrowing in silent accusation.

"Ashe will be here in a moment," I say, before

darting my tongue out to steal another taste of her blood.

Eloise hops off of the desk, scrubbing at her neck with the heel of her palm as I fall back enough for her to escape. She's at the chair, collecting her laptop, teacup and half-empty plate when the vampire in question taps a knuckle on the opened door.

"Leave the dishes," I order her as I gesture for Ashe to enter. "Someone else will collect them."

She ignores me entirely, balancing the cup on the plate carefully on top of her laptop, and heads to the doorway.

"Hello, Ashe," she greets politely. "Have you been able to check on my plants?"

The dark-haired vampire smiles down at her, and I grip the back of my chair tightly, gritting my teeth to keep back the jealous demand he never smile again.

"I have," he answers. "In fact, I'm glad you're here. I was going to suggest I bring them here, as it may be some time before Deidre returns to your apartment."

Eloise sends me a scathing and suspicious look, before turning back to Ashe, her tone full of more grace than she's ever spoken with me. "I would appreciate that. Hopefully Deidre will be back soon, but she's not the greatest with plants."

"I'll see it done tonight, Ms. Morse," he murmurs and steps aside to let her pass.

As she does, she frees a hand and pats him affectionately on his chest and the leather of my chair rends under my grip. Ashe raises a brow but Eloise never looks back, disappearing with steady steps towards the stairs that'll take her downstairs.

I want to bend her over my knee and spank her ass red until she can't sit for a week.

Without being asked, Ashe closes the door before taking a seat in one of the intentionally uncomfortable chairs directly in front of my desk. He pointedly eyes my hands on the back of the chair.

"Problem, sire?" he asks, clearly amused.

I let go of the chair, wrapping up the riotous emotions inside until I once again am the composed stone-hearted king of vampires.

"None I cannot address myself," I answer, taking my seat with casual grace. I gesture to the phone he's slid out of his suit jacket's pocket. "You have the information I requested?"

Ashe's thumb sweeps over the screen and a moment later a notification pings on my monitor. I lean forward, opening it as he presents his findings.

"Michael Garner has a clean background," he begins as I pull up the appropriate document file, my eyes narrowed on the information. "Too clean."

"So I see," I murmur.

It was the perfect resume and work history for an up-and-coming Topside politician. Good grades, no fights at his elementary schools—all of which are public, though he attended a well-respected private university, double majoring in business law and global geopolitics. His extracurriculars were tailored for government officials: debate team, civil activism, volunteering community service, and so on. He graduated summa cum laude and secured coveted internships within the Topside governing body before being offered an opportunity as an aide to a councilman. A councilman he no doubt hopes to replace when the man's term is up.

It reeks of deceit.

I close the file, leaning back in the chair, finger tapping at the end of the leather armrest. "And the other information?"

"We've collected photos, as you've requested, though the recordings will be more interesting to you," he answers without hesitation. "If I can offer my opinion?"

Ashe has been with me for nearly three hundred years. His opinions are often correct. I wave for him to continue.

He pockets his phone and crosses one leg over the other. "He might be connected to the Rapture leak, but he's not one of the big players. He visits the brothels down here, but only indulges in Rapture in the safety of his home. His personal visits to the Barrows are highly discreet and he hires a witch to create a glamor enchantment. He never thought to ask her to mask his scent, and she didn't bother to elucidate him. Humans will be fooled, but no creature with an elevated sense of scent will be."

I hum in understanding. "The people running this offense are too clever to miss something as vital as scent."

He nods in agreement. He gestures to the computer. "As for the rest of it, it's disappointingly cliché. He's arrogant, believes himself to be the power behind the seat since Councilman Silas defers most of his duties to Garner. He's single, though he'll have dinner with the right socialite. He'll fuck any woman who fawns over him and is discreet. He also has a list of women he considers eligible for marriage, most of them from high-profile or powerful families."

Ashe is correct in how disappointing Garner's proclivities are, but it makes tonight's dinner with him much easier.

"Thank you," I say, stopping Ashe before he can offer any more information. "I'll look over the rest of the files, though I doubt I'll find anything surprising."

He cocks his head, rather than leaving as I expect and after a pointed moment, I let out an irritated sigh.

"What is it?"

Ashe's face is carefully blank. "Are you certain the bargain with Ms. Morse is beneficial?"

I narrow my eyes at him, resisting the urge to snap at the inquiry. Ashe is unfailingly loyal and has a strong sense of survival. He wouldn't be asking if he felt it unnecessary. Lan, on the other hand, would ask just to goad me into a fight.

"Is there something that you've discovered since you delivered her dossier this morning?"

I combed over every word in every file Ashe had delivered in the early hours before dawn.

"No, sire," he admits, his tone still even. "I would be derelict in my duties, though, if I didn't note how you react around her."

Now I bare my teeth in a silent snarl; Ashe remains unfazed. "I can handle Ms. Morse," I say, irritation sharpening the words. "She is a tool with a purpose and once she no longer is needed, our bargain ends."

I don't say that she'll return to her life Topside and Ashe notes the omission but wisely doesn't offer further comment.

"Now, leave," I order, still irritated. "I have work to do before dinner with Mr. Garner. And get her damn plants here."

"The car will be ready at five, sire," Ashe says as he stands and heads towards the door, leaving me alone in my office.

I bite back the growl clawing at my ribs; at the agitation fueled by Eloise's blood seeping into my veins; at Ashe's question; at the reality I must face.

Eloise Morse is a threat, rushing in my veins taunting the beast within.

Chapter Nine
ELOISE

All I can think when I look at myself in the full-length mirror in the massive walk-in closet that Ambrose dubbed the "wardrobe" is holy shit. I turn from side to side, craning my neck to check out the back of the positively sinful dress that Ambrose picked for me. I wanted to be annoyed when I saw the garment bag and the attached note with only "Wear this" on it. I was almost just petty enough to pick out a different dress, and I'd made up my mind to wear something else if I didn't like it after I tried it on.

I can't even be mad about how much I love the dress.

Black as night, its thin satin straps drape down into a cowl neck to offer a generous tease of cleavage. The rest of the dress hugs my curves until my hips, where it flares out over my ass down to my ankles. It's practically backless, with the fabric gathered to drape just below the small of my back, showing off the dimples on either side of my spine. I'd look short, but there's a slit that goes all the way up to the top of my thigh and somehow it makes me look as tall as Deidre, and I'm not even wearing shoes yet.

It's a simple dress, one that I would have dismissed had I been choosing for myself, even if I could afford a dress like it. Seriously, this dress has to be at least five hundred dollars.

And it makes me want to purr like the cat who got the cream. It's sultry and sexy in a way that makes me feel powerful. Deidre is always going on about the right clothes making a woman, and damn, now I absolutely can't argue with her.

Joséphine had helped me with my hair and makeup before I got dressed. The vampire tamed my hair into a French twist then dusted makeup over my cheeks and eyes as if she knew I hated a ton of makeup. She'd laid out the ruby teardrop pendant earrings without comment, and when I asked, she simply said that I can't go without jewelry and left me to put them on and stand in front of the mirror at last.

I smooth the satin over my stomach, nerves rushing forward as I meet my own gaze. I look like myself, at least, and yet I can't help feeling like an imposter playing dress-up. Affluence has never been a part of my life.

The hairs on my neck raise and my eyes dart across the mirror before landing on him. Ambrose is leaning against the wall, his hands in his front pockets, studying me. Warmth washes over me when his eyes drag up to meet mine, my core pulsing at the memory of him standing between my legs, his desire hard against me and mouth exploring my neck.

No, not exploring, I remind myself. Feeding. He was feeding on me, because that's what I am to him.

Grasping onto the clarity with both hands, I raise a brow. "I thought vampires didn't have reflections."

He snorts and his mouth twitches, like he's holding back a smile at my goading. I don't know what it is about Ambrose that makes me want to needle and push until he snaps. I'm never like this; I can keep my attitude in check when I need to, and for the most part, I'm actually pretty nice. This man, this vampire, is dangerous and he can kill me, after making me endure incredible pain, or order someone else to do it.

Yet I still push, poking and prodding until I get under his skin, to see what he does when I finally piss him off enough.

Then, if I survive it, I'll know what type of man he really is.

"You're gorgeous, Eloise," he says, instead of responding. My cheeks go from pink to red as I have to break his gaze. I ignore the butterflies his words set free in my ribcage and make my way to the cream tuft divan that sits directly in the center of the wardrobe, opening the shoebox I'd set out. Ambrose hadn't picked out the shoes for me, which meant I'm absolutely planning to wear the heels I fell in love with that morning.

I ease one out of the box, smiling softly at the shoe as if it's a beloved pet. Before I can lower it to slip my foot into, Ambrose's hand is on the shoe. He takes advantage of my surprise, taking it from me with a serious expression.

He kneels in front of me and my eyes must almost be popping from my head.

"Allow me." His voice washes over me and I'm helpless against the effect he's having on me, frozen in place except for watching his hands move.

He guides the bottom of my calf upwards; the black satin parts as my foot rises, exposing my leg all the way up to my thigh. Ambrose guides my foot through the straps, before expertly buckling the ankle strap with a single hand. Rather than letting my foot fall, he lowers it before slipping his hand into the slit of my dress to repeat the process.

As he reaches for the second shoe, he speaks, his head bent just enough to hide his eyes from me.

"Tonight is another move in the war." His long, graceful fingers brush my ankle as he fastens the buckle. Rather than letting my foot go, he holds it gently in the middle, his fingers wrapping around my arch and his thumb presses just below my ankle bone. He meets my gaze, his eyes golden and bright, and something in them has me swallow back any retort I might have given. "Your friend is with Kasar at a safe house. Her captors had kept her high on Rapture, dangerously so. Kasar will see her through this, though."

"Thank you." I smile weakly at him, thankful that Deidre is in safe hands and terrified that she might get hurt from the very drug she was investigating. "How is this connected to tonight?" I ask after a moment, considering the first part of what he'd said.

His thumb strokes small circles, almost distracting me. I narrow my focus. I might not have known Ambrose for long at all, hell, I still don't know him, but I know enough to know he does nothing without intention.

"We will be dining with Michael Garner." —why did that name sound vaguely familiar?—"He is connected to the group who is selling Rapture outside of my control, though we have not fully discovered how. That is what tonight is about."

My heart quickens, and my mind starts working through different scenarios. Anger turns my blood hot. "He could be connected to Deidre's kidnapping."

Ambrose nods once, his eyes becoming steel. "Which is why I'm here. I need you to agree to something, or you cannot attend. I do not have time to handle you as well as Garner." He waits for me to object, but when I say nothing, he continues. "If you attend dinner with me, you must obey me without hesitation and without question. Do you understand?"

"Are you going to make me do anything perverted?"

"No," he answers. "But I have my part to play and you must play it as well, or we will not get what we need from him."

Understanding dawned over me, and I softened my gaze. "You're Ambrose d'Vil, king of vampires and the Barrows," I say, only understanding in my voice. If this man could have any knowledge about who to make pay for Deidre, I'll do whatever it takes. "What role do you need me to be? Sugar baby? Devoted follower? Aloof mistress?"

Ambrose's stony expression changes as he gives me a satisfied look. He frees my foot and stands before holding his hand out. I put my hand in his, allowing him to help me rise onto the tall shoes. He keeps my hand raised, escorting me back before the mirror so I can take in the entire look. He takes a half step back, becoming my shadow in the mirror.

I barely take in the shoes' effect, entranced by our reflection. I expected my feeling of power would diminish with Ambrose behind me, given that he dominates whatever room he's in.

Ambrose is stunning in his tailored classic black on black ensemble. Rather than clashing with different hues of black, we complement each other and the dark color isn't washing me out. The opposite, in fact.

"Black suits you," Ambrose says, and when I look up at his reflection, his eyes are taking me in.

"I can say the same," I answer. "Thank you for this."

His gold eyes meet my brown ones. "I take care of what is mine. Now, let's go. Ashe is waiting for us."

Comfort wraps around my shoulders at his words, and I sway towards him slightly. When he talks like that, being his doesn't make me feel chained. Ambrose follows me out of our supposedly shared suite and walks beside me down the flights of stairs, his hands in his pockets.

"What's my reputation, Eloise?" he asks and I look at him from the corner of my eye, my hand sliding over the banister as we descend.

"Powerful, dangerous, controlling, deals in bargains," I list off without hesitation. "You're the boogeyman of Topside, a monster not to be fucked with. You control the Barrows."

"Precisely." Ambrose places a hand near my lower back, ushering me through the rooms that'll lead to the garage. "I am a king, like those of old, and no one questions me. Especially not you tonight, Eloise. You know what power is to those who run Topside. Tonight, you are an example of my power.

I'm the king of a dark world, and to Garner you are an eager subject."

I nod my understanding as we approach the garage door.

"And, Eloise," he says. I stop at my name and tilt my face up to look at him, curious. His eyes are darker now, and I notice how close we are. My breath stills in my lungs, waiting. He tips his head closer, and I'm pinned under his look. "If you disobey me, you will be punished."

I'VE NEVER BEEN to this area of Newgate, with the ultra-modern high-rises, but before now I guess I never had a reason too. After his promise of punishment, I'm quiet. Not because I'm afraid of him. Because I'm too busy trying to avoid thinking about all the punishments and how much I worry I'd enjoy them.

The elevator doors open to the foyer of the restaurant, which takes up the entire floor of the skyscraper, and Ambrose gives me a look, a silent question of my resolve. I nod, determined to ignore the reactions this vampire is causing in my body and focus on my role. I'll play it by ear, depending on how Michael Garner reacts. On the drive, I recalled why his name was familiar. He's been in the news a lot, always for something political or for the government. Who knows, he could be as wholesome as he appears; if he's having dinner with Ambrose, though, he's probably as dirty as the rest.

Ambrose offers his arm and guides my hand into the crook of his elbow as we step out of the elevator. The host, a tall olive-skinned man with a bald head, steps away from the podium at our arrival.

"Mr. d'Vil. It is good to see you again," he says with a polite tilt of his head. "Mr. Garner is already seated. May I show you to the room?"

Ambrose doesn't offer a verbal response, just a seemingly irritated jerk of the chin. Stealing a glance at his expression before we walk through the open double doors, I see the icy mask he wore when I first walked into his office. Taking his cue, I school my features so that I'm his aloof companion, ignoring the looks other diners give us.

Because there are certainly people looking. I squeeze Ambrose's arm a bit tighter, needing his presence to ground me as we stride between tables. The restaurant is one of those low-lit places with leather padded chairs and perfectly white long tablecloths over each table. The walls are a dark reddish brown with gold fabric hanging between the massive windows that overlook Newgate. Between the lighting and warm colors, it's as if each table is secluded in its own private world, despite being less than five feet from its neighbor.

I make eye contact with an older white man, his

hair thinning and skin soft with age. From the cut of the straining suit jacket and the fancy watch on his wrist, he's full of the money a place like this exists, and it's confirmed by the slim, overly dolled up young woman across from him. He squares his shoulders as we approach, his eyes darting to Ambrose before back to me. Or, more accurately, to my breasts and then to my leg which is playing peek-a-boo with every step.

I can't blame him. My tits totally look sexy in this dress.

When he meets my gaze again, we're almost to the table and his companion turns to see what's captured her date's interest. I bring my other hand up to Ambrose's arm, and give the older man a quick up and down before looking at him disdainfully. I wait for the irritated expression to form on his face before meeting the gaze of his date. She has to be younger than me. I have absolutely no issue with sugar babies, and I meet her eyes to give her a sincere smile. I'm not after her piggy bank, and she gives me an answering smile with a quick dart to Ambrose, as if saying, "Well done."

We pass their table and Ambrose lowers his head enough to speak into my ear. "Do you enjoy emasculating men?"

I bite the inside of my lip to control my reaction, but I can't stop the light heat on my cheeks. Figuring I should just own it, I look up at him, letting out my

Cheshire grin. But then I hesitate, my smile faltering. "Should I not have? I don't want to mess this up." The consequences if I mess up are more than whatever punishment Ambrose has in mind.

The slow grin Ambrose gives me is one of pure predatory pride. "I enjoy watching you do so. Do not stop on my account, ma belle lionne."

Warmth curls in my core, but the new confidence straightening my shoulders and spine is what holds my attention as we walk into the private dining room with a single table in the middle. Ambrose reaches up and covers my hand with his cool one, giving it a slight squeeze as if to tell me our game has started.

I smile darkly, eager to see this through for Deidre.

Chapter Ten
ELOISE

Michael Garner stands, his eyes darting between us as he keeps a pleasant and placid expression. He wasn't expecting Ambrose to have a guest, that much is obvious.

"Ambrose," he greets with familiarity, holding his hand out for the vampire to take. I've never heard someone call Ambrose his first name, and from Ambrose's expression, Michael hasn't earned the right. The power plays have already started, and Ambrose counters Michael by ignoring him entirely as he pulls out the chair opposite of Michael's spot and sits. Ambrose doesn't leave me to wonder what side I'm supposed to sit on when he gives my hand a firm tug and I find myself seated on his leg, my back resting against his chest and shoulder. His left arm wraps around my waist, as if chaining me to him like I'd insist on my own chair.

Which, to be fair, in normal circumstances I would.

"Mr. Garner," Ambrose succinctly replies before snapping a finger. I keep my eyes on the white cloth in front of us, my attention on the man's reaction. He frowns, but he gets his feet under him quickly and takes his seat again, the pleasant expression back in place. A server appears at our side as if they'd been waiting for the vampire's signal. Without taking his gaze from Michael, he orders, "A bottle of Chateau Grands Arbres. Sparkling water with ice and lemon, two wedges each."

I better be getting some of that wine, I think as the server disappears.

Ambrose's hand loosens slightly on my waist, his fingers stroking me as if silently telling me to relax.

When I'd made the bargain to be Ambrose's for three months, I definitely didn't picture decadent dinners in expensive gowns with dirty politicians. It's better than just sitting in a room waiting for him to order me to him three times a day for my blood. I turn my full attention to Michael, who's looking at me with amusement. I lower my brows in a disapproving glare. He looks at Ambrose, and I get a chance to study him.

Young. Wholesome. The sympathetic and eager young man hoping to turn Newgate into a better place. When really he's just another power-hungry political snake, who is connected to the people who hurt my friend.

"If I'd known you were bringing a guest, I would have brought someone to keep her from growing bored," Michael says with a boyish grin, inviting Ambrose to join in the joke.

I open my mouth to snark, but Ambrose's fingers press into my hip as he speaks. He looks to me and, with his free hand, drags a finger possessively along my jaw and down my throat to where he's fed from me twice now. I can't stop the shiver of pure sensation as his fingers touch the spot; the area around the bite marks is so sensitive and each time he touches there, the pleasure is impossible to resist. I melt more against Ambrose, his cool body tempering my heating blood but it's not enough to extinguish it entirely.

"On the contrary, Mr. Garner," Ambrose murmurs, his voice decadent. "She is here to ensure I do not get bored."

The server returning with the requested bottle of wine saves Michael from having to respond, but I watch through half-lidded eyes as the politician's eyes flash with envy and... desire. He wants me, I realize, but on the heels of that thought another comes. It's not me specifically he wants. He wants what Ambrose has. Seductive power and adoring worshipers.

I prevent a huff of laughter by accepting the glass of burgundy wine Ambrose presses into my hand

and taking a sip. It's incredible, and despite its smooth, rich flavors, I can sense the strength of the alcohol. I need to keep my wits about me, so I reach forward and set it on the table in front of me before leaning back against the vampire again.

This dinner isn't a subtle trade of information between allies. Ambrose is taunting Michael Garner with his power, making it clear that Michael doesn't matter to Ambrose and in turn, making Michael want to get closer to the throne the vampire sits on.

Recognizing the play for what it is, I loosen my body and languidly bring up my right hand until I'm stroking Ambrose's neck. I keep my eyes on Michael, as if interested in what he has to say but making it clear that my attention is on the true power in the room. Ambrose takes a sip of his own wine, before speaking again.

"You requested this meeting." He sounds bored already, leaning his head towards my hand to encourage me. "What is it that I can do for you, Mr. Garner?"

Michael, the experienced politician in spite of his young age, doesn't let his act drop at the blunt question. He settles back into his chair, one hand wrapped around a tallboy of amber liquid, giving us an easy smile. "I believe some of our interests align and that a partnership could be quite beneficial for Newgate."

Ambrose's hand strokes upward over my side, the satin easing his way, until his fingers are teasingly close to the underside of my breast. Michael's eyes flick to the movement before he quickly recovers and continues. I'm fighting to keep my expression bored as I focus on what Michael is saying and not the sensations Ambrose's hands are building in my skin. The satin dress offers little defense against Ambrose's meandering caresses.

When Ambrose turns his attention to me again, as if more interested in playing with his pet, it's even harder to focus on what the other man is trying to suggest. Having the full weight of Ambrose's attention is as heady as it was before, and I shift, rubbing my thighs together to try to stop the ache growing there.

By the time food arrives—a thick, rare steak—Michael's calm demeanor is starting to crack under the vampire's supposed distraction. The entrees must have been ordered beforehand, and there's only one plate on our side. Like the wine, I hold back my bratty impulse, and besides, I enjoy a good steak. I wait a moment after we're alone in the room before giving Ambrose a questioning look. He turns a pointed look to the meal and back, and it takes me a moment to understand.

I pick up the fork and steak knife, cutting off a small piece of the very rare steak. I raise the fork, giving him a coy look as his golden eyes fill with approval, his face turned towards me to accept the bite.

I wrap my lips around the fork, letting my eyes close as I make a soft sound of pleasure. When I open my eyes again, Ambrose is still looking at me but the approval is gone and a different promise is in his eyes. My stomach flips and I'm so tempted to take the next bite for myself again. But I know it's not the time and bring the next bite to his lips, lungs struggling as I catch the slightest glimpse of a fang and his tongue before his mouth closes around the fork.

Despite our company, feeding Ambrose feels intimate, like this is just for us and not an act for the game we're playing.

I'm aroused and there's no way Ambrose doesn't know it.

Apparently our distraction has gone on too long when a glass is set down with a loud thump. I startle, my head snapping around to look at Michael. All of his wholesome, eager appearance has disappeared. Now he's looking at us with barely concealed irritation, his grip on his own knife and fork turning his knuckles white.

Michael narrows his gaze onto Ambrose, who is still relaxed around me, his fingers still tracing senseless patterns over the satin of my dress along my side and down to my hip.

"I've taken a great risk to meet with you so publicly, Ambrose—"

"Let me stop you there," Ambrose says, his voice indifferent as he reaches for his wine glass. He brings it to my lips, and I take a long sip, my iron will softens against the gold of his gaze. When he lowers the glass, his eyes turn threatening as he directs his attention back to Michael. Michael, to his credit, shuts up and his irritation gives way to hesitation and worry. "You need me, Mr. Garner. While your offer was enough to get me to agree to this meeting, it is simply not enough to be worth my time and money. There is one thing I want from you, and as long as you hold up your side, you will have my support when it comes to your election to the Newgate council."

I watch Michael with interest as he processes what Ambrose said. I relate to the unease and conflict in his eyes; after all, my original offer to Ambrose got a similar dismissal. Ambrose waits, and eventually Michael's desire to take his boss's place wins out. He sets down the cutlery he'd been clutching with a death grip and finally looks at Ambrose with the appropriate respect.

"What do you want?" he asks, less confident than when Ambrose delivered the same question at the start of dinner.

"It's simple enough," Ambrose suggests, his tone light. "You've been visiting the same brothel in the Barrows for months, but for the last three weeks, you've gone elsewhere."

Michael doesn't move; a mouse cat between a cat's paws.

Ambrose's voice is sinister and low. "You've been using Rapture more often, too. You see, there is nothing that goes unseen by me in the Barrows. You aren't using your usual supplier either."

Michael's face turns red. "Are you attempting to blackmail me?"

"Hardly," Ambrose says after a snort. "If I were, I would use the debt you owe to the CEO of Southbay, from the loan you needed to sweep all your ugly transgressions away during your college years. How is your son, by the way? He's what, ten now?"

There must be something wrong with me. Ambrose's delivery of precise blow after blow with such a casual tone is one of the hottest things I've ever experienced. The vampire king is displaying his power without hubris or arrogance as those in Topside expect. He doesn't need their validation, their acceptance. He's brutal and savage and the cruel glint in his eyes lets Michael and me both know he has no qualms about the silent threats in his words. No, not threats. Promises.

"You're a bastard, d'Vil," Michael growls and throws his cloth napkin on his plate before slamming back his whiskey. "Just fucking tell me what it is you want."

"When my people contact you, you will give us everything you know regarding your new associates and their supply of Rapture. If you leave anything out, the next time you're asked—I will be the one asking questions, and you really do not want that."

Ambrose d'Vil looks every part the tyrannical king with his lip curled up with disgust, high enough that a fang reminds Michael of what he's dealing with. *I want to kiss him.*

"Fine," Michael spits out and gets up, without saying another word, he storms out of the private room like a petulant hurricane.

Ambrose toys with the delicate stem of the wine glass as the room is silent, save for my breathing and pounding heartbeat. I stare at his profile, drinking in his fierce beauty. It's as if he was masterfully carved from marble, the sculptor capturing both a king of legend and a beast of infamy. When he turns to look at me, I don't let myself think.

I slide my hands into his thick, dark hair and kiss him.

Chapter Eleven
AMBROSE

I grip the back of Eloise's head, holding her to me as I take control of the kiss. The mouthwatering scent of her arousal had steadily grown throughout dinner and Mr. Garner was fortunate to have the dull senses of a human. Had he been able to smell Eloise, I would have killed him and to hell with the consequences.

Eloise's sweet musky scent of pleasure is for me and me alone.

I fist her hair, swallowing her soft mews as I own her mouth. The rich woody wine and the savory taste of steak isn't enough to hide the taste of her. She pushes her tongue back against mine, fighting me for control and I relent enough to suck her tongue into my mouth, scraping her tongue with a sharp fang. Small drops of blood only complement her flavor and

I grip her hip with my other hand, needing more of her.

She freezes in my hold, but I don't relent—I can't relent. A growl escapes me as I drag my lips from hers and down her throat. I hate how Eloise makes me feel—powerless against this craving I've had since the first moment I tasted her blood.

Her hands release me, landing on my shoulders and her blunt nails dig into my skin. She pushes against me, and I growl again at her weak attempt to separate us. I mouth her neck, tilting her head back until it's entirely bared to me. I have no physical need to feed, but I seek out the spot that I've bitten her at regardless. I latch my lips over the sensitive flesh, pulling at her hip until she's straddling my lap.

Eloise gasps out the most beautiful sound, and I yank her down against me so she feels what she does to me. She's no longer pushing me away; instead she rolls her hot core against me, separated by nothing but the thin material of her panties.

I'm drunk on the taste of her skin and the smell of her need. I sweep my hand down over her bare thigh, stroking her smooth skin before moving higher, intent on feeling her without barriers.

The moment my thumb strokes the damp lace covering her swollen folds, Eloise jolts. She pushes away from me, unable to go far before her back hits the edge of the table. Her pupils are blown wide and her lips are swollen as she pants.

"No," she gasps out, her entire body tense and ready to fight.

I look at her lips and back to her eyes, my thumb still pressing against her sex. "No?" I ask, tendrils of anger slipping out from my black heart. I tighten my grip on her hair. No one tells me no. I am the king of the Barrows.

An acrid scent fills my nose, sweeping the red haze from my eyes at the sudden rise of it. Eloise's eyes are still wide, but now there's fear in her eyes. She trembles in my hold and I snarl. Her eyes squeeze closed at the harsh sound and I curse silently.

Eloise's fear repulses me, and it cuts the anger down as something else takes its place. She should never fear me.

I release her hair and pull my hand from the place I long to bury myself. Keeping my touch light, I take her hands from my shoulders and she opens her eyes once more.

"No," I intone, a promise in my eyes. I had told her that I wouldn't take her unless she begged, and I will keep my word even if it means she never asks. The thought of bedding her with only the sick, sour scent of her fear filling my nose sickens me. I keep the maelstrom of emotions off of my face as I release her to stand, my hands bracing her waist so she can get her feet under her.

Eloise looks to the floor, hiding from me and I

step away from the chair giving her the space she needs but I loathe.

Control. I will master this craving for her, this strange weakness she creates. I've fed from countless humans and have bedded more than I can remember. Eloise can be nothing to me beyond our bargain. Even when I convince her to stay, I must keep her at a distance.

There's too much at risk otherwise. The coin smoothed from age in my pocket is my reminder.

"Thank you," she whispers and I turn back towards her, frowning.

"Do not thank me." My words are harsher than I intend and she curls in on herself, suddenly so much smaller than the confident succubus of darkness from the beginning of dinner. I cross the distance between us and grip her chin, forcing her to meet my gaze. When she submits at last, I make a point of softening my hard voice. "You should never thank someone for the basic respect you deserve, ma belle lionne."

Her gaze fills with pain. Who has hurt this beautiful woman? If she ever shares their names, I won't send my soldiers to deal with them. I'll do it myself and enjoy every moment of it.

"Come." I tuck her hand into the crook of my elbow and guide her towards the closed door of the private dining room. "Ashe is waiting for us."

She squares her shoulders, mastering herself

before we walk through the now full restaurant. This time when I sense eyes on her, I glare at every man who would think to have her for their own. They flinch back, turning their focus back to their meals or dinner companions as they wait for me to pass or strike.

Eloise walks straighter as if she realizes there is no one giving her attention. She looks up at me as we reach the elevator bay beyond the entrance foyer and gifts me a sweet, small smile. I nod once and press the parking garage floor. It's been less than forty-eight hours, but soon Eloise will learn that I will protect her from more than appreciative or perverse looks.

When the elevator doors open, Ashe is waiting for us behind the wheel. I open the door for her, waiting until she is seated before closing the door and slapping the roof of the car twice. Ashe begins to pull away as I step back and Eloise looks at me, confusion evident on her face.

She said no and I will respect that. My restraint is holding on by the thinnest of threads. Too much of her scent and those threads will break.

I ball my fists, relishing the sharp pain as my nails dig into my skin, grounding me as the car disappears from view. Forcing out a hard breath, I move in the opposite direction towards one of the parking garage's many stairwells. When I enter it, I scowl, wishing I was back in the Barrows. At least those stairwells are filled with the smell of desperation and of lives disappearing into obscurity. Here in Topside, even the damn stairwells are clean.

There's nothing to drown out the smell of Eloise lingering on my body, her taste on my lips.

Growling, I kick the ground floor door open, warping the metal door and breaking it off one of the hinges. A few human women scream at the sound, their male companions stepping between them and me, even across the street. I bark out a harsh laugh. If I wanted their women, I'd be across the street and on them before they realize I've moved.

I don't want them though. There's only one woman who my body is aching for.

Damn it all to hell and back. Anger and desire war in my veins, burning me from inside out as my blackened heart struggles to stay within the barrier of ice it's trapped within.

I need a release. I need to fuck or kill.

I run until I'm near the edges of Topside, where the city is less pristine and affluent. Where buildings aren't perfect examples of modernity. With a crouch and a powerful jump, I sail upwards and land on the gravel-covered rooftop of the two-story building. From there, I make my way over rooftops towards the Barrows. Towards my den of depravity where I can remind myself who the fuck I am.

The Barrows is closer than Topsiders like to

think. Only a wide river separates Oldgate from Newgate, but it's wide enough the Topsiders feel they can ignore us. Grim satisfaction fills me at the thought. I don't want their holy piety in my city. It used to be that Topsiders would venture into my dark streets, believing they could save my people's souls. One such woman came to me herself, convinced that she could turn my heart into something that cares. She wanted to save me.

I relished breaking her until she craved every wicked thing she once hated. She'd come to save me and, by the end, was my personal pleasure toy. She hated how much she loved it.

And then I cast her out, done with her.

Her final words damned me to Hell, cursing my very existence. I didn't bother telling her that not even Hell wanted me. Why else was I still alive when I should have died? My soul was dammed long before my sire ever turned me.

Once I'm across the river, I turn east, away from Noir and towards my club Lush instead. Even this early, people will be there, wrapped in their dangerous vices. I take my time to get there, wrestling control over the tension within me. When I arrive, the need to lash out at every male has settled down into a hum of energy under my skin. I'll need to release it eventually, but that's why I'm here.

I stride through the metal door at the front, not

bothering with my personal entrance. I want to be seen. I want to remind everyone and myself who rules this place.

The vampire at the front bows his head, taking a step back from the podium to let me pass through the second door into the massive room filled with the smell of sex, blood, and drugs. I pause in the entrance, sucking in a deep breath of the hedonistic perfume. Vampires look at me, feeling my power ripple through the room. Other supernaturals take a moment longer to sense my presence. Only the humans on Rapture finally find me, their eyes glazed over with hardly any sense.

They're waiting to see what I'll do, trying to guess why I'm here when I rarely visit.

I ignore them all and make my way through the sinuous path towards a throne-like seat half in shadow. The building was once a turn of the century theater that I'd visited more than once at its prime. Now the seating had been ripped from the floors, replaced by leather couches or chairs. Each seating area's focus was not the stage as it once was. Instead, each area is its own play area.

St. Andrew's crosses, cages, hanging hooks, and more fill this place. Spanking benches, padded tables, and devices that look straight out of medieval dungeons. As I predicted, nearly half are already in use. Most of the room is dark, the only illumination is soft spotlights on the equipment of each area, allowing the players to see and be seen. The stage's thick velvet curtains are closed tonight, their stage lighting dark. I've never taken a partner there. I'm too damn possessive to let others view what is mine.

As I sink into my preferred chair, I reach for the riding crop kept in a quiver attached to the armrest. Running my fingers over the tight leather settles me into something more recognizable. Here, Eloise cannot control me. Here, no one defies me. Not even those who are dominant in nature.

My gaze lands on a familiar vampire currently taking a bull whip to a woman's ass, sex, and thighs as she's restrained by ankle spreaders. She's bent in half at the waist, her wrists secured to the spreader. Lan pauses in his strikes, the blond man looking at me with a sick smirk. He raises an eyebrow as he tilts his head towards the woman in question. I shake my head, uninterested in playing with his toy of the night.

Lan shrugs and returns to the woman, striking her harder, the end landing right between her folds with a wet, harsh crack. She screams, and he laughs before moving closer, his hands going to his belt.

People watch him with fascination, lust, and fear as he takes her. He's a favorite here, because his tastes run only to the extreme. When Lush first opened, I forced a vow from him. At Lush, he will never kill his plaything, whether it be through violence or draining their blood.

Only the most brave, or most high on Rapture, are willing to step into his play area.

A female wolf shifter steps up to me, a tray in her hands as she keeps her head tilted down subserviently. I take the tumbler, filled with a thick liquid that is black in the shadows. The female disappears as quickly as she appeared, and I bring the glass to my nose and inhale. I scrunch my nose in distaste. The blood is clean and free from any trace of past feedings. It should be satisfying, yet I can't drink it.

It's not *her*.

My growl causes those closest to me to tense, to warily look over their shoulders, but it's not them I'm angry at. My fury is directed at Eloise Morse, who by now might be asleep in my own bed. I'd thought to torment her by forcing her to stay in my room, but I didn't expect my own torment.

I want to kick down the door and rip the bedsheets from her supple body. My gaze blurs as I imagine what I would do, and my shaft fills, my arousal at dinner returning vehemently. My ears are filled with the sounds of pleasure before me as I lose myself to my fantasy.

Eloise would be sprawled out in her faded shirt and worn-out shorts instead of the silk and lace I want to wrap her in. Her dark hair would be splayed out around her, half of it escaping the tie she'd used.

She'd glare up at me, demanding to know what I thought I was doing.

Shifting, I release the button on my fly before stroking myself over the fabric. Closing my eyes, I focus on the Eloise of my thoughts.

I crawl onto the bed and over her, trapping her under me as she starts to breathe faster, pulled in by the rapid beating of her heart. Then I rip the clothing from her and feast my eyes on her soft, plump skin. I want to punish her for making me this way, for making me need her more than I've ever needed anything.

Idly, I release my turgid member, gripping it as I slowly stroke, slouching back into the leather armchair.

Returning to my thoughts, I move off the bed once more and drag her with me until she's on her knees at my feet with defiance in her eyes. I'd free my cock and push it against her lips, ordering her to take me in her sweet mouth. My beautiful lioness can't hide how much this is turning her on, how she craves my punishment as much as I want to give it. Her lips will part and I'll sink my cock in, forcing it past her gag reflex and into her throat until her face is pressed into my body.

I'll fill her with my scent as she's filled me with hers.

Blindly, I release myself for long enough to dip my hands in the warm blood beside me, before slicking it over myself. I tell myself it's Eloise's blood that is easing the slide of my hand as I stroke.

Eloise's eyes will stay open as I make her watch me punish her throat. I'll hold her head in place as I make her take me deep over and over again until tears run down her cheeks. I'll keep going, because I can smell how badly she wants me between her legs. But this isn't for her pleasure. It's her punishment for making me this way.

I stroke myself faster, the metallic scent of blood blending in with the rest of Lush's scents. I focus on the lavender and apricot which clings to my jacket and pants from where she sat earlier. The faintest scent of her arousal where she ground down against me.

In my thoughts, I pound into her and she moans as I spill down her throat, pulling her close enough to block off her airway.

My balls tighten, then with a groan I spill over my hand as I stroke hard, wishing it was her throat.

Breathing hard, I return to the present. Those here before me continue their own entertainment, and if anyone watched me, they didn't do so now.

Dammit, I was so wrapped up in Eloise that anyone could have attacked me and I would have been taken by surprise. Scowling once more at the infuriating woman in my bed, I reach below the chair for the stash of cloths there to quickly and angrily clean myself.

The worst part is there is no relief in the tension coiling around my spine. If anything, it's grown worse now that I've allowed myself to imagine what it could be like.

Putting myself away, I stand and straighten my clothing. I leave, taking the hidden door near my seat to head out my personal entry.

Anger fuels me as I race through the Barrows. Intent on fulfilling those thoughts that had me spilling into my hand hardens my spine as I don't bother climbing into my window. When I arrive, my guards have returned. I can sense Ashe and Malachi in their respective rooms on the second floor as I stalk through the dark house with silent footsteps.

Like the predator I am, I ease the door open to my bedroom, silent and smooth enough to not disrupt the air within.

I hit a wall, unable to move past the entrance as my eyes land on the sleeping woman of my torment. She's kept the curtains open and moonlight casts a silver beam across the bed, revealing the silvery skin uncovered by her tank top as she slumbers. Lavender and apricot assault me once more, but the other scent is what transfixes me.

I close the door behind me, never taking my eyes off of her. The anger disappears, washed away by her presence in my home. In my bed. Shaking my head with a hard jerk, as if trying to dislodge her from my senses, I retreat to the wardrobe in the bathroom.

The air is still humid, though the moisture from her shower has disappeared from the mirror. With clinical focus, I change out of the clothes that reek of Lush and my own pleasure and another human's blood in favor of the gray linen pants I prefer when I choose to actually sleep.

Drawn back to Eloise, I see she's shifted onto her side and now faces away from me. The faded scent of arousal is stronger now and I climb onto the bed, over her, drawn to the source of the smell. Her hand lays across the pillow in front of her face. Lowering my head, my attention on her every move, I'm like a damn wild animal as I breathe in the scent of her hand, my cock stirring and blood heating at its implication.

Eloise may have told me no at dinner, but like myself, she was driven to fill her desire. In my bed.

I steal a taste of her, darting my tongue to the tip of her finger, not allowing myself more than that.

Male satisfaction fills my chest and rather than give in to my urge to wake her by sucking her fingers clean of her taste, I move to the other side and slide under the blankets too.

She shifts at my weight sinking into the bed, and when I slide my arm under her pillow as I lay facing her, she shuffles close enough that her head is tucked under my chin. I wrap my arm around her and ignore the heat in my groin in favor of the gentle sensation of her breathing against my neck. I tuck the duvet up under her chin, knowing it's what she prefers.

I can be patient, I think as I close my eyes. Eloise wants me, even if she's fighting it. She will give in eventually and I'll get what I want. I always do.

Chapter Twelve
ELOISE

The air is warm, the humid heat seeping in through the window panes, but in spite of having the duvet pulled up under my chin, I'm at the perfect temperature as I wake up. I try to roll onto my back and freeze at the sensation of a body against me. The smell tells me what my body already has figured out, as the scent of rich leather and frankincense fills the air around me. Keeping my breath even, and hoping to hell my racing heartbeat doesn't wake the vampire up, I open my eyes. A bare chest fills my view, wide shoulders rising above mine as we lie facing each other. His arm is on top of the duvet, lying over my waist, his elbow bent so his hand can splay between my shoulder blades.

The shallow movement of Ambrose's chest is the only hint that he's still sleeping, but his embrace is firm enough I ease my head back to look at his face.

My breath catches as my heart dissolves into something warm and soft. Asleep, Ambrose doesn't look like the intimidating tyrant vampire king of a city perpetually in shadow. He doesn't look soft or gentle. I don't think Ambrose can ever look soft. Even asleep, he's all harsh lines—a statue of a beast at rest, rather than on the prowl.

I stare at his soft, partly open lips. The urge to trace them is almost too fierce to resist but the fact that my arms are tucked up against my chest and trapped against him prevents it. My cheeks burn as the audacity I'd had the previous night slams into my thoughts. Dropping my gaze to the hollow at Ambrose's throat, I try to not think about it. Which, of course, only makes me think about it more.

We kissed. I'd started it; whether I want to blame the role I slipped into, Ambrose's possessive hands, or my rebellious nature to fuck with men of authority, it happened after that yuppy asshole left with his tail between his legs. Ambrose isn't a bad boy. No, compared to him, bad boys are just that —boys.

Ambrose is king of the underworld that makes up the Barrows.

Maybe I have daddy issues or something, but the idea of a man with that much power focusing his desire on me does something to me. He doesn't give me butterflies, that's not intense enough. It's like he's a whirling vortex sucking me underneath the water, and fighting him only makes it so much sweeter when he wins.

My core clenches around nothing as I squeeze my eyes shut. It hasn't been nearly long enough for me to want Ambrose so badly, and yet I do. The only reason why I said no last night was because of where we were. When his thumb had stroked me over my panties, I'd been so close to coming that I almost screamed. Then I'd remembered that just on the other side of the walls were strangers eating their dinners, and I'd have to walk back through them like a very public walk of shame.

Being left alone in the car for Ashe to drive home was harsh. Even with the heat in Ambrose's golden eyes and the bulge in his pants, I felt the sting of rejection.

It didn't stop me from racing up to bed to finish what we'd started. After the second orgasm, I gave up. I wouldn't have been satisfied until it was Ambrose's hand and not mine. I don't remember falling asleep, and I definitely don't remember him sliding into bed with me.

Opening my eyes again, I push away thoughts of sex, and dark lines catch my attention. I'd been right when I guessed Ambrose had tattoos. They're old, the black only so stark because of the pale skin underneath. Knot-work that makes me think of Vikings swoops down from his collarbones like a heraldic. The knots are nothing like I'm familiar with from my old school history texts. My eyes cross as the pattern they make is just out of reach. Moving on from his chest for now, I follow the art up to his shoulder where they turn into bands wrapping around his bicep to his elbow. There are different sized spaces between the bands and each one holds runes. Tracing them with my gaze, they fill me with a sense of wariness, as if something ancient and dark is near. I want to hide from it, but I'm trapped in Ambrose's embrace, and there isn't anything there. They're just ink and symbols, I remind myself, and go back to studying his chest.

"They're from my life as a mortal."

Ambrose's sleep-roughened whisper startles me, and he presses his fingertips into my back as if to keep me close. I swallow hard, my pulse already settling as curiosity toys with me.

"You weren't born a vampire?" I ask, keeping my eyes on his chest. There are the faintest silver lines and marks across his bodies. Scars, I realize.

Ambrose shifts his leg, which is trapped under my thigh. Somehow I failed to notice how our legs had tangled together with an intimacy we definitely don't have. "No," he answers, his voice smoothing out as he wakes. "I was a soldier in the city Kievan Rus."

I'm surprised at Ambrose's amiability with my question. Maybe he is a morning person, despite being a creature of the night. I decide to push my luck, keeping my voice soft and even in hopes of avoiding irritating him.

"When were you turned?" I have no idea how old he really is.

"Twelve hundred years ago, give or take fifty."

Holy. Shit. I push back from him, arching at my lower back to gaze up at him in unfettered shock. His grip relents enough to let me move, but he doesn't move his hand.

"That's..." I trail off as his golden eyes meet mine. Then I shake my head, unable to wrap my brain around it. "That's insane. Mind-boggling. And you've been a king for that long?"

An arched eyebrow precedes his reply. "Of course not. I have only been considered king of this area since I led my clan here roughly five hundred years ago."

I squeak, the secret history nerd in me giddy. "You came here before Oldgate was even settled!"

Ambrose's mouth tilts up with wry amusement. "I am, in fact, aware of that, little lamb."

My gaze goes unfocused as I try to juggle what he's just told me. Man, to him, I must seem like an infant. How mature does someone get after twelve hundred years? He's seen so much of history, of the world growing and changing. Technology evolving, kingdoms falling and turning into countries, disasters and wars. Unease wilts my wonder at his age. How many lovers has he had that allowed him to feed too?

In his long lifespan, three months with me must be a blink.

Nothing special. Just another woman to fade into the past, until he can't recall my face. Until he doesn't even think about trying.

A curled finger tilts under my chin and he moves me until I'm looking up towards him. I avoid his eyes, not daring to look higher than his cheekbones.

"Something's troubling you, little lamb." Ambrose says it as a statement, rather than a question, like he can sense the keen disappointment making my heart ache.

"It's not important," I whisper, still unable to meet his gaze. I give a half shrug. "I'm fine."

The weight of his focus presses against my skin, as if he's trying to peer into my thoughts and ferret out the truth for himself. I grit my teeth; if I thought he'd let me go, I'd try to roll away from him. Unable to lie to myself, though, I want to stay there in his arms. His body is cool, keeping me comfortable despite the humid heat, and he's solid against me, a bulwark against the world beyond this room. Around him, my thoughts don't race, jumping from one worry to the next, and the peace is as addicting as the fire he sparks inside me.

A phone rings from behind him and he scowls, twisting his head to look towards it. I finally let myself look at all of his face again, and it's endearing to see the polished Ambrose with bedhead. I fight the urge to brush it with my fingers, the memory of how soft his hair is imprinted on my skin.

He lets go of me, reaching to pick up the phone. He looks at me as he brings it to his ear, and trepidation keeps me in place. Something tells me this call is important. I know it in my bones.

"Yes?" Ambrose's voice is clipped but not irritated. Five agonizing heartbeats later, he hands the phone to me. I stare at it like a poisonous snake, worried that it'll strike out and fill me with its venom. I take it, my hand shaking, and clear my throat gently before pressing it to my ear.

"Hello?" I say, my voice unsure.

"Hey, lady," a raspy but familiar voice says.

I shoot upright, pressing the phone harder against my ear, my other hand curling against my chest. "Deidre?" I breathe out, almost unable to believe this a dream that I'll wake up from. If it is, I... I don't know what I'd do. Lose it, probably.

"Yeah," my best friend says. Deidre's voice is raspy and hoarse, and she sounds so tired.

"Are you okay?" I ask right away, heart and mind in an all-out sprint. "Are you hurt? Are you safe? Where are you? What—"

"Slow down," she requests and it's the burden in her voice that makes me snap my mouth shut, my teeth rattling from the force. "I'm...well, I'm not okay," Deidre admits with a trace of her usual humor. "But I think I will be eventually. Thank you, for going to him. I'll never be able to repay you."

"I'd do it all over again, without hesitation," I say, my voice firm. "Don't you dare think about repaying me. You being alive and home and safe is enough."

There's silence on the other end, long enough that I pull the phone away to glance at the screen. When I see it's still connected, I put it to my ear again. "Dei?"

"I need you to do something for me," she asks.

"Anything," I say before she can continue.

There's a huff of laughter and my eyes sting. Then I'm crying, pressing my hand to my lips to keep the sound back. Deidre doesn't need to hear me crying. I don't even know why I am. Happiness? Relief? Fear? All of that and more.

"Kasar says you have my computer," she begins. I don't know how the vampire knew that, but that was a question for later. "I need you to show Ambrose everything in the file on Rapture. There's stuff there that I think he'll understand a lot better than I was able to."

I nod, even though she can't see me. "Done. What else do you need? Do you want me to get you clothes? Food? The police have your purse and phone, but I can figure out a way to get it back."

"Thanks, but I'm okay for now. I just wanted to tell you thank you, and ask you for the favor." She sounds more tired than a few minutes ago.

"I love you, Dei. We'll see each other soon," I vow. Screw Ambrose if he thinks my bargain with him will keep me from Deidre now that I know she's safe. As safe as she can be in a vampire's care.

"Love you too," she says, breathless, and the line goes dead.

I clutch the phone with both hands to my chest, my eyes leaking tears, and heave in a shuddering breath. Deidre is alive. She's alive. I'm not alone in the world. She isn't either. A weight melts from my shoulders, sinking to the floor and down through the house. It's as if I can breathe for the first time.

Looking towards the windows, glowing with the morning sun, I'm not plagued with anxiety. I'm weightless, unburdened. I can face the day, strong once again because I know the most important person in my life is still here. Familiar plants line the windows, and I grin. Sometime after I went to sleep, my plants were brought to me. A touch of home, and a sound of home.

A giggle shakes my shoulders, and after a few minutes, I start laughing. I'm still crying, but it's a release. Ambrose must think I'm going crazy, laughing like a maniac in a tank top with rainbow cacti and truly atrocious bedhead. I don't care, though. Nothing, not even a king, can take this moment from me.

The mattress shifts and I twist to look at Ambrose. Instead of watching me like I'm a crazy person, he has the softest smile. A real smile, and his golden eyes aren't as cold as they have been since I first saw them in Noir.

I throw myself at him, my arms going around his shoulders, still grinning and laughing. I let his phone fall to the bed behind him and I squeeze him tight, pressing the side of my head against his. "Thank you, Ambrose. Thank you so much."

He relaxes and my laughter renews as I realize he wasn't expecting me to hug him. Then slowly, like he isn't sure what to do, he returns the hug. Ambrose oozed confidence last night, playing the powerful royal playboy, but something like a gracious hug throws him off.

I pull back just enough to press a kiss to his cheek.

He looks at me, and I swear there's a boyish wonder in him. Then I remember that I'm in bed with the vampire I bargained three months of my life to, the vampire I got myself off to last night, the vampire who everyone in the Barrows and most of Topside is afraid of.

Just as my grip loosens on him, he pushes forward, capturing my lips in his. This time I have no urge to defy him, to taunt him and push his limits. I cling to him, opening my mouth when he licks my lips, and sigh as he deepens the kiss. His arms lock around me, and I wiggle, shifting until I'm kneeling beside him, hands braced on his shoulders. The entire time Ambrose never let our kiss break.

One of his hands begins to rub my back, the other dropping low enough that his forearm is pressed into my butt as he grips my opposite hip. The touch doesn't sizzle like before. This touch feels adoring, like I'm something fragile and precious in his arms. It's a touch that promises safety and security if I just submit.

I want to. I want to so bad.

But I can't give him my heart, not until I fill my end of the bargain. Deidre is safe because of Ambrose, as he promised. So I will be his for three months, gladly. I'll enjoy what time we spend together, and share my body if he will share his. My heart, though? I'll keep it safe, tucked away where his seductive darkness can't reach.

I start to pull away and Ambrose slows the kiss the moment I do and when we finally part, I'm panting. I don't let go of his shoulders, unwilling to put that much space between us.

"I need to show you something," I say, sounding like I've just ran up five flights of stairs. "Deidre has a lot of research on Rapture that she thinks you'll be able to understand better."

He doesn't tell me that he heard what Deidre had requested. Ambrose nods once, his eyes dipping down to my lips before he slides out of bed and away from me. Bereft of his solid presence, I scramble to follow, taking his offered hand so I don't fall to the floor when my legs tangle in the duvet.

"Then let us start the day, ma belle lionne," Ambrose says with the poise and gravitas of a king assured of victory, even barefoot and only wearing sleep pants. "We have work to do."

Chapter Thirteen

AMBROSE

"How the *fuck* did a human, junior investigative reporter find this much intel and we didn't?"

I want to throw my chair through the window, but the last time I did that, Joséphine dressed me down for it like she'd been the one to raise me and not the other way around. I have my inner circle gathered in my office except for Kasar. Malachi stands at ease towards the center of the room, unfazed by my fury. Ashe simply crosses his leg over his knee, his finger beating out a steady tattoo as he stares at the wall behind me, deep in thought.

A harsh huff of amusement has me curling my lip in irritation as I direct my gaze to Lan, where he leans a shoulder against the window, ankles crossed and hands in his pockets like he can't be fucked.

"Care to give me the answer, Lan?" I don't even try to contain my irritation.

He gives a half shrug. "It's obvious, *sire*," he drawls. I curl my fingers at the disrespect in my title; Lan has never liked authority. I'll have to remind him to heel soon. He continues before I can act on the impulse to throw him through the window instead of the chair. "She's an attractive warmblood, and she's a woman. All she would have to do is bat those pretty eyes, show a bit of tit, and act oh-so fascinated, and most males would feed her information without realizing it. And if she never took Rapture before, like your pretty little blood donor insists, that's another angle she could play up."

A snarl tears out of my chest at Lan's mention of Eloise, and I straighten to my full height of six foot four inches. Rage and the instinct to protect Eloise, even from petty slander, lines my very bones. Malachi and Ashe focus in on me as the tension thickens the air to sticky molasses. Lan pushes off the window, his hands sliding from his pockets as he shifts into a deceptively casual pose, the embers of blood rage flaring in his eyes.

"Landon Polastri, you watch your tongue, child," Joséphine says with a sharp look as she carries in a tray with tea, coffee, and water. Ashe rises smoothly to his feet and reaches for the tray, which she gives him with a sweet smile before turning her glare back to the blond at the window. "You are not too old for me to bend you over my knee and paddle your bottom until it's red. Disrespecting your grandfather like a wildling." She shakes her head, her hands on her waist.

"Yes, Matka," Lan says, his defiance melting from his shoulders at the reprimand and the blood rage disappearing into the depths of him once again.

"Ms. Eloise is a wonderful guest," she continues to chide him like an erstwhile child. Seeing as he was, in fact her child both in the human sense as well as vampire, Joséphine is the only one Lan won't gnash his teeth back at. I could do without the reminder that Lan is my vampiric grandson, however.

"She and her friend Deidre have been a boon to the Nightshades, and you will mind your tongue about her, do you understand? If Ambrose doesn't get to you first, I will have your hide if it happens again. Do you understand?"

"Yes, Matka," Lan says with a nod, his hands back in his pants pockets. He strides the short distance to her, and she offers her cheek, which he presses a gentle kiss to. "It won't happen again."

She clasps his shoulders, all irritation gone from her face and replaced by the adoration that only a mother can give. "Good, now apologize to Ambrose."

Lan turns to face me, a look of indifference on his face. "I apologize for referring to Ms. Morse as a blood donor." *Even if that's what she is,* goes unspoken except in his eyes.

I give a sharp nod, sitting down in my chair. The sheer need to just *hit* something practically vibrates my bones as I stare at the files Ashe transferred from Deidre's computer to our private network.

"Malachi." My soldier straightens to attention. "Go to the Blackfang Barons. Tell those wolf shifters that remnants of the Latian pack are in Newgate and ensure we have permission to take them out. I don't fucking need any more political shit fucking this up. Draven will agree, but I refuse to take chances."

The Nightshade vampires and Blackfang Barons are tenuous allies after having a common enemy for so long. Wolf shifters and vampires do not get along, perhaps because of our similar primal natures. It's been a beneficial relationship for both of our territories, but it's still a new alliance. If Draven, Kade, or Bishop take issue with me ordering the extermination of the Latians within my kingdom, our ties will be severed.

Considering they now have an exclusive deal with Rapture in their city, I doubt they want to risk it either.

Wolves can be unpredictable though, and their mate, Jemma, has personal history with the Latian pack.

"Ashe." I lean forward and move the mouse until I can drag the folder into the network drive that only Ashe has access to other than myself and Kasar. "I want you to go over this with a fine-tooth comb. I want every piece of information we can get out of this. I want to know how the Latians got to Newgate and how Michael Garner is connected. It seems he has a greater part to play than even he realizes."

"Sire," Ashe agrees with a tilt of his head. He rises and, together, he and Malachi leave the office. Now it's only me, Lan, and Joséphine. The latter who has taken a seat across from the chair Eloise has claimed as her own.

"And what do you want me to do, sire?" There's not a hint of defiance or mockery in Lan's voice now. Not after Joséphine took him to task. I give it six months before Lan is back to pushing boundaries. Something he and Eloise have in common, it seems.

I watch him, considering. Lan, in spite of his violent and extreme nature, is a highly skilled asset to me. It's the only reason why I haven't put him down yet. He's the Nightshade's reaper, and no one can deny his dedication to his duties.

"Have Ashe send you a list of targets. I want you to follow them and learn every fucking detail about them. I want to know what toothpaste they use, what's past the expiration date in their cabinets. Every. Fucking. Thing."

Lan gives a short bow and strides from the room with his orders.

I pinch the bridge of my nose, pressure building behind my right eye. One would think that being a vampire would prevent migraines, but alas even the undead can get them. Migraines are the bane of all creatures, natural and supernatural alike. I doubt even spirits are able to avoid them.

The fucking Latians. Goddamn piece of shit wolf shifters who worked with Markus and his fanatics. Bishop will be furious that some of them have escaped their justice. The head alpha, Draven, may consent to my vampires killing the rest, but it'll be Bishop who I need to concern myself with. The sociopathic shifter will want to see the bodies, no doubt. I make a note to tell Lan that if he has to kill one of them to leave them identifiable for the shifter.

It seems like we aren't the only vampires to bridge the animosity between our races for an alliance. Deidre's information doesn't reveal what vampires are associating with the Latians, but Kasar will have information on that by now.

There's so much I need to consider; Deidre was able to gather fragments and she was right to believe I'd make more out of it than she ever could. It's been a week since Eloise showed me everything and I'm still fuming and piecing all the parts together. These Latians are much more cunning than their former alpha. They're willing to move in small increments, to hide in the shadows and blend into the background of the Barrows. Tyrion was flashy, needing to wave his dick around, claiming power that wasn't ever his.

Brash arrogance does not a king make.

Joséphine is still in the room, the weight of her all-too-seeing gaze on my shoulders. I drop my hand to the armrest and look at the woman I consider a daughter straight on. She's never held her opinion back, something she gets away with when I'd tear the throat from others for such an act. Even though I turned her when she was fifty-two, I still see the malnourished five-year-old girl wearing a bundle of rags. She hadn't been afraid of me then and she's never been afraid of me since. When the Naples Plague broke out in 1656, her mortal body had swiftly broken down. I offered her the choice and she agreed on the condition that I never abandon her like her family and late husband did. It was a bargain I happily agreed to.

A year later, Lan had come home to find his mother changed. He'd changed too, and when her once peaceful son had been stabbed multiple times and left for dead after getting into too much debt, I gave her my blessing to save him. He'd been unconscious and when he woke, there was so much anger in him. All transitions from human to vampire are difficult. The hunger is torturous, and the world is overwhelming to the much keener senses. It was more than that for Lan, however. He resented being saved and blamed me for it. Only his love for his mother kept him from ending his new life.

The anger and violence he'd returned to Naples with became worse after he'd been turned. In those early years, we cleaned up after his killing sprees across continents. When he'd finally gone too far, I gave him a choice. Pledge himself to me, not just as my vampiric grandson but as a soldier in my army and stay in control of his rage, or I would kill him and end Joséphine's torment.

"I know you have something to say, piccola," I murmur when she stays silent.

Joséphine tilts her head, continuing to observe me before heaving a sigh and shaking her head. "Oh, papà, why do you do this to yourself?"

I force back the instinct to snarl. She's referring to Eloise, whom I've avoided since she showed me the research. It's been two weeks of silent agony, but it was necessary. Waking up with her in my arms was too much for me, and that was before she embraced me with such genuine affection and gratitude. I still feel the press of her lips against my cheek, the smell of her sleep, the sharp taste of arousal from her fingers.

She's consumed my thoughts when I should be focusing on dealing with this issue with Rapture and the Latians.

I can't even bring myself to feed from her, afraid of breaking my threadbare restraint and taking her for my own.

Joséphine tuts and the sound brings me out of the spiral that is Eloise Morse. My gaze lifts to meet hers again and she's smirking at me.

"See what I mean?" she admonishes more gently than she had her son earlier.

I let out a long breath, slouching back into my chair and running my hand back through my hair. I want to groan and bitch and do anything other than think about why I'm avoiding Eloise. My head rolls against the padded leather, my neck stretching to the side as I look out the window Lan had stood against.

"Has she said anything to you?"

"Beyond asking about you for the first two days? No. She is a smart girl. She knows you're avoiding her, but she doesn't know why. The little lamb acts as if she did something wrong."

My gaze darts to Joséphine at the tone of reproach, but she's not wrong. Joséphine may have never allowed me or my men to call her the princess of the Nightshades but she sits as regally in the armchair, flanked by deep bookshelves, that it might as well be the original throne from Versailles. She isn't in my inner circle, officially, but not for the lack of my frequent requests and offers. She is the mistress of my household and thrives with it.

"What do you mean?" Why on earth would Eloise believe she offended me? Doesn't she realize I'm a predator ready to snap and devour her body and soul?

Joséphine snorts with amusement, a smile deepening the lines of her face. "Oh, papà. You can be so stupid sometimes."

I roll my eyes, but don't disagree. Casting my senses beyond the room, I make sure we can't be overheard. I lean forward, elbows on the desk in front of me, my fingers laced together as I look out the window again.

"I feel like an untried boy, piccola," I confess in a quiet voice. There's no need to risk speaking any louder than necessary. "No woman, vampire or human, has done this to me. Especially in such little time. I even considered if she was working for someone, meant to seduce me, even though I knew the idea was preposterous."

She raises an eyebrow, the damn exact copy of the same look I give, and it's hard not to tell her to stop acting like me. I splay my arms out, as in invitation as exasperation floods my veins. "What would you have me do, Joséphine?" I ask, a note of desperation in my words. I barrel onwards. "She's a human, and in her twenties. She came to me because she wanted to save her friend, and I forced her to my side in a bargain. She hasn't chosen to stay at my side, and why would she? She has an entire life ahead of her. One that shouldn't include staying with an overbearing vampire who can barely control the urge to fuck her or tear out the eyes of any male who looks at her."

I push up out of my chair, unable to stay still any longer. I pace towards the windows, glaring out at the sliver of a view of the Barrows. "I want her, piccola. I know what it means when a vampire reacts to someone this way but I can't—I won't force that on someone. I've told you what happened last time."

I hear the soft swish of a cotton skirt and then Joséphine's arm is around my waist. Habitually, I raise my left arm and she presses against my side, her head just above my shoulders. She lets me stew in silence, fighting against memories of my ancient past. I cannot recall her face, but I can still hear her screams. I've never let myself forget the anger and pain and shame that tore through me that day and the following years. I reach into my right pocket, my fingers brushing the smooth metal circle that was once a coin. It's my constant reminder of why I keep myself apart from anyone, how it's safer for everyone that way.

"She is not Kalina," Joséphine says at last. The compassion in her voice has me squeezing my eyes shut. "And you are not the same man you were then."

I let out a rough, humorless laugh. "No, I'm so much worse."

"In some ways," she concedes, never having been sheltered from my actions. "But in the ways you fear? No, you are not that man, not that vampire. You know what it is like when a man becomes a vampire, how hard one can struggle for control for years."

I jerk my head, refuting her words. "I should have been better. I could have been."

That's my dark shame. That I had mastered my

new abilities and strengths so quickly but let myself lose that control so easily.

Joséphine doesn't say anything. She lets go of me and pats me affectionately on the back before going to the tray we'd all ignored. I watch as she pours me a cup of tea and sets it in my usual spot. She picks up the tray and heads to the open door before pausing to look back at me.

"Talk to her, at least," she requests, brooking no argument. "Be brave, sire. And if it bothers you so much that Ms. Morse hasn't chosen to stay at her side, you know what you can do to fix that. If you have the courage."

She leaves without another word and I stare through the empty doorway at the blank wall across the hall. Of course I know what I can do. I could release Eloise from our bargain. Joséphine doesn't know everything about that black day, though. No one does, not even Kasar and he was the one to find me and pull me back from the edge.

I want to hate Eloise for making me feel this fear again. For turning me into a coward. I won't let her out of our bargain. I'm too fucking selfish. Because this way, at least, she has to be with me. If I let her go, she might run. And then I'll burn the entire city down until I catch her.

Chapter Fourteen
ELOISE

I got the message real fast. Ambrose didn't want to see me. For the first couple of days, I asked Joséphine about him but stopped when I couldn't stand the look of sympathy in her eyes. Apparently I'm too much for the vampire. It seems I have my answer. A man that's over a thousand years old is still as immature as a teenager.

I hate, hate how I feel guilty for trying to show him gratitude. For thinking maybe I could act on the feelings he stirs inside me. I was so stupid. I should have known the moment he put me in the car all by myself that I'd stepped over a line. Maybe if I'd given in, let him take what he wanted in that restaurant, he wouldn't be avoiding me. But fuck that and fuck him if that's what it is. No, don't fuck him is more appropriate.

Two weeks, I've been drifting through the house,

about to go insane. At least Joséphine spends time with me, and the other vampires won't leave the room anymore when I walk in. I've learned their names, other than Ashe, of course. The dark-haired, olive-skinned Italian one is Malachi. He doesn't talk much but when he does, he's got a wicked dry sense of humor that took a bit to catch on. There's Lan too, who was the one that touched my arm and creeped me out when I was at Noir. He's Joséphine's son, both by blood and vampire standards apparently.

I have no idea how such a sweet woman could have such an off-putting son. Every time I see him, it's like he's a chained, drowsy velociraptor just waiting to wake up and rip everything to shreds. Only when he's with Joséphine does that anger seem to settle. Otherwise, every time his eyes are on me, I wonder if he's deciding whether or not he's hungry enough to strike.

Ambrose told me if anyone else touches me, he'd kill them—but is that true if he's avoiding me?

Every desire to submit to Ambrose has relented. Now I crave to push him, to piss him off and make him react. I don't have a death wish, because while he's been avoiding me, I've caught glimpses of him as he comes and goes. Sometimes he's as clean and sharp as any Topsider CEO. Other times, he's bloodied though a sick sense tells me none of it is his own.

I hate it when I catch a glimpse of him walking

through the first floor or up the stairs and he has blood streaking across his mouth. Goddamn envy and anger simmers hotter each time I see it. I agreed to give myself to him for three months, to let him feed on me whenever he wishes, and now this fucking vampire isn't even letting me fulfill my end of the bargain? He's feeding from other people, maybe even other women.

It's chilling and unfounded how I hate the women I picture. How these beautiful, perfect women slide their hands over his shoulders and bare their necks to him. Does he fuck them too? It's a good thing he hasn't made me go anywhere with him, because I'd turn into a jealous hellcat if one of them approaches him. I might only be a human, but high school as a foster kid is a trial of hell and violence. I know how to be a scrappy bitch when I need to.

I've claimed the room with all the plants as a type of workspace for me, since I wouldn't want to offend his majesty with my presence. I don't even eat in the dining room anymore, and not just because Joséphine still confiscates my laptop—resorting to taking it with her into the kitchen. At least there, I can just eat toast and drink my tea while scrolling through my empty email inbox.

I don't have any projects and no potential clients have reached out. It's not unusual, and the last project I wrapped up the day of the dinner had a large enough payment to last me a couple months. Which means I'm bored out of my mind.

And there's nothing to do except think about Ambrose and Deidre. She's answering my texts, from a new number, but not often. She doesn't tell me anything and it's scary because she stonewalls when something is wrong. She keeps putting off another phone call too. I don't like it.

I haven't felt this rudderless in my own life since my dad died. I won't let myself go back to that. Never again.

I close my laptop, irritated but not enough to risk breaking my main source of income, and head towards the stairs. It's past dinnertime but I'm not hungry. Not hard when you're forced into doing jack-all. When I turn the corner into the room full of bookshelves and the stairs, I halt in place as Ambrose and Malachi are coming down.

Ambrose doesn't stop as my irritation at him snaps at his indifferent look.

I bend at the waist, sweeping my free arm out dramatically. "Oh, excuse me, your majesty," I ooze out, not bothering to hide my disdain. I step out of the way, ensuring I'm far away from the landing. "Please forgive this lowly human for intruding on your divine presence."

Straightening, I meet Ambrose's glare with one of my own. A small part of me recognizes the slight lift of Malachi's lips, his amusement plain to see.

Ambrose blinks and my world narrows to him as I see the thick red rings in his eyes. He's hungry. Really hungry. My stomach twists and I slide my foot forward before forcing myself to hold back. He's the one that's been avoiding me. If he wants to feed from me, he's going to have to ask. I won't offer myself; I never will, bargain or not.

Besides, no doubt he's heading out to find someone else to slake his needs.

"Eloise," Ambrose rumbles and his voice vibrates through me. My sex clenches at the tone, even though it's detached and chilly. It doesn't help that my anger doesn't help me ignore how sexy the vampire king is. Black tailored suit, pristine white button-down, two undone buttons in place of a tie. He looks damn good, the expensive clothing working overtime to show off his broad shoulders and solid strength.

"Oh!" I gasp theatrically, and press my hand flat to my chest. "You do remember who I am."

Malachi is grinning now, and it softens his harsh look. He's attractive, in his tailored black on black suit. He's maybe six foot two, an inch or two shorter than Ambrose. If I'd never met Ambrose, I might think Malachi is the most beautiful man I've ever seen. A demon from the dark of hell, promising sinful delights.

"I have business to attend to this evening,"

Ambrose states, ignoring my jibe. A wicked thought occurs and I give him a sweet-as-cherry-pie smile.

"Of course," I say, just as sweetly, before turning my attention pointedly to Malachi. I take a few steps closer to the pair, my hips swaying. I have moves when I want to use them. "Maybe Malachi can entertain me tonight?" I don't look at Ambrose even though his gaze is stabbing into me like daggers. "I've been so lonely lately."

Just before I step around Ambrose, a vice grip digs into my bicep. I look at where Ambrose grips me and make sure he can see me roll my eyes. I don't try to tug away from him, knowing all too well he'll let me go when he decides to and not a moment sooner. I meet his gaze, and the entire world narrows down to the space between us as he lowers his face to mine. A cruelty I've never seen snarls his lips and the red and gold clash violently in his eyes that a moment before were ice cold. Now they burn, flay my skin and burrow down to boil my blood.

I should be the little lamb he called me and cower before the dangerous monster.

I don't, though. I welcome the heat, letting it bellow within me until I burn just as hot.

"Do not test me, Eloise." Ambrose's voice is fire and ice, and pure threat. "You will never win that fight."

Every sense of self-preservation burns away and I

raise an eyebrow like he's so fond of doing. "Are you sure about that?"

The snarl that rips from him hisses through the air like paper ripping, harsh and loud but I don't flinch. I push on, stepping closer to him and never losing his gaze.

"You want to know what I think?"

We must look ridiculous. I'm all of five feet two inches, the top of my head barely coming up to his pectoral muscles, and I've refused to wear any of the clothes he's provided. I'm in my faded leggings with a hole in the thigh, a too big knit yellow cardigan, and a graphic tee with a bear drinking coffee that says Bear Necessities. My black hair is in the same messy bun it's been in for the last week. I've already ditched wearing bras too, not seeing the point with how empty the house always seems to be. Basically, I look like the hot mess freelancer who gives no fucks and prefers comfort over fashion.

Ambrose, on the other hand, is the complete opposite. Despite him being from the Barrows, and me from Topside, he's the one that oozes wealth and power. He's the one who looks like he belongs in the sunny, modern city that prizes itself on its aesthetic, and I look like I should be stuck in crappy, cheap apartments rife with drugs and violence.

When Ambrose says nothing, I push further. I poke him in the middle of his hard chest. "I think you are all talk." I laugh, a bit because of my own audacity and the rest because of how Ambrose's eyes widen the smallest amount before his brows narrow with renewed irritation.

Now I pull away from him, and he lets me go with a pointed release of his hand. I move past him and Malachi, whose face is once again undecipherable and stoic. As I reach the landing, I look over my shoulder at Ambrose, and toss out, "Go take care of this business of yours. You're looking peckish."

I walked the rest of the way to the bedroom—the one he hasn't entered while I'm in there since that morning—with my head held high.

I kick the door closed behind me, locking it out of sheer pettiness, and set my laptop on the dresser before making my way to my plants. I still haven't figured out who brought them in while I was asleep. Maybe it was Ambrose, but I doubt it at this point. More likely it was Joséphine or Ashe. Regardless, they'd also brought in a small watering can as if they knew I'd prefer to tend to them myself. Hooking my finger under the thin handle, I fill it in the bathroom before beginning to water them.

I trail my fingers across the large leaves of the Monstera as I let my mind empty as much as I've ever managed by myself. Testing the soil of each one before pouring water in their pots, I move from Monsteras to my Devil's Ivy and ferns. They're flourishing here in the Barrows, to my surprise.

"I almost thought it'd be the same for me, Charline," I murmur as I run my fingers through the delicate, evergreen fronds of the fern. Deidre always teases me for naming my plants and then talking to them, but I swear it helps them grow. And they're great confidants when I need them. "I guess I was just caught up in the rush that Ambrose gave me, you know?"

I move on to Sandy, a string of pearls succulent that I've had for three years. The muted green color of the plant fits perfectly in the aesthetic of the room. I let a few drops of water fall into the soil in her pot before returning the can to its place and go back to stand between my plants, looking out the window. I don't want to look behind me, at a room that is Ambrose's, or at the bed that I remember waking up in his arms in.

"Am I just a stupid girl for being attracted to him?" My plants never answer, but that's okay. "He must have women throw themselves at his feet all the time. He had a woman to feed from before. Did he bring her here too?"

The sun is setting over the city, and it's beautiful. Unlike Newgate, where tall buildings are monoliths of reflective glass, straight uniform lines and the comfortable appearance of an unburdened life, the Barrows has personality. The buildings are old, like the true name of the city suggests. When Oldgate was built, it was a small port town at first. Over decades, buildings were designed by whomever commissioned them, meaning nothing looked uniform or similar. It was a chaotic kaleidoscope of architectural styles, with winding streets and pocket neighborhoods. The residents didn't seem to particularly care about preserving the history of the city, but nor did they seek to erase it like Newgate had.

A terrible idea makes me smile and I rush into the wardrobe before I can talk sense into myself. I know it's stupid, but if I stay in this house for another minute, I'm going to scream. Embracing my anger at Ambrose, I yank through the clothes I've been ignoring. Dresses land on the floor in heaps as I hold up different ones to me in the mirror at the end of the wardrobe and discard them until I find the perfect one. Tugging it on, I don't even hesitate to lose my panties when the dress makes it clear there's no way of hiding the lines of even a thong. My blood is humming with excitement as I sit on the tufted bench where Ambrose put my shoes on for me.

Scowling, I abandon the strappy fuck-me heels I love and wore that night and opt for boots I would have never dared to wear before.

Fuck being a little lamb, though, I think as I tug up the black velvet boots on up over my knees. They're wedge heels, and when I walk up to the mirror, I can't help but feel a bit attracted to myself. Thick thighs may save lives, but finding a pair of thigh-high boots that don't roll down or squeeze my thighs enough to give me muffin tops is like trying to find a unicorn. Usually girls with curves like me have to settle for one or the other. These, though?

These are fucking sexy as hell, and make me want to stroke my own thighs without shame. And the dress? Deidre would be proud of me. In fact, I yank out my hair from the tie and finger comb the black locks until they look more sultry-messy than lazy-messy. A couple of bobby pins, bold maroon lipstick, and mascara later, and I'm back in front of the mirror, phone in hand with the camera pulled up.

After a few snaps from different angles, I send the best ones to Deidre. Looking at the phone, I'm giddy. The boots are black, and combined with the obscenely short silver dress, I look ready to make men fall to their knees. It's a silver, glittery halter top dress with the neckline sweeping down low enough that I'll need to make sure I don't bend over too far or I'll lose a boob. It drapes my curves and ends just a couple inches above the top of my boots, giving a sexy tease of skin. Even better, there's a slit that goes all the way up past my hip, hence my lack of panties. It's like someone took a sexy nightgown, dumped it in silver glitter and called it clubwear.

I figure if Ambrose didn't want me to wear something like this, he shouldn't have put it in the closet.

And the best part? I look and feel like a boss bitch.

No, a goddamn queen.

My phone beeps and I jump, my heart leaping

into my throat as if Ambrose somehow has figured out my plans and is condemning me. It's Deidre, though, with a response that is her normal self.

🔥🔥🔥🔥 *Slay, bitch. Ambrose isn't going to know what hit him!*

Biting my lower lip in a smirk, I use both hands to type out a reply.

Fuck him. This isn't for him. If I'm going to be in the Barrows, I'm going to enjoy it.

Satisfied, I bare my teeth to make sure I didn't smear any of the lip color but the bright stain is perfect and my teeth are clear. One last plump of my hair and a quick spritz of hairspray, and I set off to find someone in the house. I definitely plan on needing a designated driver.

I'm not to the point where I'm familiar enough to knock on the bedroom doors on the second floor, so I keep going downstairs and start prowling through the house. I don't know how long the staff stays before heading home, so my best bet is to find one of the vampires who stay here. If I can't, I'll check the kitchen and see if Joséphine is around. Even though the idea of asking her to take me to a club makes me feel like asking my grandma to take me.

Ashe isn't around, and I'm about to chance calling a rideshare. It's not like I've had anything to spend money on lately. Before I can pull my phone from the tiny black clutch I grabbed, I find someone.

Lan.

The vampire looks me up and down, a wolfish grin on his face. "Going somewhere, sweetheart?"

I roll my eyes and cock my hip with a hand on it. "Don't call me that. And yeah, I'm going out. I'm sick of being stuck here like Ambrose's forgotten toy."

Maybe Lan isn't the best choice, but there's an understanding look in his golden eyes. I study his eyes as circumspectly as I can, and I don't see a hint of red. I don't have to worry about him taking a bite of me at least.

"Ambrose won't like that," he says as he crosses his arms. He doesn't say it like I'm getting in trouble. Oh, no, he says it like he wants to help piss his king off.

I shrug. "Ambrose can fuck off seeing as he's ignored me for the last two weeks. I'm bored and I want to have fun. Are you going to help me or not?"

Lan's golden eyes brighten with perverse glee and my heart thuds in my chest but I stand my ground even as his grin turns into a smile made sinister by the point of his fangs becoming visible. He's dressed more casually than I'm used to seeing the vampires, with black jeans and a gray fitted tee underneath his black leather jacket.

Oh, yeah, this is a really stupid idea. But I'm not going to back out just because Lan looks like he's ready to fight or fuck.

"I know a place Ambrose would hate to know you went to," Lan purred, his voice like gunpowder and smoke. "You game?"

"Always," I bite back, the thrill of angering Ambrose rushing down my spine and spiking my adrenaline.

He jerks his permanently disheveled blond hair towards the garage before turning. I follow at his heels, practically skipping. In a few minutes and with only a minor hesitation, I'm pulling on a helmet and swinging my leg carefully over the back of a black motorcycle behind Lan. He doesn't let me second-guess my decision and I squeak and cling tight to him as he lets out the throttle and we race out into the early night of the Barrows.

Lan pushes the bike ridiculously fast, hugging corners and weaving between vehicles and even market carts at one point. I have half a mind to remind him that I'm human and can, in fact, die, unlike him and his no-helmet ways, but the thrill is too perfect.

By the time we pull up to an unfamiliar club, the music is so loud I can feel the beat from out here, I'm goddamn high on adrenaline. Lan hits the kickstand and gets off before I can process it and he picks me up off the bike like a child, saving me the risk of flashing my crotch at the people staring at us from the line. I take off the helmet and shake out my hair again as he takes it and stashes it.

I see a few humans in the line passing around neon blue lab vials and side-glance Lan, who seems to be waiting for my lead.

"Do you have any Rapture by chance?"

A smirk twists his face, and he slides his fingers into a narrow breast pocket in his jacket before pulling out a light, bright glass vial. I snag it from his fingers and pull my camera up on my phone and hand it to him in a silent order. I bring the vial to my lips with one hand and flip the camera off with the other.

Lan hands it back with a dark chuckle and I trade him back the vial. I don't actually want the stuff. He looks over my phone as I pull up Ambrose's contact for the first time since I saw it added to my phone. I send him the photo without hesitation.

"Oh, I think I like you," Lan murmurs and I watch him slip the newly stoppered vial back into its pocket.

"Yeah?" I turn and march towards the line, but Lan guides me to the door, the bouncer opening the velour rope and letting us pass without comment. "Then you can buy my drinks."

Chapter Fifteen
AMBROSE

Acrid copper overwhelms the brine-heavy air as the last body drops from my hand, the thick warm blood from his neck rolling down my chin. The nameless demon isn't the only one's blood that has wet my fangs this evening, but even after the slaughter, the blood I've tasted only increases my hunger.

I survey the docks, half lit by the tall stadium lights that shine bright every thirty feet. Malachi secured permission from Draven to deal with these outcasts and Lan had tracked them here, to my fucking docks, where their supply of Rapture was skimmed off of the Nightshades'. When I'd seen my own workers turn their backs and ignore the three creatures with duffle bags, I'd fallen on them with rage and destruction.

Eloise is right. I am hungry.

"Too bad we couldn't keep any alive," Malachi says dispassionately, as he uses his foot to flip over one of the bodies. He's got his phone out and takes a picture. It's one of the Latians, but not all of them are here. And this dead demon was working for them. They'd grown their network with whispers and toxic lies.

Malachi is right though. I should have left one alive for questioning. The one wolf shifter, his head almost fully detached from his torso, is the only Latian shifter here. Along with him, there was the demon and a vampire I don't recognize.

"ID that one." My voice is vacant as I point to the unknown. I make it a point to know each creature in the Barrows, and I don't forget faces. That one was new. My shirt sticks to my chest, soaked with blood and I look down at it in distaste. This suit is ruined now, all because my hunger is setting me on edge. I can't bring myself to feed, especially not from the creatures I've been killing each night. Their blood is tainted with drugs, whether it's coke, heroine, or Rapture. The small amounts that make it into my mouth burn my tongue and I spit whatever I can out as I fight. I've drunk tainted blood before, so I know I could if I had to.

It's not her blood though. The only blood I crave. I know what my eyes look like, how those around me watch me with more care. I've been snapping more, quicker to fight, to kill.

"Get a crew down here and clean this mess up," I bark out but Malachi knows better than to offer commentary. His phone is still in hand and he starts sending out orders. "And get a team down here to finish the offload. I want every single glass vial accounted for."

My phone vibrates as Malachi brings his own to his ear with a sharp nod. He's less bloodied than me, having stayed further back and covered me with the rifle now slung behind his back. I never drew my own handgun. I shake my head in disgust at myself. Shucking off my jacket, I find a relatively clean spot on my shirt to wipe the tacky drying blood from my hands. Pulling out my phone, I go to absently swipe the notification from Malachi's text away but my thumb hovers over the screen.

It's an image notification from Eloise. The first text message she's ever sent me. My rage reignites as well as my desire. Her sheer disrespect and attitude earlier in the night nearly pushed me to the edge. I wanted nothing more than to throw her over my shoulder and haul her upstairs where I'd show her exactly why I'm the fucking king.

The rage is why I will not let myself close to her until I master it.

Opening the image, the world around me freezes as time stands still. She's outside of Tooth and Claw, a fucking dive bar of an excuse for a club. A place I would never allow her to step foot in, a place I've considered razing to the ground for all the violence and danger towards women there. Only the balance of the Barrows keeps me from acting. And she's there, wearing nothing but the fucking slip of a dress I couldn't resist picking out. A dress meant for my eyes only.

More than that, though. I don't give a fuck that she's flipping me off. It's the fucking neon blue vial at her lips, her head tilted back as she stares at me in direct challenge. Fucking Rapture. The drug that Deidre is currently going through withdrawal because of. A drug that should never have made it into her hands.

My phone shatters under my grip a moment before I let out a guttural roar of death and throw the crumpled phone into the ocean. It disappears into the night long before my hearing picks up the soft splash of it hitting the water.

"Sire?" Malachi is at my side, his brows narrowed and his rifle in his hands, ready to go to battle.

"Stay fucking here," I snarl, as the final threads of my tenuous control start snapping like violin strings.

I'm running before my words have finished, darkness roiling around me as I make my way through the twisted roads and alleys of the Barrows. Creatures, even humans, sense me as I run, the former diving for cover and the latter cowering in place.

A small part of me tells myself to calm down, that I can't go to Eloise like this, but I fucking *warned* her.

I halt at the curb in front of the seedy nightclub, right in front of a familiar motorcycle. Regardless of the stares of the terrified creatures, I sink my fingers into the seat and gas tank, the metal buckling under my grip. I slam it into the ground, the machine crumbling into pieces as it dents the asphalt. Screams accompany the sound of the blow, and the smell of terror cuts through the scent of blood in my nose.

Then I smell her: lavender and apricot. Strong enough to know she hasn't been here long.

I stalk towards the door, the crowd fleeing from my bloody visage. Not even the bouncers try to stand between me and my goal. I step over the pathetic velvet rope and kick the door off its hinges, sending it flying inside. Harsh music violates my ears as a cacophony of screams and scents washes over me.

Unlike the crowds outside, everyone in here is too fucked up on something to recognize death has arrived. The prickle of a vampire's stare itches in my skull and I locate them—fucking Lan. He will pay for bringing my mate here. She's pushed me too far to ignore the truth of my connection with her. She's my goddamn mate and I will bring her to heel.

The only reason I don't rip Lan's throat out is because of his stance and proximity to Eloise. It only takes two heartbeats to scan the situation, and see he's sober and ignoring the women around him. His glare is the only thing keeping a small circle of space around the dancing woman.

If I found out anyone touched her, I will have their hands.

I stalk through the crowd, shoving dancers out of my way. Strangled shouts or insults are cut off when they realize who and what I am. The closer I get to her, the more people realize what's in their midst and they're faster to clear the way.

She has her back to me, her arms up and bent over her head, her hips swaying to the music. Her back is on display, though fortunately for everyone around, not as much as the dress I'd picked for the dinner. A bead of sweat rolls down her spine, and I want to lap it up. She's sultry in her movements, the plump bottom of her ass playing peek-a-boo as she gyrates, her thighs taunting me above the boots.

I ignore the dancers who watch us with horror and press right up against her back. I grip the front of her thigh with one hand and capture her loose flowing hair in the other, yanking her head back and making her cry out. I want to lick the sound from her mouth.

She looks up at me, her eyes clear and only the faint hint of vodka on her breath. She didn't take any Rapture. Eloise fucking played me. Dared to manipulate me, thinking she could get away with it. My lip twitches into a snarl, my fangs bared as the lights of the club pulse and flash around us. She grips my forearm near her thigh with both hands, as if she could rip me away from her.

Her eyes widen as she recognizes me and then takes in the blood smeared across my face. I bend my lips to her ear and her fingers dig into my arm.

"I told you that you would lose if you tested me." She shudders against me, her gasp only for my ears before it's drowned out by the music. My fingers dig into her thigh, my thumb sliding up just under the hem of her dress as I pull back to relish in her regret.

Except my little lamb is smirking at me, pressing her lush ass against my hardness without shame. "Are you sure *I'm* losing, Ambrose?" Her words are lost in the music but I hear them all the same.

I sweep her into my arms, spinning on my heel as she wraps her arms around my neck. Then I'm racing us back to the house, back to my office, the door slamming shut behind us. Only the ancient fear deep inside keeps me from taking her to my bed. If I got her there, I'd ravage her body, breaking it under me.

Eloise is breathless from being carried so quickly, and I drop her onto her feet and shove her against the wall before she can get her bearing. I keep her there with a hand wrapped around her throat and finally I smell the sweet and sour scent of her fear.

"Is this what you wanted?" I growl as I move my head closer. The room is dark and the only light comes from the windows, casting us into shades of gray. "To see what I really am? To be bled dry, begging for your life?"

Something clatters to the floor at our feet as

Eloise grabs my forearm again with both hands. In response, I dig my fingers in harder, her lips popping open as she gasps for air. I haven't cut off her airway entirely, but it's enough for her eyes to widen.

Then Eloise's ink-black brows narrow, her maroon-painted lips opening. "Fuck you," she rasps out, the toes of her boots slipping against the floor. There's a heat in her brown eyes that mirrors mine and I vibrate with restraint. My fangs burn, sharp pain lancing through my head to my stomach demanding I strike and suck her dry while my cock strains against my pants.

A sharp, musky scent morphs my fury into something else entirely. Eloise's chest heaves, the dress barely containing her breasts and taunting me with a delicate sliver of her areola. This is turning her on. I knock her legs apart with my knee and cup her sex with my free hand, hissing at the lack of barrier between my fingers and what I want.

"Really, my lamb?" I purr before ducking my head to drag the tip of my tongue up the side of her face. "Your audacity knows no bounds, does it?"

I loosen my hold on her throat enough to let her speak. The defiance and lust in her eyes have me licking my lips.

"I was wondering what it took around here to get your attention," she answers. "Guess I figured it out."

Leaning my forehead against hers, I imagine my eyes reveal the extent of which I've denied myself. "I assure you," I whisper against her lips, "you have my complete attention now."

I capture her lower lip between my teeth, scraping a fang along the delicate flesh and bringing a bead of her precious blood to the surface. Eloise's sex clenches against my hand as I hold her gaze and capture the drop with my tongue. My own shudder runs through me and I grip her harder, making her gasp for air, and my fingers slip between her slick folds.

Brushing my lips against her skin, inhaling the sweet smell of lavender and apricots, I taunt both of us as I angle her head to the side and move my lips down her throat to her bare shoulder. The pale moonlight makes Eloise's dress glow, turning her into the dark goddess that I'd gladly offer my soul if I still possessed one.

"Ambrose," she whispers, her breasts taunting me, her blood rushing up to the surface. It begs me to sink my fangs in as I tug her pebbled nipple into my mouth. Her voice is thready, her eyes half-lidded and I ghost my lips over her.

"Little lamb," I murmur, still fascinated with the thump of her heart and the blood pumping through her veins, so damn close to my lips.

"Why—" she gasps as I lap up a bead of sweat that'd collected in the hollow of her collarbone. "Why have you been avoiding me? Did I do something wrong?"

I still at her timid question, pulling away from her skin and meeting her gaze. I release her neck and she settles on her feet as I slide my hand up and into her hair, cupping the side of her head.

"No, Eloise," I say, willing her to believe me.

She swallows, and I drop my eyes to follow the bobbing of her throat before looking back up. "Then why?"

"Do you really wish to know the truth?" My voice is sinister now, my fingertips digging into her scalp. She doesn't wince at the pressure, nodding. I move my hand enough to trace my thumb over her lower lip, enraptured by her softness. "Because all I've wanted to do since that night is fuck you until you beg me to stop." I meet her gaze, forcing my thumb into her mouth. "And I won't stop until I'm done. I'll feed from you too, drawing your life essence into me."

Eloise looks beautiful like this, bracketed by my body, her sex growing slicker as I undulate my fingers against her. I don't think she even realizes that I'm doing it, or that she's moving her hips, seeking more.

"Is that so bad?" My thumb muffles her, but the question is clear enough.

My black heart freezes as I look at her. Her pupils are blown wide, her arousal is coating my hand, somehow I've missed her hands clutching my blood-stained shirt at my sides.

"It is when I will never have enough of you," I

snarl before ripping my thumb from her mouth and crushing my lips against hers. I stifle her yelp, shoving my tongue between her lips, tasting every part of her mouth, marking it as my own. I kiss her, deep and desperate, my hunger free at last.

She tries to push back, to return the kiss with her own fervor but I won't let her. Not after the stunt she's pulled tonight. Sliding my fingers through her folds, I lap at her lips, taunting her as she's taunted me since the first night she walked into my office. Eloise shamelessly ruts against my hand, trying to get more pressure but I move with her, keeping my touch firm enough to make her angry.

"Ambrose," she groans, her voice half frustration, half desperation.

I speak against her lips, keeping her head against the wall with my grip in her hair. "You get what I give you and nothing more, little lamb. Be good and after I get what I want, I'll reward you."

Her tongue wets her lips, briefly touching mine, as I wait for her answer. "Yes, *sire*."

Fuck, this woman will be my downfall. I bare my fangs and angle her head away. The moment my fangs slide into her neck, I push two fingers into her hot, wet channel. She moans with pleasure and pain as I suck the blood from her veins. Each time I pull, I push my fingers into her, crushing her clit with the heel of my palm. She feels divine, her muscles fluttering around my fingers, sucking me in greedily even while I drain her of blood.

When Eloise begins to rut against me once more, I force my mouth from her. My hunger isn't the least bit satisfied. My fingers still inside her, I lick at my lips, unwilling to miss any drop of her blood even if it means I have to taste those I killed earlier.

I need more of her. So much more.

I let go of her head and trace the thin silver strap of the dress. "Tell me no and I'll walk away." It'd be worse than hell, but I'd figure out a way. For her, I'll always figure out a way.

She tilts her hips towards me, brushing against my dick. "I trust you."

"You shouldn't," I tell her. It's the absolute truth.

"I know," Eloise agrees but doesn't pull away. "I still do, though."

With a snap of my teeth, the dress falls down her body in a shimmering wave until it pools around her feet and over the dropped clutch. I step back, holding her at arm's length, my fingers still buried in her.

"You're beautiful, little lamb."

She's a vision of hedonistic beauty, a sin I want to slake my desires with. Her thick thighs are encased in black velour, and the rest of her is bare to me at last. She leans her shoulders back against the wall as I drink her in. The dark patch of curls over her sex, the silvery stretch marks decorating her hips and soft stomach, her luscious curves and heavy, full breasts with peaked nipples. The narrow trails of blood running down her pale neck.

Eloise stiffens, her eyes clearing as she finally takes me in. Even in the dim lighting of the room, her human eyes can see the dark stains that have dried into my clothing. This is when she'll reject the monster I really am.

"What happened? Are you okay?"

It's my turn to be shocked as she reaches out for me, real concern distracting her from the pleasure I've been giving. She is never what I expect. I catch her entreating hand and bring her fingertips to my lips where I press a gentle kiss against them.

"I had business," I remind her. "None of the blood is mine, my little lamb."

Her breath hitches at my claim, and I'm on her again. This time I let her have her hands, and she's ripping at my shirt even as our mouths battle for dominance. I growl, pumping my fingers faster, fluttering them inside when she succeeds at ripping the shirt open. It was already ruined, and her touch is a pain I'll always welcome.

She clings to me, her arms wrapping around me under my shirt, her nails digging into my back. I relish the pain, fucking her with my fingers harder, and scoop her right breast into my hand, guiding it to my lips as I curl down around her. Her hands grip my hair when I suck her pert nipple into my mouth, a sweet cry spilling from her lips. It's quickly becoming my favorite sound.

I lash at her with my tongue in time with my thrusts. Her breathing hitches, her walls clenching down on my middle and ring fingers as I push her to the edge. I stroke her clit with my thumb as I curl my fingers inside of her, finding the fleshy spot. She keens, her knees buckling and I catch her by shoving my thigh between her legs, never letting up the torment. Three more strokes and I give into the temptation I was presented with earlier. I gentle my hold on her breast and prick the flushed skin around her areola with my fangs.

Eloise's back arches off the wall, a silent scream parting her lips as her channel tries to crush my fingers as she climaxes. I don't let up, drawing it out, needing more of her pleasure. My cock burns with the need to be buried inside her, but she tastes too delicious.

When she wiggles against me, oversensitive, I let go of her tender, bitten nipple with a wet pop.

"Holy shit," she breathes out, her eyes still closed.

I growl with male pride at her blissful expression. "More," I snarl out and her eyes fly open as if she finally realizes I've given over most of my control to my instincts.

"Wha—Ambrose!" She cuts herself off with my name as I pull my hand from her and grip the back of her thighs and lift her upwards. She scrambles to get a hold of something, finally slapping her hand out to catch the top of the antique bookcase beside us as I bring my face level to her sex. I drape one of her legs over my shoulder, gripping her ass with one hand, and use my other to brace her thigh and open her wider for me.

Her folds are drenched, the scent of her pleasure dizzying. I fall on her like an animal, needing to taste every last drop of her. I feast, spurred on by the nectar slicking her and the sounds she can't seem to help making. Surrounded by her scent, her blood on my tongue and in my veins, I'm close to the edge myself. Shoving her other leg over my shoulder, I urge her to lock her ankles behind my back. The moment she does, I reach down and free my aching cock. My hand is still slick from her pleasure, and I stroke hard as I ravage her with my tongue.

She starts grinding against my face and I growl my encouragement as I pump my fist faster. She's so close, and so I am. With snake-like speed, I tilt my head and push a fang into her swollen lips around her clit. She jumps, hips pulling away before slamming back into me, both of her hands gripping my hair and tugging me against her. I suck her clit into my mouth, the blood flowing freely from the engorged flesh and mixing with her slick.

"Fuc—" Eloise's curse turns into garbled sounds as she comes hard. I shudder, staggering against her as I drink up her blood and pleasure, and then I groan into her, spilling into my fist.

With iron will, I pull my mouth from her sex, heart racing and breathless. I press my forehead against her mound, her thighs growing lax against my head. For a few long moments, all that fills the room is our heavy breathing. When she taps my head, I huff with disappointment, making her giggle. A beautiful sound that is a new contender for my favorite sound. I ease her legs off of my shoulders and down until I'm able to brace her on my forearm and kiss her. I tease her lips, taking my time.

Eloise's eyes flutter open and my black heart clenches at the emotion I see in her warm chocolate and honey gaze. I'm undeserving of that warmth, but hell if I won't hoard it close and do whatever it takes to make her keep looking at me like this. She brushes her fingers over my cheeks and I press into her touch, unable to help it. This is the woman who is meant for me, created by whatever fucked-up god that made my kind.

Proving herself too good for me, she tilts her ear towards her shoulder, offering her throat. I wait for her to guide my head down, needing her to be as involved in this as I am. This isn't her letting me feed because it's a part of the bargain, this is her telling me to feed, taking control. It's a revelation of sensation, having someone look at me with an affection I dare not hope for and having them guide my fangs to their blood.

I feed, keeping her braced on my arm and trapped between the wall and myself. She sighs, her body loosening as I drink more of her in. In this moment, in the moonlight in the dark world of the Barrows, I'm at peace with my mate.

Chapter Sixteen
ELOISE

When I drift awake, I'm still cradled in Ambrose's arms, his tall, lean body curled around mine. It makes me feel precious and cared for, delicate and small in a way I've never had a man inspire in me. Warm puffs of breath tickle my scalp and I nestle back against his hips, needing to steal a few more moments before the sun finishes its arrival.

Last night was another roller coaster in the amusement park that Ambrose and I have found ourselves creating. Avoiding me for two weeks and then making me come twice, first with his hand and then his tongue, feeding from me all the while... I think I would have shattered apart if Ambrose had carried me to bed and abandoned me. Breaking into pieces I'm not sure I could put back together.

I'd been afraid that was his intention as he laid

me down on the cool sheets before sliding off my boots. But he promised to return before disappearing. When he was gone long enough I began to worry, he returned with a plate in one hand and a sweating glass of orange juice in the other.

Something must be wrong with me, because he was covered in blood still, his shirt half tucked in his waistband and hanging open. He'd dealt death then given me pleasure. I should have recoiled from him, but when he sat at the edge of the bed, one leg tucked under him and opened his arm, I crawled right up against him.

I ate what he pressed against my lips, which turns out to have been chocolate toffee chip cookies. Whoever made them, I had wanted to propose. This morning, remembering how good they tasted, I still want to propose.

Ambrose had taken care of me, a much more intimate version of the volunteers at the blood donation centers. When I'd eaten enough to satisfy him, I could barely finish chewing, I was so ready for sleep. All I remember is pressing myself against Ambrose's chest and him rolling us towards the center of the bed.

He didn't fuck me last night like I'd expected… like I wanted. Now, with his hips cradling my butt, I learn that male vampires have the same physical response as human men have. My stomach twists with desire and heat pools between my thighs as I remember the sounds he made last night. Ambrose had come after I had, his mouth on me, and something about that is really, really hot.

I push my hips back just a little bit, afraid if I move too fast I'll disturb the sleeping vampire. He's not hard as a rock, but even at half-mast from sleep, he's large. I'm bombarded with memories of watching supernatural porn with Deidre, both of us curious as hell but too intimidated to look alone. Ambrose said he was turned into a vampire, which meant he'd been human before, so I guess his cock is what I'm used to working with. There are no knots or moving ridges or...multiples of them as there are with other supernaturals.

Unless becoming a vampire changes his shape?

I press back harder, shifting, my face bunched in concentration as I try to feel him up without actually feeling him up. Each little movement makes it firmer, and even though my curiosity is half academic, knowing that I'm arousing his body is heightening my own arousal.

What will he feel like in my hand?

I'm like a damn curious cat, but curiosity gets cats killed. My ardor cools. Curiosity got Deidre kidnapped and hurt. I know Rapture and Ambrose's dick aren't the same thing, but I'm out of my element here. I might have given in to the temptation of Ambrose, but I have to remember we have an expiration date. I'll keep booking clients and going with

Ambrose whenever he needs me somewhere, but this isn't a fairytale.

Ambrose isn't a savior, isn't a prince charming, even if he has wealth and power and insists on the best for me. I can't let myself get used to it.

"Where are your thoughts at this morning?"

It's so hard, though. Because I can really, really get used to that sleepy, husky voice murmuring in my ear.

I lean back against him, looking over my shoulder through my messy hair. "I was thinking about how you are not Prince Charming," I say with utter honesty.

Ambrose's lips—lips I know are so soft and wicked now—tilt in a grin. "God forbid anyone ever accuse me of such."

I roll my eyes and tug away from him, my bladder making its needs known. He lets me slide out of his arms and it's so hard to get up out of the cocoon of warmth and safety. When I start to pull the blankets off, I realize I'm still totally naked and yank them back to my chest, staring at the floor in consternation.

Letting Ambrose see me in the buff in a dark room last night was one thing, but it feels entirely different to walk across a dawn-lit bedroom. He'll see every bounce and jiggle of my butt and thighs.

"Is there a problem?"

I twist around to glare at him, the thick white duvet still clasped to my chest. Words die on my lips as I take Ambrose in. After I fell asleep, he must have showered and changed since there's no sign of blood —mine or what he'd had on him when he came to the Tooth and Claw. He's spread out on his back, one hand lazily behind his head and the other splayed out on his abs. A dusting of dark hair trails from his navel to the waistband of dark gray sleep pants, which are slung low enough that the trail of hair spreads out enough for a taunting tease.

Is this what it's like for guys when a woman's top is so low cut, you just know the nipple is barely staying covered? Because hell, I'd never thought a thin smattering of pubic hair would make me want to yank a man's pants down, but here I am all the same.

Especially since his pants are tented enough to know his morning situation hasn't entirely dissipated.

Realizing I'm staring at Ambrose's crotch like a crazy person, I yank my eyes back up to his golden ones. There's no trace of red in them this morning, and my heart thuds because I'm the cause of his satisfaction. Pale gold and orange from the sunrise warm his skin, and his brown hair is tousled from sleep. The biggest surprise of his appearance, though, is the lack of lines on his face. This is Ambrose, the man, before he takes on the mantle of vampire king. This is him without the crown of blood and night he insists on wearing.

I can give my body to Ambrose, leader of the

Nightshade vampires, king of all Vampires, and ruler of the Barrows.

It's Ambrose, the man, that I truly have to protect myself from. Everything is telling me to give this man my heart. And that's terrifying. Because I might be able to trust Ambrose the man to never break it, but Ambrose the king will never put me first.

His forehead wrinkles and he reaches out, but before he can touch my face, I jerk back and he halts. I can't let him touch me with tenderness, not when he has no barriers up right now. I'll dive headfirst into him and that can only end in misery.

"Can you look away?" I ask, hoping he mistakes my shaky voice for modesty instead of the emotional battle raging between my heart and my brain. "I'm not wearing anything."

"And deprive myself of such beauty first thing in the morning?"

I cast my eyes down at the bedsheet, biting the inside of my lower lip to keep from looking at him. Where is the dramatic asshole that I'm used to? That's who I need right now if I'm going to keep it together today. Thinking quickly, I force my eyes into a roll.

"You'll survive considering how long you stand in front of a mirror." I yank the rest of the duvet off him and twirl it around my shoulders and head as I finally stand up. I know I look ridiculous, but who hasn't wrapped an entire blanket around themselves like a wearable tent? The hardwood floors are chilly against my feet, another sign that the seasons are turning. The air is cooler this morning than it was a week ago. I rush through the bathroom door, closing and locking it behind me. If Ambrose really wants in, the lock won't stop him but it makes me feel better to have something solid between us.

As the water is heating, I abandon the white duvet on the floor and look at myself in the mirror above the sink I'd claimed as my own. I'm paler than normal, but that's not surprising given how much blood Ambrose drank from me last night. My fingers find the new bites on the side of my neck, the set from the first time he fed no longer sensitive. They're healed but send just as much pleasure through me as the first set had. Around my nipple is bruised, and my core clenches at the memory of his lips and tongue on my nipple. Peeking down, I try to balance with a leg up to see if I have a bruise near my clit but my knees prove too wobbly still. A tentative touch makes me bite my tongue to stop the moan from slipping out.

Holy shit, if I thought the bite on my neck is sensitive? The punctures on either side of my clit feel both heavenly and torturous from my touch. It'd be so easy to get myself off right now, but Ambrose is on the other side of the door. I bet he could hear me with his super vampire senses that he's so proud of.

Deciding I'm not brave enough to push his

buttons this morning, I jump into the shower and don't linger. By the time I'm done and dressed for the day, I've got enough of my shields up to face Ambrose again.

Except when I open the door, he's not there and the bedroom door is open. Telling myself I'm relieved, I head down the stairs to the dining room. Joséphine has finally accepted that I don't eat more than a few bites of any breakfast she makes and doesn't overwhelm the table with so many choices. This morning there are egg muffins with spinach and I blush, while chiding myself. I shouldn't be embarrassed that Joséphine knows I need iron-rich foods this morning; she's a vampire herself! It's probably a totally normal thing—

Oh, shit, did they hear us in Ambrose's office last night?

Groaning, I steal the plate and mug of tea—since I put my foot down on using the delicate china—I scurry away, head bowed. I don't even realize I'm heading towards Ambrose until I'm in the doorway of the office, startled to a stop because of who is in there with Ambrose.

Forgetting all about the fact that less than twelve hours ago, Ambrose had me braced up near the top of the bookshelves eating me out like a starving man in this room, I charge in and set the plate down on the table between the shelves.

"Where's Deidre?" I ask, not apologizing for

interrupting Kasar and Ambrose. My stomach turns and a cold sweat breaks out as I look back out the door, as if she might come in at any moment. "Is she okay? Is she here or home?"

Kasar gives me a bored look, and it's then I take in his attire. The last, and only, time I saw him, he wore the suit and tie look I've come to accept as the Nightshade standard. It's stranger to see a vampire around here in anything other than a suit. Kasar is wearing black cargo pants, combat boots and a gray t-shirt that has to be a size too small. Combined with his olive skin and ink-black hair pulled back in a messy bun, I want to snort.

Deidre must be panting like a bitch in heat, because Kasar like this is her dream man. Sure, her dream man has always been human, but now that I've experienced Ambrose's supernatural strength—I've gotta say human dudes are looking a bit lackluster.

"Deidre is in a safe location," Ambrose answers, and there's enough warmth in his voice that it makes me emotionally stutter to a stop.

"Oh," I breathe out, a tide of relief pulling my panic away as quickly as it'd washed over me. "Good. That's really good."

I wrangle my hands, the fact that I interrupted the two men in what was most likely an important meeting hitting me. Ambrose is dressed as clean as I'm used to, though he's foregone the coat and tie and has even pushed his sleeves up to his elbows. His hair isn't as tidy as it usually is, and there's no helping the blush as I realize he's just smoothed it down from when I'd gripped it like a crazy lady.

The warm mahogany office seemed too warm now, except for the chilliness radiating from Kasar, who hasn't moved except to cross his arms over his chest.

The vampire is ripped. He's definitely Deidre's type.

I point with my thumb over my shoulder. "I'm just going to go now," I say and take a step backwards, feeling awkward. I turn, about to quick-step the hell out of there when Ambrose calls my name. I halt, shoulders tensing like that time one of my better foster moms walked in on me doing karaoke in the bedroom. I'm like a glacier, barely able to turn back around but I do. "Yeah?"

Ambrose's statuesque face is placid, but when I meet his golden gaze, I get a brief glimpse of the warmth from this morning. "You'll be joining me for a late luncheon. Be ready by one."

I give him a finger gun and a wink before feeling horrified. What the hell, El? Are you back in middle school with a crush for the first time? The man had his tongue in you last night, and you gave him a finger gun? I speed around when he stops me again. I don't turn this time. Because, god, what if I offer him a high five or a coolio?

"Your breakfast?"

Tempted to abandon it, I hurry over to collect it, my head down and cheeks burning. Kasar is like an ice yeti full of disapproval and Ambrose is definitely laughing at me.

I flee out of the office and up the stairs. I haven't explored much on this floor but last week I did find the door to the wrap-around porch on this level. I'll take annoying bugs over embarrassing myself any day. Using my hip, I open the door and the cool air fans my face. The temperatures are dropping, but the humidity is still as thick as the height of summer. One thing the Barrows and Topside have in common, neither city can escape the humidity.

On this side of the porch, there's a roof, and two massive fans spin lazily, giving enough of a breeze to be comfortable.

"I don't know how you humans handle the heat," an unfamiliar woman's voice says, irritated.

I freeze just before I turn to sit in one of the white wicker chairs and see... well, I'm not entirely sure what I see. I eye the door and she scoffs.

"Please, I know better than to touch Ambrose's toys before he's done with them," the stranger says, waving at me dismissively with an elegant hand with a really sharp manicure.

"Okay," I say, voice neutral as I sit down, keeping my eyes on her. The porch is whitewashed and the railing is wrought iron. Each side of the house has the same furniture: white wicker chairs and benches with gray cushions, glass tables with votive candles, and hanging flower baskets set over the railing.

The supernatural—and she's definitely supernatural—is lounging in one of the wicker benches, her back tucked into the corner of the armrest and back, one leg bent with her booted foot braced on the other armrest, the other leg off the bench. She's wearing all black leather, from the knee-high biker boots to the painted-on leather pants with ties along the side from the top of her thigh down into her boots, showing off diamonds of bronze skin, to the leather corset halter top. She's bronze-skinned with long black hair that glows red where the sun catches, and she has a face and body that belongs on lingerie billboards.

Seriously, wealthy women in Newgate pay tens of thousands of dollars to look half as sexy and sultry as this woman.

She also has three-inch nails that look like metal and are sharpened to wicked claws. I look at her eyes again, not even bothering to hide my curiosity. Her eyes are gold, like vampires, but her pupils are slit like a snake's and when she winks, her eyelids close horizontally, startling me enough I jostle my tea and burn my hand.

Hissing, I break away from my study and set the mug and plate on the low glass table between us.

"Name's Eris," she says with a click of her tongue

and cheek, dropping her foot to the ground as she spins and sits upright.

"Nice to meet you." It really isn't. I want to run inside and hide under Ambrose's desk, but I think if I run, she'll chase and I won't even make it through the door. If I thought Ambrose feels dangerous, this woman oozes chaos and danger.

She gives another disconcerting wink. "Liar."

"Eris." Ashe's angry voice snaps her name and my heart starts beating again. "You were told to meet me in the garage."

The vampire who always has a smile to offer me is transformed in this... creature's presence. Malachi and Kasar always give off vibes of "fuck around and find out," but I'd put Ashe in a bit of a cinnamon roll category. Now, though, he looks like hell incarnate and I'm glad it's not me he's directing that fury at.

Eris, whatever she is, looks at me with mock repentance. "Oops. Looks like I'm caught." She stands up and is tall enough to almost look Ashe in the eye. She walks by the enraged vampire, tapping her nails against his clenched jaw in a mockery of an affectionate touch.

Each nail draws a drop of blood to the surface, but Ashe doesn't flinch or push her hand away.

She opens the door to head inside and tosses me a sultry grin. "If you ever get tired of Ambrose and want to play, come find me at the Acropolis."

Ashe growls something too low for me to hear,

and it makes her toss her head back and cackle before striding back into the house, not in the least bit intimidated.

A huge breath leaves me in a whoosh as I wilt against the wicker chair, my heart racing like I just had a brush with death. I really need more of Joséphine's cookies. And when I'm sure my legs aren't water balloons, that's exactly what I'm going to do.

Chapter Seventeen

AMBROSE

Kasar watches Eloise hurry out the door with a wry—for him—expression. Only those who have known him as long as I have are able to read the amusement in his otherwise blank face.

My second has been with me since almost the beginning. We share a sire, though we were turned months apart and had no knowledge of each other before then. We were Sir Mhichíl's first children and we bonded through the hell that transition can be without guidance. Mhichíl was a true-born, descended from the first Children of the Night, our forsworn ancestors from before history. They were legends by the time man first put a chisel to a stone tablet, and now only the oldest of us remember our history at all.

Modern vampires, as we're called now, have no reason to care about a history so far in the past even I struggle to comprehend it. Little does anyone know that this history and the fallout of our kind becoming forsworn are the reasons why humans are able to be turned into weaker Children of the Night.

Kasar looks at me, his passive face dropping as he cocks his head. "So, that's the way it is, hmm?"

I snort and lean back in my chair, in too good of a mood to let Kasar's ribbing irritate me. Had it been anyone else, maybe I'd growl and snap. But not with my oldest friend, who's stuck by me through hell and death and traveled the globe as we survived a practically immortal life with me.

I roll my head to the side, glaring without any heat behind it. "It is. Haven't told her yet," I confess. It's too soon to tell Eloise that she's my mate, the one soul meant for mine for the rest of our lives. She has the genetic trait to be turned into a vampire, but the older the human race is, the more recessive the gene becomes. If she's turned, she'll become a vampire—whether or not the gene is strong enough for her to survive the transition is another thing entirely.

"Never thought I'd see the day," Kasar says as he drops into the chair on the other side of my desk, reaching into his pocket for a cigarette. Even if we don't have to worry about lung damage or cancer, I don't understand his penchant for them. At least he keeps to the pure tobacco rather than the shit ones sold today with all sorts of chemicals. He lights up and doesn't bother offering me if I want one. He gestures to my office with the antique lighter. "This place reeks of sex."

I bark out a laugh and gesture towards him. "You're one to talk. Sex, blood, *and* Rapture." I smirk. "Your job was to rescue Deidre and return her home safely. Not fuck her."

Kasar, to my surprise, looks away towards the window, his gaze unfocused. He inhales deeply, the glow of the cigarette flaring to bright orange before cooling. When he breathes the slightly sweet smoke, I stiffen as I pick up the trace of Rapture's tart scent. I lean forward, pushing aside the keyboard and resting my forearms on the desk, my fingers laced together. It's not as if Kasar hasn't done Rapture before. Hell, we all have, but Kasar cut himself off when he found himself using it too much.

"Brother." I keep my voice low, not wanting to let anyone else overhear. Ashe is prowling in the garage; Joséphine is in the kitchen; and Lan is holed up in his room upstairs. "Should I have Malachi take over?"

The snarl and dark look Kasar sends me, pure fury and defiance in his golden eyes, almost makes me snarl in response. A challenge like the one lining every muscle in Kasar's tense body has the primal beast in me rearing up, wanting to leap across the desk and squash the challenger and prove myself the victorious king.

But this is Kasar, and he isn't a threat to my position. Never has been. I breathe out, forcing calm, and Kasar does the same. I watch patiently as he squeezes his eyes shut and pulls the Rapture-laced cigarette from his lips. If Deidre is pulling Kasar back into the world of Rapture, a world he made it clear he never wanted to return to, I will do what it takes to protect my brother.

"I'm managing it," Kasar says at last, his eyes half-opening. He stubs the cigarette out on his thigh without flinching. "I told you they doped her up. I'm helping her get through withdrawal, and you know what that means." He holds up the stub. "This helps me keep my own shit together and from reaching for the shit myself."

I nod, understanding, and look towards the open door, thinking about Eloise. I'm not surprised my thoughts are more concerned about her well-being when she learns about Deidre's condition, instead of the status of our bargain. Still looking away, as if I can conjure Eloise back to me by will alone, I ask what I need to know. If not for me, for my mate.

"Will she live?"

The thing about Rapture, and one reason the Nightshade vampires control it so fiercely, is that humans, once truly addicted, deteriorate fast. It's not like human drugs, where the withdrawal will be hell on earth but there's hope on the other end if you hold out. Rapture, by its supernatural components, alters the body. Indulged in, it's safe enough and humans will never feel the side effects and their bodies will heal, none the wiser of the risks.

If Deidre was forcibly addicted, which is entirely possible given enough Rapture, it means her human body is battling the evolution to the supernatural. Kasar has to keep giving her the Rapture to keep her alive, lessening the doses each time; but the most important step is after it's in her system, he has to feed from her. To drain her blood and force her body to create new, pure blood. Forcing it to return to its human nature.

So he's ingesting Rapture to save Deidre, and battling his own demons as he does so.

"Fuck," I bite out. Kasar just nods. The situation is fucked. I hate this goddamn drug, but it's better in my control than rampant on the streets.

"You have news," he says, waiting expectantly. It's why I called him here.

The garage door slams and we tense as Ashe blitzes through the house and up the stairs. He's following the path Eloise took, and I rise, panic skittering across my arms. Then I hear him say *her* name, and I snarl, but force myself to sit my ass down. Ashe will handle Eris, and she might be a chaos demon but

Cassandra is still in there enough to control her from harming humans.

"I still wonder if we'd have done him a favor by killing her," Kasar says, entirely serious.

"He'd never forgive us." I shake my head. If my family killed Eloise, even if it was the right thing to do, I would slaughter them all. "You know why she's alive."

"Whatever." Kasar dismisses the sore subject. "The Latians. Malachi says we're clear to take them out?"

I open one of the large drawers in the desk. Ignoring the handgun, I grab a manila envelope and hand it to him. I explain as he opens it, inspecting the contents with an experienced eye.

"They were out of the city when the Blackfang Barons took them and Markus out. Showing a modicum of intelligence, they stayed away. Bishop knew of them, but they were all low enough pack members, he figured monitoring was better than sending his men into my territory to kill them. I'd have allowed it, naturally, but they were too busy with their mate and by the time they cared, it didn't seem worth the effort. Since they're not posing a threat to their pack or Jemma, they don't care what we do to them."

He flips through the surveillance photos from Lan's work over the last two weeks, committing them to memory. "They're sticking to Topside," he mutters, and I nod even though he isn't looking for a response. "This Garner man, the politician, does he know what he's getting into with these guys?"

I don't answer right away. The Latians had distanced themselves from the name, choosing to go by the Kusheriri instead. Someone as arrogant as Michael Garner wouldn't have his people dig in too deep, especially considering the image the pack has carefully crafted. Enough money to be considered respectable in Newgate, with the right connections to Oldgate. The pack's residence was just across the river from the Barrows, and thanks to Lan, we know exactly how they're getting access to our supply of Rapture.

"I believe he understands, but perhaps not to the full extent," I say at last, steepling my fingers under my chin as I muse. "He's arrogant and young. He's also very intelligent, but still a man driven by greed for power. Our information shows he's skeptical enough of the Latians to not entirely trust them."

Kasar frowns as he reaches the last page and I wait for his response. Has he put everything together the same way I have, the same way as Lan? Ashe and Malachi have yet to see the dossier, and they won't if Kasar disagrees with my opinion. I do not move my pieces on the grand chessboard of the Barrows and Topside if my second doesn't support the moves, not with something on this scale.

His golden eyes meet mine, his ink-black brows

narrowed with indignation. He shoves the papers and photos back into the folder before tossing it to my desk with disgust.

"Garner is trying to make a new family," Kasar says; his voice drips with disdain. "He's a fuckin' human and thinks he can get enough supernaturals to follow him? What, like some fucking golden boy mafia boss for the Topsiders?"

I collect the folder and put it back in the drawer, eyeing the handgun. I've used guns many times to kill since they'd been invented, but for something like this, I want my knives. The knives I've had since Kievan Rus, from my human father.

"It's what Lan and I suspect," I agree. "He's gathering support from other cities. Newgate is one of the few cities that human crime organizations haven't been able to get a foothold in."

"Yeah, because this part of the country is ours," he snarls, territorial. His heel bounces, agitation running through him. Eloise was right when she pointed out, quite obviously, that I've been in Oldgate since before the town was formed, let alone Newgate. Kasar was here too, as well as the vampires we'd sired and the other supernaturals we fought to create a haven for. Oldgate has always been called The Barrows. My followers gave it the name when we buried the last of our pursuers and built our settlement on their grave hills to stake our victory. "Send Lan in and kill the bastard."

"That's where it gets complicated. He's built too much of a public political persona. If he dies now, no matter how, there will be questions. Lan's on him now." Indignation burns my stomach as I think of him sitting across from Eloise and me, his interest in her before turning his irritation on me. I had made a mistake and it rankles me. He wasn't some lowly connected pawn in a greater player's pocket, but a carefully scheming opponent.

And I put my mate on display for him.

"So you're going to bring him in?" Kasar stands, yanking his hair out of the bun before resecuring it again. "Think that's wise?"

I hum. "I've yet to decide. I'm sending Ashe and Eris to observe. If the demon will let Cassandra take control, she could get into his head. Plant a geas without the risk of him dying at an unfortunate time just for Eris's amusement."

Kasar stared at the ceiling and I know what he's thinking. Thinking about the witch who'd saved us all but lost her body to a demon. How Ashe had raged and hated us. He hadn't forgiven us in the past hundred years and I suspect it'll be another hundred years, given that Eris refuses to leave Cassandra's body.

"He's going to be useless for a while," my ancient friend warns and I grimace.

"Ashe will handle it if we need him," I counter, tugging on the responsibility of a king and letting any compassion I might have for a fellow vampire disappear. I have too much at stake to let the feelings of one vampire stop me from protecting my kingdom at all costs. It's why I gave Cassandra what she needed that night, and why I'd sacrifice her and anyone else all over again.

I don't give a fuck if I live until the world crumbles into space, but the haven I have created in the Barrows must live on. My atonement is far from complete. It will never be complete, but I will continue to try. Karina deserves that much. And it's the biggest fuck you I can give to my sire. The mad Child of Night who wanted to rule over a city flooded with the blood of all creatures.

Kasar was gone; must have left while I was stuck in my own dark history.

Shaking the morose and unproductive thoughts from my mind, I use my new phone to send messages to my soldiers. Names of creatures and humans who owe me favors, and orders to deliver them to Noir that evening. Michael Garner may believe himself powerful and clever enough to create a seat of power to rival mine in Topside, but relying on the weakest survivors of a traitorous wolf shifter pack is a mistake. By the end of the night, the Latians and those who have worked with them will be eradicated.

I will dismantle the foundation he's built, brick by brick, and he will know what true power is.

My phone rings and a perverse grin twists my

lips. Those who know me would know what the expression means, while others would be terrified. Swiping the screen, I bring the phone to my ear.

"Mr. Garner," I greet, before running the tip of my tongue over a fang. "What can I do for you?"

Chapter Eighteen

ELOISE

Excitement hums underneath my skin as the car pulls us into the garage connected to Noir. Ashe isn't driving us tonight, and our driver is a vampire that's unfamiliar to me. He seems young, and not just because he looks barely old enough to drink, but I mean young even for a vampire.

He puts the car in park and slides out of the seat at a normal speed, making me tick another box for evidence of his youth. The vampires I've been around seem to use their abilities as their primary nature, whereas this kid is still acting like a human. If it wasn't for the golden eyes and the supernatural stillness of his being, I'd think him human. I like him, though. It's good to not feel like the only one out of place.

After opening the door for me, he falls into step

behind me as I make my way to the familiar door that'll lead us towards Ambrose's office. I should be nervous about what I'm walking into, considering the last time I was here, but instead I'm excited to see Ambrose. When he went down on me, covered in blood, something came alive in me. Maybe I'm way kinkier than I ever suspected. Another part of it is how damn good it made me feel to know that someone as literally powerful as Ambrose was going to town on me like I was in the one in control. That I could bring him to his knees if I want to.

Tonight, I definitely want to.

The service hall is empty, and I feel the muffled sound of the club beyond more than I hear it. Last time I was here, I'd borrowed one of Deidre's dresses and felt awkward. This time, in a tease at the smart suits the Nightshade vampires always seem to wear, I'm wearing a two-tone outfit. It's my own power suit, though it'd never fly in Topside at an actual business. I'm rocking a pristine white, long-sleeve bodysuit that hugs my curves like a race car but the best part is the massive V-neck that goes almost down to my belly button, and it has lapels like a dress shirt that released its repressed sexuality. My black skirt is tiny but high-waisted, starting just below the deep neckline and only going as far as mid-thigh. If I drop anything, it's lost forever because I definitely will not be bending over in this.

The best part that has me swaying my hips and

feeling like hot shit? I'm wearing the fuck-me heels *and* a borrowed pair of Ambrose's suspenders.

I don't even bother keeping the giddy smile hidden; I'm too excited to see his face when he realizes I'm wearing something of his.

With my black hair hot ironed and in a high ponytail and maroon lipstick on, I feel like I belong here at Noir. I'm one of the Nightshades, something that so many humans in the Barrows, here on the dance floor, wish for each time they come.

The kid—I really should ask his name again—uses his superhuman speed to get to the door and open it before I can, and the music is louder now as we step into the dimly lit hall leading towards Ambrose's office. Before we get too close, Malachi steps out, closing the door too swiftly for me to get a look inside. Is there someone or something in there I shouldn't see?

Seriously, what's wrong with me that I'm getting disappointed that I don't get to see Ambrose in his element?

"Ms. Eloise," Malachi greets with what I've learned is his warm voice. "Ambrose is downstairs."

"Oh!" I perk up and studiously ignore the knowing look in Malachi's dark gold eyes. "Is he busy?"

Malachi gives a nod to the vampire behind me and raises his arm to guide me towards the stairs that'll take us down to the actual club.

"Ambrose is never too busy for you," he answers in an incredibly dry tone. I shoot a look over my shoulder, but not for too long. Even though Malachi would probably catch me, I don't need to lose the power chic vibe I'm feeling by almost breaking my ankle falling down the stairs.

"Is he meeting with anyone?" I ask just before we reach the door at the bottom. I step aside, knowing not to try to open it myself. I only need to be glared at once by one of the vampires for me to know that they take their protection duties very seriously.

Malachi opens the door, his back to me as he practically fills the doorway and waits for a long moment before stepping aside and letting me follow. I look around the more sedate side of Noir, the deep booths filled with patrons even this early in the night, but I don't see Ambrose. In fact, I don't see any of the vampires I'm familiar with.

Malachi gently grasps my elbow and turns me the opposite direction, towards the packed dance floor and pounding music. The music I could feel earlier now surrounds me with heavy beats, sensual rhythms, and intoxicating energy. I want to lose myself in the music, still craving that feeling from last night. Ambrose caught me too soon—all I'd had was one drink and danced for two songs before he'd swept me into his arms.

The room would be pitch black if it weren't for the swinging colored lights, bright strobe lights from different angles, and hazy, glowing fog swirling overhead. On one side of the room is a huge stage where a DJ dances that's lit by a backdrop of mind-bending images projected on the wall behind him. Opposite him is a bar stretching across the entire wall and filled with people pushing up to get their next order in. In between alcoholic bottles are the familiar ultraviolet blue vials of Rapture, glowing as if under a black light.

If Malachi answers me, it's lost in the music as he shifts in front of me. I press my hand to his upper back as he stalks straight through the dancing crowd. They part before him like schools of fish fearing an orca whale; some look at us with foggy gazes, while others move away by instinct alone at the aura of danger Malachi puts out. A few weeks ago, I would have been terrified of the vampire in front of me. Even now, my spine tingles with repressed nerves. But it's hard to be terrified of a vampire after seeing him squabble with another vampire over the last croissant at breakfast.

For all that Ambrose, Malachi, Ashe and the others are powerful and rightly terrifying—they're incredibly human. Perhaps it's because they were all turned, rather than born as vampires?

Even in the middle of a dance floor filled with humans high on Rapture, vampires feeding, shifters gyrating and howling—I'm not afraid anymore. Not when I know the most deadly creatures in here would kill to protect me simply because I'm the human Ambrose has chosen to feed from.

It makes me want to be wildly dangerous.

We make it through the dance floor and Malachi nods towards the mezzanine level of booths and private bar. To my surprise, Eris is leaning against the short handrail, watching the dancers with rapt fascination. Her strange gaze flicks over us before dismissing us entirely. Malachi steps to the side and gestures for me to go ahead. Before I can ask where Ambrose is, he's melted back into the dark and left me on my own.

Wary of Eris, as distracted as she seems, I take the three steps up to the sitting area. The flashes of light and colors give me a slightly disorienting view of the area and I pause, trying to see what booth Ambrose might be in. It's impossible to see anyone in the booths, with lights pointing out towards the dance floor shielding each booth in darkness. The part of me, the one that purrs and melts whenever Ambrose is near, tells me to go right.

After a few steps, I'm more confident. I haven't seen him, but I know he's in the furthest booth. Focused on him, I don't see the two male vampires appear in front of me until I practically run into them.

"Aren't you a tasty one," the brutish bald one on the left says loud enough for me to hear clearly. His eyes have the faintest red ring, but instead of being afraid, I'm more pissed off.

"Not interested." I cross my arms, glaring at the two. There's no way I can shove myself between them and keep going.

The other—not a vampire, shifter maybe?—has ragged, long black hair and is wearing a black leather trench coat. All he's missing are dark glasses and he'd be the ultimate stereotype of bad guys from the Barrows, and not in the sexy way.

"We could make you interested," the ragged one says with a smirk and pulls out a vial of Rapture. "Got more where this came from. Won't even charge ya. Just have a good night with us, sweetheart."

I roll my eyes. The bald vampire is wearing street clothes, so I don't think he's with the Nightshade vampires. Then again, I only know the inner circle. For all I know, he could be a street runner for Ambrose, and I doubt the king sends out a bulletin each time he has a new human to feed from. Either way, I know if I shout Ambrose's name, he'll be here with the hearts of these men in their hands before they've realized they've died.

Embolden with confidence, I change tactics. I'm not the nervous human I was before, and I cock my hip out and tilt my head at them. I don't miss how both of them give me hungry looks, the shifter's eyes stuck on my tits. He still has the vial of Rapture in his hand and I bat my eyelashes at him but I don't reach out to take it. Pitching my voice loud enough to be heard over the music, even with their supernatural senses, I shoot them both smirks. They trade smarmy grins and I have to resist rolling my eyes again.

"Is that right?" I ask, moving closer to them. They're tall, but not as tall as Ambrose. As if thinking of him conjured him, my skin prickles with awareness. Peering over the brutish vampire's shoulder, I see the narrowed gaze of the vampire king. His golden eyes meet mine and I wink. His shoulders loosen, and he leans against the mezzanine railing with idle curiosity replacing the irritation in his eyes.

"Sure is, sweetness," the brute growls and puts his meaty hand on my hip. I look down at it in distaste before leaning closer to his ear, making sure the shifter leans in to hear me as well. Ambrose is snarling, glaring at the vampire's hand.

"Unfortunately for you, I have plans for this evening. And I doubt you can give me half as enjoyable a time as he can." As I say the last bit, my eyes find Ambrose's once more and my stomach warms with the promise in my words.

The brute snorts and squeezes my hip. "Ya sure about that? What's his name, maybe we know him?"

I pull back and pinch his thick finger to pull it off of me, my nose scrunched. "Oh, you absolutely do know him." I cock my head and look between them. "Why would I settle for two mangy street curs when the king is waiting oh, so, patiently for me?"

They both freeze, their muscles tensing, before the shifter lets out a nervous laugh. "No fuckin' way the king is botherin' himself with a human chick like you."

Rather than be insulted, I put a hand on one of their shoulders each and push. This time they fall apart as if I have the same strength as Malachi. As I step between and past them, I look over my shoulder.

"Bothering? No," I say. "Supplicating? Absolutely."

I stalk towards Ambrose, who hasn't moved from his spot at the rail, ignoring the disbelief coming from the two men behind me. My vampire looks at ease leaning against the rail, ignoring the males and only having eyes for me. When I stop just in front of him, his eyes don't have any sign of red but there's a hunger there. Hunger that burns me, and drives my own higher.

"I hope I didn't keep you waiting," I say, knowing we still have the attention of the other two males. I hold Ambrose's gaze, challenging him, as I offer my hand to him. Will he make an example out of me in front of these two peons and make me submit or will he indulge me in my display, letting me maintain the power I've claimed?

"Never, ma lionne," Ambrose says with a toe-curling purr and takes my hand, dipping his head to press a kiss and nip to my fingertips. "Shall we?"

I nod once, and as he holds my hand as if we are

at court in the sixteenth century, I look back at the males, only to laugh when I see they've disappeared.

"Riffraff should recognize royalty when it nears them," Ambrose whispers in my ear, his sensuous voice somehow drowning out the overwhelming music. He steps behind me, still keeping my hand in his, and wraps his other arm around my waist, pressing his front to my back. Molten lava pours between us and the hard length of him presses into me.

"Did you like watching that?" I ask, tilting my head to the side, arching my neck for his gaze.

Ambrose takes the offer, running his lips up the column of my neck, the barest scrape of his fangs making my knees weak. "Absolutely." Ambrose nips the bottom of my ear, and I moan. "Watching you act like the queen you should be is now the second favorite thing I've seen."

I twist in his arms, only enough to meet his gaze as he holds me with insurmountable strength. "The second favorite?"

The grin that spreads across Ambrose's mouth is lewd and perverse. "Oh, yes. Watching you shatter in pleasure against my mouth is absolutely my favorite."

The damn vampire pulls back, walking me the last few steps to the booth. "Mr. Garner and I have nearly concluded our business," he says, his gaze going to the politician already seated. Surprised, I raise my brows and the man raises a half-filled tumbler in salutation.

"Eloise," he greets and at my confusion, he takes a long sip as I sit. Ambrose slides in after me, his arm coming around my shoulders and pulling me close. "I remembered where I'd seen you before. A reporter interviewed me a month or so back, a Desiree —Denise—"

I don't realize I'm gripping Ambrose's thigh until his hand covers mine. "Deidre."

Michael Garner uses his tumbler to point at me, his face open with recognition. "Deidre! Yes. She was asking about my plans for community support in the Barrows. We got on the topic of her, and she showed me a picture of the two of you." He finishes his drink and slides out of the booth. "If you see her again, tell her hi from me. I always like having reporters as friends. Ambrose."

Not waiting for Michael to be out of sight, I turn towards Ambrose with wide eyes, heart in my ears. He presses a finger against my lips, stilling my questions, and glances towards the retreating politician. Stomach twisting from Michael's comments about Deidre, I try to keep the questions from erupting. After an eternity, which was likely no more than a few seconds, Ambrose drops his finger.

"He knows Deidre—"

"I know," Ambrose says, his face close to mine so I can hear. My fingers dig into his thigh again, urging him to continue. "He's more involved with her abduction than we first believed." When I try to stand, my thighs hitting the underside of the table and rocking it, Ambrose grabs me by the shoulders and forces me back down. "I'm handling it, Eloise. He may be a rising star of Topside politicians, but he will not go unpunished for Deidre or his other transgressions. Can you trust me?"

I chew my lip, searching Ambrose's face. With the strobe lighting, I only see him clearly in quick flashes but what I can see tells me he isn't lying. I nod, looking down at the table as I try to force the anxiety from my stomach. He releases me, but leaves a hand on my back, rubbing comforting circles there. It doesn't take long for my body's natural response to this man to replace the anxiety with a different type of nerves.

"Do you want a drink?" he asks, a lock of dark hair falling out of place. I reach up and smooth it back into place before tracing his sharp jaw with my fingertips. How I ever thought I could resist the pull Ambrose creates in me, I have no idea. Right now, I don't want to resist it. I don't want a drink and I don't want to dance.

Leaning forward, I brush my lips against his in a ghost of a kiss before moving to his ear. "I want you, Ambrose."

Chapter Nineteen
AMBROSE

I barely stop myself from sweeping Eloise into my arms and racing through the crowded dance floor. Instead, I settle for holding onto her hand and charging through it like a madman. If the dancers had swayed and flowed out of Malachi's way, they're racing and leaping out of mine. When one dancer doesn't move fast enough, I grab him by the shoulder and fling him to the side with a snarl.

Eloise's laughter, so distinct to my ears despite the music, makes my cock throb. I pull her faster, ripping the door up to my office open, uncaring that it bounces off the wall. Hell, I don't care that I'm making a spectacle of myself and ruining my black-hearted statue image. All I care about is getting Eloise alone before she can come to her senses and change her mind.

When I get her in my office, I pin her against the

door, my mouth devouring hers even as I lock the door. Using the sharp pin in the mechanism, I let the lock take a drop of my blood, the blood runes ensuring that no one will interrupt us. It's strong enough it'll keep a damn army out. Which is what someone will need if they want to try to come between me and my mate in this moment.

Eloise grasps my shoulders, sighing into my mouth. When she arches against me, I wrap my arm around her, needing her closer still.

"You drive me crazy," she murmurs between kisses and she doesn't know the least of it. My scalp burns as she tugs on my hair and it only makes me ache harder. "How can you make me this way?"

I grip each of her wrists and pin them to the door above her head, my mouth going to her delectable neck. I can't get enough of her and I growl against her pulse point. "You have no idea." I nip her there, but don't sink my fangs into her. Her blood won't satisfy the need gouging me apart within. "The moment you walked in here, all I wanted to do was pin you on my desk and fill you with my cock."

"So inappropriate," she teases, breathless, and I huff out a laugh as I hold her wrists with one hand and give in to the temptation of her.

"Me?" I run my finger over her shoulder to the suspender strap. My suspenders, the minx. I was hard the moment I recognized them when she stepped up onto the mezzanine. "You're the one stealing from me. I should punish you for that."

Eloise turns her face towards me, her eyes half-lidded with lust. The smell of her arousal overwhelms my senses and it's all I can do to stop myself from taking her right against the door.

"You wouldn't dare." There's a glint of challenge in her eyes, a plea in her tone that sings to the wickedness inside of me.

I still, pulling on the mask of the vampire king, the beast she responded so beautifully to the night before. A shiver rolls through her as I turn an icy glare onto her and release her hands.

"I wouldn't, would I?"

For all that my beautiful lioness chafes at the chains of authority, I'm beginning to understand how much she desires to be overpowered. To be forced to give up control and submit. I am more than willing, eager in fact, to bring my mate to heel. To break her down until she spills everything to me and only me.

Eloise gasps when I grip her long hair, so conveniently pulled back, and she stumbles forward as I march her to the center of my office. The lights are off, but there's more than enough for me to see by from the dance floor below. To her human eyes, though, how dark must it be? It's been too long for me to remember, but from her wide blown pupils and spike in arousal, it's dark enough to be tantalizing.

"Knees," I bark, yanking her hair down when she refuses. Eloise gives another token resistance before falling to her knees so perfectly. Releasing her, I move to lean against my desk, the memory of her here overlaying with the sight before me. I'm thankful for my decision to have the carpet cleaned. I wouldn't want the stench of that foul creature's blood mixing with the delicious scent of Eloise, who, even on her knees, glares at me with a mixture of lust and defiance. Her nipples are pebbled against the white of her top, the barest shadows begging me to twist and bite them.

I palm my length lazily, considering all of the punishments she would enjoy but I know there's only one thing I want to do. My sensitive hearing picks up the gentle hitch of her breath as I push off the desk and stalk towards her again. When I'm close enough she has to strain herself to look up at me, I catch her chin in my hand.

Running a thumb over her lower lip, I smirk. "You love to mouth off, Eloise. I think I'd better put this pretty mouth of yours to better use." I release her and slide off my jacket, tossing it to the side of the room, before beginning to roll up my shirt sleeves. When she doesn't move, I arch a brow. "Take out my cock, little lamb."

Her small hands reach for my belt buckle without hesitation and I take in the view of her, so pretty on her knees, her breasts barely contained in her devious choice of a top. It'd be so easy to slip my hand in her shirt and free her breasts. I hold back, for now. My little lamb craves punishment, so that's what I'll give her.

A groan rumbles from my chest as she wraps her hands around my cock for the first time, her fingers and thumb not touching, I'm so thick compared to her. When she leans forward, too eager to take me in her mouth, I catch her by her hair again, keeping her from her goal. She whimpers and shifts on her knees, but she doesn't let go of my cock.

"Hands behind your back, little lamb," I order, my heart beginning to speed up. Only this woman has ever enthralled me so quickly. "You thought I wouldn't punish you, and now you're about to learn how wrong you are."

Slowly, as if considering how far she might be in over her head for the first time this evening, Eloise grasps her wrists at the small of her back. The position has the added benefit of thrusting her breasts out, and this time I don't resist the temptation to cup one in my hand. She hisses when I pinch her nipple harshly before kneading the supple flesh. With another hard pinch, I let go of her breast and guide my cock to her red painted lips.

"Take your punishment like a good girl, and I'll tell you a secret." I'm rewarded with the intrigued glint in her whiskey dark eyes and she opens her mouth obediently. I don't give her time to accommodate my girth before I thrust in, anchoring her in place by my grip on her hair. She groans and winces around my cock but doesn't pull away as her eyes close.

"Look at me as I fuck your mouth," I order, pulling out and thrusting back in. Her eyes fly open, finding mine, even as she gags around the head of my cock. I thumb her lower lip again, a satisfied snarl on my lips. "This is the proper use of your mouth, little lamb. Each time you think of mouthing off, I want you to remember this."

Eyes watering, Eloise stays still as I slide out of her mouth and back in. This time I push past her gag reflex and her eyes smart as I push in until my balls are pressed against her chin. Her nostrils flare as she struggles for breath and I relent at last, letting her gasp in air. I wait, my cock resting against her lips and she opens her mouth obediently once more.

"Good girl," I praise. Will she ever not impress me? I doubt it.

I fuck her mouth and throat until tears spill over her cheeks, but Eloise never releases her wrists and never tries to pull away. She takes me like I ordered, her eyes staying open as I abuse her lips, and every passing moment I can smell how wet she's getting because of this. It would serve her right for me to spill down her throat and deprive her of what she wants, but I'd be depriving myself too.

Eloise isn't leaving this office until I've fucked her and filled her cunt with cum.

She's panting after I take my cock from her, her lips swollen and even darker red. Unwilling to resist the desire, I bend down and kiss her, my tongue replacing my cock in her mouth and she whimpers and eagerly returns it. In a swift move, I pick her up and carry her around my desk before setting her on her feet. Once she's steady, I sink into my chair and give myself a moment to appreciate her. I reach out, tangling her fingers with mine as I drink her in.

"You're gorgeous," I breathe out, entirely sincere. She blushes, even after letting me fuck her mouth. Letting go of her, I grip the armrests of my chair. "Undress for me, then sit on my desk. Leave your shoes on."

The brat in Eloise emerges again, much to my secret satisfaction, but she complies, pushing down the excuse of a skirt before reaching towards her sex. Then she's pulling the bodysuit up and over her head, dropping the top between us. Obediently leaving the shoes on, she hops up onto the desk, leaning back on her palms with a fierce look in her eyes as if she refuses to be embarrassed by her nudity.

Good, my little lamb should never doubt herself.

I take myself in hand, stroking slowly and catching her attention. When she sucks her lower lip in, I still.

"Spread your legs, little lamb," I chide, and am

rewarded with a shy grin as she does so... barely. Growling at her malicious compliance, I lean forward and force her legs as wide as she can go. "There we go," I murmur as I drag a finger up between her slick folds, coating myself in her arousal. Holding her gaze, I lick my finger clean. "Delicious."

"Ambrose," Eloise whimpers so beautifully, her chest rising and falling rapidly with her breath. "I want you."

I stand, nudging my way between her legs. I grip her thick, soft waist with one hand and stroke myself against her sex, teasing her clit.

"Remember what I told you in this very office, little lamb?" I murmur before dipping my head down and capturing a nipple between my lips. Her head falls back, moaning as she reaches for my shirt. When she doesn't answer, I release her nipple with a wet pop and tug her chin down until her lust-glazed eyes meet mine. "I won't fuck you until you beg, little lamb. So say pretty please."

Her nostrils flare and then she's leaning up towards me, her heels digging into the back of my thighs as I narrowly keep my cock from sliding into her eager channel. She wraps my tie around her fist, holding me tight.

"Won't you fuck me, pretty please, my king?" she purrs with a flutter of her eyelashes.

Ignoring the defiant sarcasm, I fulfill her request. Slamming into her, I snarl and squeeze my eyes tight against the onslaught of her body. If I thought her mouth was divine, her cunt is beyond words as it pulls me in, pulsating around me and threatening to send me to the edge already.

Holding her fast to me, I grab the back of her head and our mouths meet in a desperate collision as I begin to thrust. Eloise clings to me, her hands scraping over my shirt until I finally rip it from me, needing to feel her skin against my own. Her laughter blending with sweet moans taunts me as I shove down my pants and kick my feet free before shoving the computer monitor to the floor. I don't give a fuck if its broken or not; I can get a new one. But I'll go mad if I can't cover Eloise's body with my own.

Laying her out lengthwise, I palm her ass and lift her hips as I thrust back into her. Our hands are frantic, touching and grabbing and holding on to one another as our bodies continue to collide.

Eloise's moans become shorter, higher, and her channel clamps down harder around me. She's teetering on the edge, and I'm nearly there with her. I slide a hand between us, seeking out her swollen clit with my thumb, but I can't bring myself to ease her madness yet.

Baring my teeth against her chest, right above her heart, I groan as my fangs elongate. The need to claim her as my mate squeezes the air from my lungs.

"You're mine, Eloise. Tell me you're mine." My words are so guttural I'm amazed when she responds.

"Yes, Ambrose. I'm yours." Her words are so broken, I raise my mouth from her heart vein and I'm astounded at the vulnerability in her eyes. Vulnerability and desire and hope and an affection I've done so little to be worthy of. An affection I will spend the rest of my eternal life earning.

"Do you want to know my secret?" I ask, slowing my thrusts to long, steady strokes, keeping the both of us dancing on the knife's edge of pleasure. When she nods, I shudder and hide my face by brushing a kiss across her racing heart. Dropping the guise of the cold king, I burn for her when I speak. "We were made for each other, little lamb. You're my mate, and I can never, never let you go. Not in a few weeks, not in a year. Never. To lose you would be to lose myself."

She tenses when I first speak, and I'm close enough to hear her heart beating harsher against her ribs. I wait, a terror that she'll refuse me tracing a cold finger down my spine. Her whiskey eyes widen as her vulnerability recognizes my own and a ferocity overtakes her. She grabs the back of my head and pulls me to her mouth, kissing me harshly.

"You're mine, Ambrose d'Vil," she says against my lips. "Even if you could let me go, I won't let you go."

I snap my hips into hers, both of us raggedly

breathing as we kiss, sloppy and desperate. I make my way down her neck to her heart vein once more, dragging my fangs against her skin.

"Bite me," she whimpers, arching harder against me until my fangs prick her skin. "Please."

Sinking my fangs into her heart vein, I strum her clit with my thumb as I drink in her heart blood. The fresh blood of her heart, forever marking her as mine and only mine. Eloise shatters around me, her nails digging into my back and drawing blood. I'm glad of it, hoping she cuts deep enough so I can wear her mark as she now will wear mine.

Her pleasure still milks me, pulling me closer and closer towards following her into bliss, I take one last swallow of her blood. Relenting on her clit, I cut a gash across my chest, against my own heart vein and guide her mouth towards me.

"Drink," I beg, ragged. When she hesitates, I shake my head. "It won't turn you. Claim me as yours, ma belle lionne."

Her lips press against the bleeding wound, and the sweet pull of her mouth sends me over the edge with a roar. I spill into Eloise, my heart-marked mate, with a growl that shakes the bulletproof glass wall. Then her core clenches around me as she comes again, dragging out my own pleasure until I'm weak and she slumps back against the desk. Braced on my forearms on either side of her shoulders, I rest my forehead against hers and she clings to my waist with limp hands.

As my heart begins to settle, I run my nose against hers, reveling at the sensation of... happiness filling my chest. Eloise is my mate, and she's claimed me as her own—vampire or not. She's drank from my heart vein and there will never be another for either of us.

Chapter Twenty
ELOISE

I could never have imagined how giving into the primal craving for Ambrose would change my life, or how quickly. To be honest, after we finally combusted in his office, I don't think either of us thought of anything other than each other for the next two days.

Ambrose took me home—the place I truly feel is home—and we didn't leave the bedroom for two days. I've never been more sleep-deprived or sexually satisfied. I had no spare room in my thoughts for anything except getting my hands on Ambrose, taking him into me, getting as close as I can since I can't physically burrow my way into his chest and live within his skin.

The part of me that always sensed him is stronger now. I can sense more than his presence or what direction he's in. Now I have a seventh sense that is specifically Ambrose. In the few stretches of times we were awake and able to keep our hands to ourselves, he explained what mates are. To be honest, I expected to panic, and I'm still waiting for it to hit.

I've bound myself to an ageless creature, and he's bound himself to me. It's like going from a simple infatuation to way more committed than marriage, skipping all the steps in between. Considering how I've avoided committing to anyone relationship-wise, other than my friendship with Deidre, then combined with Ambrose's sheer radiance of authority, I should be clawing at the walls, desperate to escape.

I'm not though; in fact, I'm so chill about it I'm wondering if this is some sort of dream. The sense that connects me to Ambrose is wholly and utterly content with the change in our relationship. The skeptical voice inside tries to shame me for giving in to him before our bargain is complete, but it's easily rebutted. Maybe I'd be concerned if it was only Ambrose who claimed me, but he assures me that my mark on his heart vein is evident to other creatures even if it isn't as strong as it'd be if I were a vampire.

That's what I'm wrestling with as I stand in the shower, soaking in the hot water by myself for the first time since we marked each other. It's silly to already miss Ambrose, when I know he has work to do and he's just downstairs, but I do. I can't say that I love him right now, but I'm sure as hell falling hard and fast, and it won't be too much longer. The bond between us tells me that this feeling isn't going to fade after the honeymoon stage of any new relationship. Like Ambrose, this bond between us is immortal.

I'll grow old eventually, I consider as I begin to shampoo my hair. My scalp is sensitive from how much Ambrose enjoys pulling my hair, and my core tightens and slickens at the thought. Before he left the bed this morning, we'd taken our time with each other but he still made sure I saw stars twice before finding his own completion deep inside me.

Praise the doctor who came up with the IUD.

What would Ambrose do after I pass away, being mortal? What about when I grow old and wrinkly and my body is saggy and weak? He will still look the same, a beautiful, ageless sculpture of primal power, not a gray hair or wrinkle in sight. He'd said there would be no one else ever again for him, but if I'm honest, I'm terrified that he'll come to resent me. How would it look to have an old lady at the side of the vampire king?

Sighing, I rinse out my hair. I don't want to think about tomorrow's problems, but that's not who I am. I'm the worrier, the one who has to overthink everything. I don't make split-second decisions, like binding myself to the vampire king on his desk when he's balls deep in me.

A small tink and draft of cool air lets me know

the shower opened, and the bond between us tells me it's Ambrose who's stepping inside just before his hands touch my waist.

"You're worrying, little lamb," Ambrose says against my damp shoulder and tugs me back against him. I melt against him with a sigh, my world feeling right again now that we're in physical contact. I've never been clingy, but now I'd glue us together if I could.

He's naked, and his length is half hard against my back. Through our new bond, I sense his concern and his growing arousal. I wiggle my butt against him, having learned just how much of an ass-man Ambrose is. He growls playfully against my ear, gripping me harder against him to keep me from moving.

"You can't distract me that easily," he rumbles, and starts to stroke my stomach with his broad hand. Warm fuzzies bundle up around my heart as I think about how he's never once made me hesitate about my body around him. My stomach is soft and round with evidence that I prefer cookies and ice cream over lifting weights or running. Yet Ambrose touches every inch of me with reverence, and I'm swiftly getting used to it.

"A girl can try," I say with a pout and another tiny wiggle. I think I've won when he moves, his length fully hard against my ass now. One hand dips down to cup my sex while the other slides up between my breasts and wraps around my throat.

God, I love how it makes me feel when he holds me so possessively.

"Good girls get rewards, little lamb." Ambrose undulates his fingers against my sex, enough to tease the arousal into burning coals but not enough to give me the pleasure I want.

I turn my head as much as I can in his grasp, wanting to kiss him but he's keeping me out of reach. I give him a heatless glare. "And if I don't want to be a good girl?"

Ambrose's golden eyes turn cold, and his smirk is a match with its iciness. Without warning, his hand vanishes from my sex and I whimper at the loss.

"Then you'll be punished," he promises. "I won't give you what you want."

I hate that Ambrose means it. He has a thing about control, and I'm a sucker for it. Which means if I want his fingers in me, his cock in me, in the next five minutes, I have to play nice. I consider refusing out of spite, but the topic is going to come up eventually. I might as well get it over with now rather than let it fester in the back of my mind until it erupts like a nasty infected boil.

Turning to stare straight ahead at the white marble shower wall, I slump against his chest and bring my hands up to hold onto his arm. As if sensing my compliance, Ambrose slides his hand back between my thighs, his fingertips teasing my entrance with gentle pressure.

"I was just thinking about the future," I admit quietly. Anxiety digs its claws into my stomach as I face the issue head on. "About how I'm going to grow old and die," Ambrose stiffens, but I push on, "and how you'll end up resenting having an old lady at your side. It won't be good for your image."

"Fuck my image," Ambrose says with considerable heat. "I will adore and cherish you for the rest of my life, Eloise. You are a part of my soul, and if you die, I will follow without hesitation or regret."

I turn in his arms, heedless of his hold on me, and press my palms flat against his tattooed chest. Tattoos that I've spent hours tracing with my tongue now. Ambrose's expression is fierce, his eyes full of intimidating determination as he looks at me. His dark hair is still dry, but water drops run down his shoulders where the shower sprays over my head. My own hair is plastered to my head and back, and I have to blink away random drops of water that run down my forehead.

"No," I say adamantly, aghast at the idea of Ambrose dying. "You can't die. I forbid you. Even if I'm dead. I'll—I'll figure out a way to come back and haunt you or refuse to see you if there's an afterlife."

His gaze doesn't soften as he gently grasps the side of my head, his thumb stroking my jaw. "Mates are new to you, Eloise. But not a single creature would wish to outlive their mate. You were the missing piece of my soul, as black as it is, a piece I never knew existed. If you leave, I will be a broken creature. It will be a hell unlike any other and you cannot ask me to suffer that."

Tears burn my eyes at the sincerity in his words, and I hide my face against his chest. His arms wrap around me, and we stand there under the water together, existing with each other and ignoring the rest of the world. The slow, steady heart beat under my ear melts the worst of my anxiety away, and when one of his hands begin to stroke along my spine, all but one small part disappears.

Unable to look up at him, unwilling to see his reaction, I ask the question I've refused to consider until now. "Could I be turned into a vampire?"

Ambrose stiffens against me and fear that isn't my own radiates down the bond, before it's entirely cut off. I look up, concerned, but he's got his mask firmly in place. My heart aches for him; no one feels that much fear unless they've experienced something to cause it.

"Talk to me, my king," I murmur, hoping to give him the same safety as he gives me.

Ambrose turns me until my front is pressed against the cool marble wall, making me yelp from shock. His hands grip my hips like vices and his cock is heavy against the cleft of my ass.

"You can't distract me like this," I throw his words back at him, even if my sex is burning with anticipation.

"Can't I?" Ambrose tilts my hips and cool air wafts against my back as he moves. He grips one of my thighs, lifting it up and opening me up to him. "Fuck, you smell delicious, little lamb."

Giving up any pretense of resistance, I push my hips back in a silent plea. Then his mouth is on me as he pins me against the wall. I groan, unable to say anything that makes sense as his tongue delves between my slit and teases my clit. I want more; I need more. I will always need more of Ambrose.

His growl vibrates through me, and I belatedly realize he can sense my desire through our bond. Then he's moving us, manipulating me like a doll until he's lying on his back and I'm kneeling over his chest. He palms my ass as I look down at him in shock.

"Come here," he demands, his voice rough with arousal, his eyes staring hungrily at my core.

"But—I'm heavy," I protest weakly. There's a reason none of the guys I've ever hooked up with wanted me to ride their faces.

Ambrose lifts a brow as if I've insulted him, and then he literally picks me up and brings me directly over his face, leaving me to squeal and throw my hands out to try to brace myself. I end up with one hand behind me on his abs and the other slapped against the wall. I can't resist his pull as he sets me on his mouth, my back arching as his depraved tongue resumes its self-appointed task of my pleasure.

With Ambrose's encouragement, I end up leaning back against him on both hands, transfixed by the erotic image of him greedily gorging himself. When his eyes find mine, I gasp, my hips thrusting forward, from the sheer lust there. He pulls me tighter against his face, never breaking eye contact, and then one hand is sneaking between us. Two fingers slide into me embarrassingly easily, but what makes me pause in my thrusts is the pressure his thumb puts against my ass.

I meet his gaze, and between the amusement in his eyes and the challenge I feel through our bond, I refuse to pull away. It's not like I've never considered butt play before, and even had one short-term boyfriend try to introduce me to it. It was always weird with him, but right now with Ambrose? It feels decadent and sexy. I push against his fingers and almost crumple when he sucks my clit between his lips.

Ambrose is drowning me in sensation and I don't want to be saved. I give myself over totally to the instinctual part of my brain, the part that only cares about chasing my pleasure. When his thumb slips deeper in, I groan at the indulgent feeling of having him in both my holes. Now if only I had the mental capability of getting his cock in my mouth, but I can barely keep myself upright as my hips jerk back and forth and he pumps his fingers into me.

When twin sharp pains lance through my sex,

the familiar bite of my vampire lover, I'm catapulted into oblivion. My hoarse, incoherent scream echoes in the massive shower as Ambrose keeps sucking at my sex, dragging my pleasure on and on and on. My orgasm slams into a second one, and only when the pleasure begins to turn to pain does Ambrose relent. I flop over him, totally useless, much to his amusement.

With one last lick, he shifts me again until he's able to stand up, with me all limp noodle in his arms. The last thought I have before I doze off in his arms is why I ever thought I'd be too heavy to ride his face, with his supernatural strength and all.

Vampire lovers are definitely the best lovers.

Chapter Twenty-One

AMBROSE

Tonight, we will be meeting Mr. Garner to put him back in his place. Eloise requested to go, wishing to see me mete out justice on Deidre's behalf. The vampire I was before meeting her wants to deny her. She's a human and has no right to make requests from a king, especially one that will put her life in danger.

But I'm her mate, heart vein marked and sworn, and I cannot find it in myself to deny her. I could never have imagined how different the bond would make me. Since she's human, she only gets a fraction of the experience. Only extreme emotions make it down the bond to her. For me, though, and how powerful I am, everything she feels and even trace whispers of her thoughts assault me constantly.

I wouldn't have it any other way, though.

Steeling myself, I slide my hand into my pocket

to find the item that has kept me company throughout my long life. At this point, it's inconceivable to go without it. It is as much a part of dressing for the day as are my usual suits and ties.

Studying the ancient coin in my palm, worn smooth by time and my constant need to touch it, I consider again the reason I bear it.

Karina. The woman I wished to make my wife before I was turned.

The woman I killed in blind rage and desperately tried to save by turning her into a vampire. I injured her too greatly to survive the transition and bore the shame since. When I first learned of mates, and how even turned humans may have one, I wrapped my heart in darkness and violence. Karina would have been my true mate, I believed.

Opening the box with my other hand, the ancient daggers nestled in velvet call to me. They know blood will be spilled tonight and they want to taste it.

Before I reach for them, I set the coin, my past, on the velvet between them. Karina was my past, hundreds of lifetimes ago.

Eloise is my true mate and my future. It's beyond time to let Karina go.

It's as if a knot releases and loosens within me, my breathing easier, my thoughts less edged. Had the guilt and pain of Karina's murder truly affected me so much?

I collect the daggers, and take a few minutes to secure them on my belt at my lower back. It's a comforting, exciting weight that has my heart rate elevating. Weaponry may have advanced over my lifetime, but there is nothing more satisfying than the feel of a blade entering your enemy's flesh.

Snapping the box shut, I head towards the garage, knowing Malachi will be there with Eloise.

He's pulling up as I walk in and I open the door for Eloise.

"We're taking my car," I explain as I offer her my hand. "We must play the game and appear as if we've arrived on our own."

"That makes sense," she says as she accepts my assistance. She's a vision, with her favored black leggings paired with an evergreen silk tunic that only covers half of her ass. She has her hair pulled back as if she couldn't be bothered with it and a pair of ballet flats. An entirely casual outfit for a meeting between powerful rivals.

I want to fall on my knees and worship her. It is likely unintentional, but her choice of wardrobe is a display of power. She wields the entire might of the Nightshade vampires through me, even if she doesn't fully understand what her position as my mate is.

I reach past her and close the door after giving Malachi a nod. He will move into position around the meeting place.

"Can I drive?" Eloise bounces on the balls of her

feet, her hands clasped in front of her, pushing her breasts enough to tease me with the V-neck. I thread my fingers into her hair, gripping her tight and tilting her head back.

"If you are a good girl, I will let you drive us home."

Arousal, bright and hot, radiates down our bond as Eloise's cheeks pinken and her breathing quickens. Her eyes are wide and hold mine as I tilt my face towards her and nip her plump lower lip with a fang and capture the bead of blood that wells up with the tip of my tongue.

"Can you do that for me, little lamb?" I ask, my tone more serious. The urge to drive her home and lock her in my—*our* bedroom claws at my insides. "You have to follow any command I give you."

She swallows hard, her lips pressing together in a firm line as the fires of determination brighten her whiskey brown eyes. "I can." Her need to see this through resonates to me and I press a kiss to her forehead.

Only for Eloise will I temper my jagged edges.

I take her hand again, leading her to my WRX. Ashe gave me so much shit for getting one, letting me know exactly what most humans think of those who buy them. But unlike many human street racers, this vehicle is purely for its functionality.

And I like how it looks.

Helping my mate in, I crouch beside her and reach for the racing harness, making her giggle.

She tries to take the strap from me, saying, "I can buckle myself."

I nudged her hand away. "I know that, ma belle lionne. I enjoy taking care of you."

She doesn't say anything as I finish up, tightening the straps until I'm satisfied. Warmth fills both of our chests and I cup her chin, running my thumb over her lips.

I pull away, shutting the door and moving to the driver's side before I can give into the temptation of her lips.

With swift efficiency, I secure my own harness and turn the key over, the car humming to life. Pushing in the clutch, I check the mirrors and catch Eloise looking at me with a smirk.

"Yes?" I shift into gear and we head out of the garage, the door closing behind us.

"I'm just thinking about how much you liked strapping me in," she says, her voice husky. Amusement ripples from her, but I scent her arousal.

"Naughty," I tease, squeezing her thigh before returning my hand to the gear shaft. "Behave yourself and I might just tie you down and have my wicked way with you."

One day, I will need to take her to Lush. One of the private rooms. But something tells me my little lamb will enjoy the experience.

"Fine," Eloise huffs and settles into her seat. Then she sends me another taunting look. "I know old people drive slow, but really, sire?"

I growl playfully before pressing on the gas, shifting into a higher gear and launching us forward. Eloise squeals with delight, and I laugh as I turn, hugging the sharp corner. If I can't make my mate scream with pleasure before this meeting, I'm more than happy to have her scream with delight as I discover just how much she enjoys fast cars.

To ASSUAGE Mr. Garner's paranoia, I've agreed to meet with him in Newgate at a location of his choice. He will believe himself in control, and I will maintain that illusion until it is time to rip it out from under him. He'd only sent the location two hours before we left, as if that would leave me little time to prepare.

Considering the meeting is supposed to be only the two of us, I gave no objection. Besides, Lan had done his job well. Lan had harried the young upstart all across the city except for three specific areas to create a false sense of security in Michael. The fool had played right into our hand, and picked a warehouse near the river on the north side of Newgate.

Michael will not be foolish enough to arrive without some sort of concealed security, just as I will have my trusted men around the building in spots of their preference. Malachi will blend with the shadows in the eves, Lan will be on the rooftop of a building one street away with sightlines into the open warehouse, Ashe and Eris will be in an SUV staying on the move and waiting for my call.

If Garner wants to survive tonight with his rising political career intact, he will bend to the superior power.

Eloise's nerves flare as we walk towards the building's open bay door. I take her hand in mine, threading our fingers together, and tug her to a stop. She looks up at me, one side of her lower lip caught between her teeth.

"All will be well, ma lionne," I say before leaning to rest my forehead against hers, my eyes closing briefly. I inhale her, wrapping myself in her scent, in her very being. "I have promised you justice and it will be done, one way or another."

She squeezes my hand, and I admire the strength in them despite my hand nearly engulfing hers. Her nerves lessen, but do not disappear entirely, although along with her anxiety I feel her strength and fortitude.

"Let's do this," she says, and I step away but don't drop her hand.

As we approach the modern warehouse, made of wood and stone and tiered roof with ceiling windows, I cast my senses out. When I was first turned, I couldn't sense who was in the room beside mine, but now my power has grown enough that I can seek out living creatures in a three-mile radius. Kasar can sense up to five miles, but he's honed that skill as he's become my most lethal enforcer. Each of my vampires are in place, and the few supernaturals I sense flee when my mind brushes against theirs. There are mortals in place around the warehouse, which I'm not surprised. I do think it's strange that Garner has only hidden away human guards.

The more fool, him.

I let go of Eloise's hand just as we step into the yellow light spilling from within. The place only carries legal goods, which lends credence to Mr. Garner's public image. If he's seen walking in here, no one would question his business. Oh, how people only see what they wish to see. The warehouse is neatly organized with three rows of shipping transport boxes, stacked only two high. No debris or trash litter the floor, as a warehouse in the Barrows would have. Then again, the warehouses in my kingdom are also made of sheetrock and corrugated metal roofing.

"Stay by my side," I order quietly, and to Eloise's credit, she doesn't roll her eyes. I've only told her this multiple times, but the amused frustration aimed at me settles her nerves more. In one stride, I assume the heartless monster that is the vampire king and we come to a stop at a crossroad in the warehouse. The rows of transport boxes are before us, to our left are forklifts and other necessary machinery, and to our right is a bay of desks as if the operators preferred to work close to their goods rather than in the offices making up a second floor along one wall.

Garner began his walk towards us the moment we crossed the threshold and it's not long before he joins us. Like me, he's wearing a suit and tie, though his is a deep navy rather than black. His hair is slicked back, and when Eloise notices, she snorts. A snippet of her thoughts brushes my mind, too quick for me to hear them clearly. From the rest of what I sense from her, I gather she's amused at how Garner is trying to match me in appearance, and perhaps puts too much credit into mafia movies for crime lord fashion.

I care less about his appearance than his emotions. His heartrate is too steady, and no scent of fear or trepidation comes from him. In fact, I can't smell anything. His eyes meet mine, a pleasant camera-ready grin on his face that reveals nothing. I narrow my gaze in at the leather cord at his neck, and his grin grows wider as he comes to a stop.

"Ambrose," he greets and raises his hand to hook the cord on a finger and tug it up from under his tie. A pale stone carved with a bindrune hangs there. "Do you like my new amulet? Cost a pretty penny but it seems to be worth it from your reaction."

Whatever witch had created that for Garner has signed her death warrant. Bindrunes or protection amulets are not forbidden in the Barrows; ones that erase the traces of a being are though. To younger vampires and creatures who haven't come into their full power, Garner is invisible to them. The amount of magic it takes for such a spell to maintain its power beyond a few hours is staggering.

"Ambrose?" Eloise whispers, but I don't respond. I'm scanning the shadows, catching signs of the few human guards I'd already sensed.

Michael Garner lets the leather cord drop, the pendant sliding back under his tie, and shoves his hands in his front pockets. He cocks his head, making a pointed effort of studying Eloise. I bite back the growl building in my chest, forcing myself to freeze my heart once more. An impenetrable wall of ice armors me, and from the hitch of Eloise's breath, she feels our bond being blocked off. I cannot send her away; she's already a player in the game we've begun and must see it through.

I meet Garner's eyes, and his pupils dilate a fraction. I may not be able to scent his fear, but his body language is clear enough.

"An expensive trinket," I say at last, and Michael's smile becomes a touch forced. I keep my hands at my side rather than in my pockets, my blades a comforting weight at my back. "It is too bad the witch who created it will have to die. They know my laws."

Michael laughs, and Eloise shifts her weight

beside me. I'll have to teach her to master her emotions and not display them for all to see. He's shaking his head. "*Your* laws? When did you become an elected official? Did I miss the fundraising and campaign?"

I only allow a slow blink of my eyes, though my ire is quickly rising. "I have been here since before the fou—"

"Yes, yes, I know," Michael interrupts me and cocks his head. "Sorry, did I interrupt your grandstanding?"

"It doesn't matter." Though I'm already tempted to make him suffer for such disrespect. He believes he has something keeping him safe, not just the protection amulet. Something I've missed. "We have business, do we not?"

Michael's body language changes, squaring his shoulders he looks at Eloise instead of me. I let out a soft growl, unable to stop it. Michael's eyes dart to me, satisfaction in them, and I tamp down my temper. Instead of snapping at him, I reach out with my senses and brush up against Malachi's, letting him sense my anger enough that he will set the others on high alert.

"Eloise, right?" he continues without letting her answer. "Your friend Deidre was a fighter. I wish I could have brought her over to my side, but she refused. Called me a dirty politician just like the rest of them. As much of a fighter as she is, she's still human. Couldn't fight back against the vampires."

"You're a fucking asshole," Eloise snaps, rage infusing her voice. "And she's right about you. But you're not getting away with hurting her."

"Hurting her?" Michael shook his head. "I didn't hurt her. I set her free." I wait, preternaturally still in the way only vampires can achieve, as he reaches into his coat pocket and pulls out a vial of Rapture. It's different, though. Any human wouldn't be able to tell the difference, but I can see the glowing blue is undercut with green. "With this. Shame I didn't get to see the final result, though. Maybe when this is over, I'll go find her and that Kasar of yours. I owe him anyways, considering how many of my men he's killed."

"What do you mean, you set her free?" Eloise asks, taking a step forward with her fists balled. "That's just fucking Rapture."

Michael holds it up in the light, inspecting it with false curiosity. "Is it though?" He muses, before shrugging and lowering it. He nods his head towards me. "Did he not tell you then? About what she was like when that savage took her from me?"

Eloise stares at him for two long ticks before turning just enough to see me. I meet her gaze, cold and unflinching. "What is he talking about?"

"She was forcibly addicted to Rapture." I'm blunt and when a part of me wishes to wrap Eloise in my arms after I see the pain in her eyes, I force myself to be cold once more. "It's being handled. We had a bargain and I keep my word." I turn my attention back to Garner, who is smirking now. If that was his trump card, he has much to learn about surviving at the top of the criminal world. "Enough of this. You are establishing a crime syndicate in Topside with supernaturals and humans alike. I'm prepared to offer you terms to allow it. If you don't agree..." I shrug.

Garner fucking tsks at me, shaking his head again. "So predictable, d'Vil. You know what your problem is?"

"I have the feeling you're going to tell me," I droll, bored.

"Arrogance. Hubris. Being in power for too long," Garner lists off as he begins to pace. He's becoming riled, excited, unable to stay still until the perfect moment to strike a death blow. "You believe you have no challengers because you've ruled with fear for so long. You couldn't see what was right in front of your face, but an upstart human could."

I drop my head back, as if exasperated, but in doing so I see the dark form of Malachi slipping into the building through a window. I drop my gaze back to Garner. "And you're that challenger, I presume? The one who will take my seat from me?"

Garner raises the vial of altered Rapture as if toasting me. "Right in one. Did you know Rapture can do more than just give a taste of power to humans? With the right additions... well, let me show you."

Garner uses his thumb to unscrew the cap with a swift flick and then downs the entire drug. I'm dragging Eloise behind me before the liquid hits his tongue. The garage bay door slams down behind us, and she whirls to look while my eyes stay on Garner.

He drops the vial and rolls his neck, his nostrils flaring as he pants. Something is happening, but the damn bindrune amulet stops me from sensing him. When his eyes open, they're the same color as the Rapture.

"Ambrose..." Eloise trails off and that's when I see them. The human guards I'd dismissed are coming out from the shadows now, their eyes honed in on us, the same blue-green glow to their eyes. Fucking hell, the man had been right about my arrogance regarding the guards. But it's the last mistake I'll make tonight.

Garner takes a step forward, a macabre grin on his face. "Killing you is going to be so fucking satisfying."

As one, they launch toward us, death in their eyes.

Chapter Twenty-Two
ELOISE

One moment, a dozen guards are stalking towards us with creepy-ass glowing eyes, and the next moment I'm on the ground, Ambrose standing over me. I scream as one of the beefy dudes in black tactical gear soars through the air from a jump that is definitely not natural for a human. Then Ambrose has caught him in midair, faster than my brain can process, gripping him by the shirt. In the same second of time, Ambrose throws him towards the transport boxes, snarling and hissing in a way that might be funny later.

Right now, though, it's really fucking scary... and hot.

Curling up in a ball, I've got to get my shit together; right now is the worst time to get all turned on by my mate going full vampire on these drugged-up humans' asses.

"Get her out of here," Ambrose orders and then someone grabs my waist.

Out of some instinct, I kick out before I realize it's Malachi. He doesn't seem to care, and my kick probably felt pathetic to him anyways. His eyes are straight red, though, and fear sinks its claws into my heart. I trust Ambrose, and know even if his eyes were fully red with hunger, he wouldn't hurt me. Malachi isn't my mate, though…

"It's the fight," Malachi snarls, his deep voice raspy with restraint. He yanks me onto my feet before I can object or thank him for clarifying that he's just hyped up on vampire adrenaline and not hungry. "Let's go."

We don't even take a step before another of the guards is behind him, his hands going to Malachi's head. I can't do more than scream before the guard begins to jerk his hands to the side. I don't think I'll ever understand how powerful vampires truly are. Because Malachi just fucking twists to the side with the guard's movement and then punches through the man's chest. When he jerks back, Malachi has his fucking heart in his hand.

The guard doesn't drop, though. His eyes glow brighter and he manages two steps before he finally falls, his drugged body catching up with the fact that it was dead. I stare in horror at the dead man, wincing when I hear the wet squelch of Malachi crushing the organ before dropping it.

"Shit," he grunts, moving to my side and taking another hit meant for me. "Take my fucking gun," he orders as he grapples with the guard. I must be in shock or maybe he compelled me, but I don't hesitate. I move towards him, ignoring the fact that he's trading punches with someone and crouch low to avoid swinging elbows. I don't remember unhooking the strap on the holster, or even sliding it out, but the heavy handgun is in my hand.

Looking down at it, I say, "I don't know how to use it."

Ambrose is in front of me, blood splattered across his face. "Point and shoot," he barks. "Safety off. Now get your ass somewhere else." He's gone just as fast and all I can think is he's somehow already lost his suit jacket.

One of the guards is thrown past me, jolting me into action. I run towards the desks, hoping I can make it to the stairs and hide upstairs somewhere. Blood fills the air, I don't even need to have heightened senses to smell it. I weave between the desks, trying to put anything between me and the fight.

I yelp, and slip backwards when one of the guards is suddenly there in front of me, snarling. "What the fuck," I eke out as I stagger backwards. "What the fuck is that shit?" I bring up the gun but before I can raise it more than a few inches, the guard's head snaps backwards. Like the other one, he's able to bring his head back up and snarl once more before he crumples to the ground, blood oozing out of the bullet hole between his eyebrows.

"Thanks, Lan," I say, not sure if he can hear me, but grateful all the same. I jump over the dead man, but two more guards appear. I skid to a stop, my flats slick with blood now. "How many of you *are* there?" Not sticking around for their answer, or for Lan to pick them off, I book it towards the rows of boxes. I just have to keep moving and stay away from the fight.

There's a gap in the row wide enough for me to slip between, and from all the movies I've watched, I know I can't stay put. Looking up the crates, I don't even process my thoughts before I'm climbing up them. Somehow I scramble up to the top. It isn't graceful, especially while holding a gun, but I make it to the top and flatten myself on my stomach.

Safety off. "Right," I mutter to myself and inspect the gun. I find the safety and switch it off, muttering about how I should have gone with Deidre to the firearm workshop back in high school. At least I hadn't really needed Ambrose's helpful advice of "point and shoot." I'm not that inept, for crying out loud.

I inch forward, trying to keep low and just glad of the crates having lids. It'd suck right about now if I had to do an awkward obstacle course of shoeboxes, computer parts, bags of rice, or whatever the hell is in these things. I finally get a clear view of the fighting area and almost vomit out my heart.

Ambrose and Malachi are separated, each one fighting off at least five guards. Both of them are saturated with blood, and I slap a hand over my mouth when one of the guards lands a punch to Ambrose's face and sends him staggering back a step. Ambrose roars as he strikes back, a knife in each hand, and cuts through the guard's head before delivering a kick right to the man's chest. His headless body goes one direction while his head goes another. The man's body staggers backwards, as if somehow still able to try to catch itself before death catches up with it.

"This is some insane shit," I mutter. I narrow my eyes. Michael disappeared, and all the bodies are wearing the same black uniform. The box shudders as something slams on top of them, and I look over my shoulder. "Fuck. Ambrose!" I scramble to my feet as Michael Garner, bloodied and crazy-eyed walks towards me with a very pissed-off expression. "It's Michael!"

There are only a few more boxes before the end of the row, and there's no way I can jump to the next one. I turn around, gripping the gun with both hands and raising it.

"Don't come any closer." Later I'll be impressed with how confident I sound and how my hands don't even shake. "I don't want to shoot, but I will and you fucking deserve it."

"You're on the wrong side, Eloise," Michael replies, walking towards me without hesitation. "Deidre was so close to being transformed. She would have thanked me for it. Fucked me for it, even. But you had to steal her away too soon. Now she must be in terrible pain if she isn't already dead."

"Eloise!" Ambrose's shout comes just before the stack of boxes shudders from a huge impact. I have to throw out my hands to keep from tumbling off the boxes.

Michael has no issue and keeps walking towards me, quickly lessening the distance between us. Fuck it, if Michael Garner dies and people ask questions, I'll tell them the truth. Raising the gun again, I pull the trigger. The recoil sends my hands up, but Michael stops. He rotates his arm, inspecting the bullet hole in his bicep. Holy shit, I actually shot him. And it isn't worth anything as he shoots me a creepy grin.

"This is why we humans must become a better version of us. We have the potential in our DNA. This wound? It's already healing. Don't you understand how this will change our world?"

"You're fucking crazy, dude."

A blur fills the space between us and then a blood-drenched and very, very pissed-off Ambrose is standing between me and Michael.

"Ah, the soon-to-be late king."

There's an eeriness about Ambrose that sends a

chill down my spine. I'm not afraid of him, not exactly, but in front of me is a vicious, deadly predator, greater than any apex mammal on Earth. When my mate speaks, it's with such a deep cold that it burns.

"You are a child in this world," he says, as if each word is being written in stone. "You are playing with a power you have not earned, that you do not understand. You claim I have arrogance from ruling too long? You have the foolish arrogance of a child who still believes themselves immortal."

Michael snarls something, and then they're fighting. It's wild and unrestrained, but I can't look away. Ambrose is no longer using his knives, and he isn't striking to kill. How the hell is he still willing to keep Michael alive? I stagger to my feet, needing to get down in case Michael pushes Ambrose back towards me. Scoping the area, I realize there's no one left on the ground. All that remains are piles of bodies all wearing black.

And blood. So much blood. My gorge rises and I slap a hand over my mouth to keep from vomiting.

Someone stalking along the top of the other row has me looking towards them. The briefest panic disappears as I recognize Lan. Then Ashe and Eris drop down from the open window above, both landing with enviable ease like cats. Ashe meets my eyes and gives me a nod before looking at Eris. She grins and leaps from her spot to behind Michael.

I scream when Malachi is beside me without warning, flinging myself away. Before I can topple over the side, he catches me deftly in a gentle but secure grip.

"Apologies," he murmurs and plucks the gun from my hand.

"Jesus, dude," I shake my head but look back at my mate. Ambrose was right. Michael fights with sheer power, trying to muscle his way to victory. Yet he isn't as strong as Ambrose, though it may not seem that way. Ambrose fights with precision borne from centuries of experience.

Michael is a bumbling bear, and Ambrose is a savage wolf, striking only when necessary and delivering critical blows. Ambrose could have killed Michael by now, and from the growing fury on the man's face, he knows it.

"Is he just... toying with him?" I ask, unable to look away from the display of brutality in front of me. With the other Nightshade vampires at such ease, I find myself relaxing too.

Michael lunges with a guttural roar, a last-ditch effort at violence. Ambrose steps aside and under Michael's arm, letting the man stumble past him. Ambrose's expression is one of poised cruelty, and he grips Michael's hair with one hand as he slams a knee into the man's back. My stomach twists at the sound of bone breaking and Michael's scream of pain. It's the same scream that a cornered rabbit cries before the fox strikes.

"Eris, now." Ambrose barks, glaring down at the man now on his knees. I think he's only on his knees because Ambrose is holding him up by the hair. I'm utterly hypnotized by the scene in front of me.

Eris, dressed as badass as when I first met her, strolls up and around Ambrose like she's out for a sunny stroll in the park. There's even a bounce to her step, and when she meets my gaze, she gives me a jaunty wink before spinning on her leather-booted toes and gripping Michael by the chin. He moans in pain and thrashes against Ambrose's hold as her metal nails pierce his skin.

She begins speaking, and I think it's Latin. Whatever it is, though, sends another wave of goosebumps over me. I've never seen magic done before, but this is definitely magic and very powerful magic at that. As she continues, Ambrose joins in, speaking in tandem with Eris for a few lines before falling silent, leaving her to finish it alone. He's not the only one silent. Michael Garner is glassy-eyed and still, as if his soul has been drained from his body and now he's just a living husk. I wait for him to fall dead as the others did, but when Ambrose releases him, he stays upright.

"Leave us," Ambrose orders Eris, who bows dramatically before dropping down the side of the crate. Ashe goes to follow, but halts when Ambrose snaps his head to him. "Stay."

I think Ashe is going to argue but then he stands with his hands clasped in front of him, his hard gaze trained on Michael. Looking over my shoulder, I watch Eris pick up one of the bodies and I have to look away as she brings it up to her mouth.

Ambrose is crouching in front of Michael, who's now slack-jawed but his eyes follow Ambrose's every movement.

"Throw yourself to the ground," Ambrose bites out unexpectedly. My eyes widen as Michael does exactly what he says without hesitation, and I flinch at the wet thud at the impact. Ambrose doesn't look back at me as he steps off the crate and into the empty air.

"Come on," Malachi says softly, opening his arms.

Speechless, I let him scoop me into his arms and squeeze my eyes tight as he jumps to the ground below. It's not even jarring when he lands, and when he sets me back down on my feet, it's in time to see Ashe and Lan land in tandem. They may as well have just taken a step forward for all the impact they showed.

They approach Michael, lying limply on the floor. A groan lets me know he's not dead. Together, they lift him onto his feet, and turn their attention to Ambrose. Soldiers awaiting their king's orders.

"Michael Garner,"—Michael twitches at Ambrose's voice. Holy shit, is he *healing*?—"You will never struggle against the Nightshade vampires. You will allow them to escort you home. You will tell no one of this night. You will give these two vampires all the information about the Rapture you have had altered. Then you will recover and continue your life until I have further instructions. Do you understand?"

Michael's jaw pops back into place as he opens it to speak. "I understand."

Ambrose nods to Ashe and with Lan's help, the two drag Michael out of the reopened garage door. Ambrose still has his back towards us and I take a step forward. I freeze when he says Malachi's name.

"Sire?" Malachi responds without hesitation.

Ambrose turns his head to the side, enough I can see his sharp cheekbone and the streaks of blood on his face.

"Leave us."

Malachi hesitates, looking at me so fast that if I hadn't been looking at him at the same moment, I wouldn't have noticed it.

"I will not repeat myself," Ambrose says with a low growl.

"Yes, sire," the vampire beside me says with a sharp bow despite Ambrose being unable to see him. Then he's gone and it's just Ambrose and me in a warehouse full of dead bodies and blood.

I wait, unsure of what I should do. I still can't feel him inside me, not the way I normally can. He's still there, but it's like when a hose gets bent and the water is cut off.

"Ambro—oof," I end with a grunt as suddenly I'm surrounded by him. He's gripping me tight, squeezing me against his chest as his fingers dig into my skin and his face is pressed into my neck. He's holding me so tightly, I can't even bring my arms up to return the embrace. "Ambrose?" I try again, my voice quieter. I don't know what to do with this Ambrose.

He shifts and pain lances through my neck as he sinks his fangs into me. I groan at the unexpected intrusion, and how it morphs from pain to pleasure. He's gulping at me greedily, his lips on me so fiercely that I'm definitely going to have a hickey from it. When he doesn't stop after a few mouthfuls, I'm afraid he's been hurt.

He stops as suddenly as he started but this time his forehead is against mine, his face contorted in pain as his chest heaves with ragged breaths. Worry turns into real fear and I fight against his embrace. He loosens just enough that I can squeeze my arms up between us and catch his face in my hands.

"Ambrose." Fear makes my voice harsher than I intend. "You're scaring me. Are you hurt?"

He flinched when I said he was scaring me, but his eyes open when I ask. His golden eyes are still clouded with red, but streaks of gold are glinting through.

"No, my little lamb," he murmurs, his voice hoarse and rough unlike moments ago while speaking to Michael. "I'm already healing from the fight."

I search his eyes, wishing he would just spit it out and not make me pull the words from him one by one. His mouth quirks up in a smile, his eyes softening as he cups my cheek with one hand, stroking it with his thumb.

"I am in awe of you, Ms. Morse," he whispers. "Rather than run from me, you fear for me. I do hurt, though."

My mouth parts in shock and I try to step back to look for his injury but he laughs. A true, unexpected, loud laugh.

"I hurt from how I could have lost you tonight," Ambrose says, his eyes still the blended swirls of red and gold. "I've been hurting since the moment you walked into my office with your chin held high."

Ambrose dips his head, capturing my lips in a gentle kiss. I don't even care that he has blood on his mouth and down his chin. He doesn't deepen it though, and steps back again, my heart pitter-pattering and my stomach doing flips. "I hurt from how much I love you."

Tears burst from my eyes, this breaking the dam that'd held back all of my emotions from what we'd just experienced. And then I can feel him again, deep inside me. It's warm, and stronger than it's ever been. I'm a blubbering mess, but I throw my arms around his neck and I kiss him hard.

"I love you, too," I say between sobs before kissing him again and holding him as tight as I can as a human.

We stand there in the shadows of the transport boxes, stinking of blood and the air filled with death. But it doesn't matter because I'm in Ambrose's arms and he's in mine. I'd offered three months of my life to Ambrose and I will give him so much more. Forever, if he will turn me. For him, I'll do it.

He loosens his embrace and looks down at me with the broadest smile I've ever seen on his devilishly beautiful face. "Let's go home, ma belle lionne." He sweeps me into his arms, carrying me so I don't have to walk through blood or around bodies.

When we get closer to the car, two SUVs pull up. I look at Ambrose, who nods in their direction. The SUVs back up so the back ends are right in the garage bay opening. Ambrose doesn't even look back as the doors open and I decide I don't care either. As he sets me down in front of the car, I realize there *is* something I care about though.

He tilts his head in silent question, waiting patiently.

"I know this is really stupid, considering what just went down, but..."

He cocks an eyebrow. "But?"

I bite both of my lips before blurting my request out. "Can I still drive home?"

For the second time that night, Ambrose fills the air with his laughter. It's officially my favorite sound, and I vow to make him laugh more just so I can hear it. I even feel the gazes of the vampires from the SUVs and when I glance at them, they're watching Ambrose in shock. Then one of them looks at me and smiles, as if in gratitude. I smile back and give my attention to my mate.

He reaches into his pocket, pulling out the key. I don't know how they stayed in his pocket in the chaos, but I grin up at him and hold my hand out flat. He drops the key with a softer smile on his face. "It's probably better that you do."

I race around to the driver's side, and maybe it's because he can tell how excited I am, but he doesn't beat me there. He lets me fling open the door and jump inside. He gets in the passenger seat, and I'm giggling as I watch him loosen the harness straps while I have to tighten mine considerably. And move the seat up as far as it can go. Pushing in the clutch and brake, I turn the key and when the car engine purrs to life, I seriously have the biggest grin. I don't think I can smile any harder.

Ambrose's hand lands over mine on the gear stick, and I look at him. He's leaning his head back against the rest, looking at me indulgently. My blood-covered vampire king. Ambrose, my mate. And the vampire I love.

"Take us home, little lamb."

As I slide the shifter into gear and ease off the clutch, I realize I was wrong. I can definitely smile a lot harder.

EPILOGUE

ELOISE

Tonight I will be leaving my human life behind. I should be scared, but I'm not. I'm more than ready, and Ambrose is too. After things settled down with Michael Garner, and later when Deidre finally came home with Kasar, my mate had opened up about his past. About Karina, the woman who he'd planned to marry before he was turned. How he'd believed for centuries she would have been his mate and because of the volatile nature of newly turned vampires, he lost control when he found her with another man.

He'd learned to forgive her, considering she'd believed he was dead and women at the time needed marriage for security. Ambrose had wanted to be explicitly clear about how he'd attacked them both in his pain at her apparent betrayal, and when he'd seen how brutally he'd injured her, he'd tried to turn her. She had looked at him as a monster as she died in his arms.

It's taken these two years for Ambrose to forgive himself enough to be willing to try again with me. With modern technology, vampires have been finally able to understand why some humans are able to survive the transformation and others are not. It all comes down to genetics in the end, and vampires sense the gene in the blood of those humans they bite.

I have the gene, and I've relented to the rigorous health examinations Ambrose insisted on. If he suspects I have so much as a cold tonight, he will postpone it.

At this point, I'm ready to ask someone else to turn me if Ambrose can't. I'd probably ask Lan, since he's the only vampire who would dare go against Ambrose. Then again, Josephine won't approve so maybe Lan wouldn't. I find it equally amusing and heartwarming that Lan is more obedient to his mother than his king and vampiric grandfather.

It's definitely strange when Lan teases me by calling me grandmother in front of Ambrose. How can I be the grandmother of someone who's been alive for centuries?

I'll save those thoughts for later.

For right now, I'm in the spacious master

bedroom in the large country estate Ambrose owns outside of the city. Public records claim it's been passed down between d'Vils since the land was first deeded and the house built. In truth, each inheritor has been one of Ambrose's numerous names throughout his lifetime.

Unlike our home in the Barrows, this estate's master bedroom oozes masculinity with its warm browns, dark grays, and burgundy colors. The massive bed is even larger than the one back home, with a wooden frame nearly black from age. There's only a single picture window, currently hidden behind thick brown drapes.

Tomorrow, I'll have to worry about the sunlight. As a new vampire I will be sensitive to the light, but Ambrose assures me that since he will be my sire, I will be much stronger than any other newly turned. Ambrose's blood is powerful and he walks under the sun without fear of burning. When his blood replaces all of mine, it will grant me some of the same power, though not entirely. We won't know how sensitive I will be until I'm turned, but his other children were able to walk in the sun so long as they were entirely covered and carrying a parasol.

I'll have to ask Deidre for her advice on fashion.

Ambrose will not be turning me in the bedroom, considering how messy it may end up being. And even though I'm ready, my stomach is filled with nerves. I never pictured myself getting married, and frankly, I don't know if Ambrose and I ever will. We're mates, our souls claimed by one another. What is getting married compared to that?

Still, Deidre insisted we shop for the perfect gown and, looking at myself in the mirror, I'm glad I gave in to her urging. Despite Ambrose's obsession with my health, he's never once pushed me to lose weight. In fact, from all of his spoiling, my body is softer than it was two years ago. I've never felt so sexy or desirable in my life.

It's impossible to have self-doubt or let judgmental stares get to me when a vampire who exudes power and dominates sexuality worships every curve and dip of my body with his lips, tongue, and hands.

Inspecting the dress, I get a kick out of it that we went with white. It's not what I'd consider bridal, though I guess it could be worn as one. It's an unlined satin dress with a scoop neckline and thin straps, and it hugs my breasts before draping loosely around my hips and fluttering down around my ankles. It's simple and modest, yet it makes me feel positively indecent with how the fabric caresses my skin and ripples around me as I move.

I've braided my hair to keep it out of the way, though knowing Ambrose, it won't stay braided for very long. As for makeup, I've gone without. When explaining what to expect, Ambrose made it clear that there will be plenty of mess. And while I know he won't care if I have mascara all over my face, I will.

Holding my reflection's gaze, I wonder, not for the first time, what I will look like with gold eyes rather than deep brown. How long will it take for me to get used to it?

I can stand here for hours, studying myself and thinking about all the ways I'm going to change or I can hurry my ass up downstairs and start this new journey.

Since it's just the two of us in the house, I forego shoes and leave the suite barefoot; the satin warm from my body heat teases my hips as I walk.

When we first arrived, I was too excited to take in the details of the country estate but now I take my time as I stride towards the stairwell. The walls are white, but rather than the old-world elegance that our Barrows townhome has, this place is full of intimidating extravagance. Crown molding lines border the ceilings and massive art pieces in gilded frames dominate the walls. This is a place where the wealthy elite would gather in the summer for expensive parties and debutante balls, if vampires did such a thing.

Though, Ambrose did warn me that once I've become his blood sworn heart mate, we will host a large gala in honor of me as I take my place beside him in the Nightshade Vampires. I would never have guessed my search for help with rescuing Deidre would lead me to eventually being considered a vampire queen.

A queen who will continue to run her own graphic design business, thank you very much. I shouldn't be thinking about work as I make it to the lower level of the estate and turn towards the ballroom. Yeah, the place has an honest-to-god ballroom, with a garden terrace and everything. Ambrose's collective wealth will never not astound me. But it's another reason why I insisted on continuing my freelance business, and when I first discussed it with him, I'd expected him to try to fight me on it. I don't know why I did, though, because he's always been supportive of me.

His only so-called stipulation was that I have a proper office and not take over the indoor garden room. Within an hour of our discussion, one of the spare rooms in the Barrows House had begun its transformation into my ideal office. Now I have enough clients through my new connections with the Nightshade Vampires that I've had to take on three employees, one of them being Tara, the human assistant who helped me with being fitted for an entirely new wardrobe.

I force the thoughts away as I sense Ambrose's presence growing ever closer. My pace quickens and in moments, I'm pushing through the double doors into the room where Ambrose will drain me of my blood and capture me in the moment between life and death. Yet another reason I'm eager to become a vampire at last is to feel our mating bond the same way he does. Over time, it's grown stronger but I can only catch snippets of Ambrose's actual thoughts. When I'm a vampire and claim him once more, we will be bonded closer than ever.

My eyes find my vampire mate instantly. He's standing in the center of the expansive room. It's empty save for the soft lights overhead and the wide platform covered in black fabric. I have no space in my mind to process the bare walls, the color of paint slightly different where paintings hung less than twenty-four hours ago. All I have room for is Ambrose, who watches me with his slight smile I've come to adore.

Around everyone else, that smile disappears, but I'm the one that breaks through the black-hearted vampire's icy walls and brings a smile to his lips.

Unlike his usual wardrobe choice of clean, smart suits, he's opted for something more casual. Like me, he's barefoot as he stands beside the platform, one hand in the front pocket of his dark jeans. He's bare chested, his sculpted chest and stomach on display along with his ancient tattoos of a life from medieval history. His jeans hang low on his hips, and my mouth goes dry as I appreciatively drink in the sharp V that leads down to his glorious fucking cock.

"My beautiful lioness," he greets me, his golden eyes dark with hunger. His gaze glides down my body and back up, leaving a searing path in its wake and making my nipples harden while my sex flares with warmth. Our desire has never waned for each other, and something tells me it never will. His smile turns into a smirk when he scents my arousal. It used to embarrass me, but now I know how to use it to taunt him. He holds his hand out for me and I step up, putting a hand in his, and he draws me into his embrace.

"My vampire king," I reply, tilting my head back and offering my lips to his.

He doesn't deny me, bringing his lips to mine and kissing me slowly. I open my mouth, eagerly inviting him in, and Ambrose slides his tongue in against mine, tasting of whiskey and blood. My blood. A shiver runs through me as my anticipation returns.

One of my only hesitations about becoming a vampire was not wanting to see Ambrose feed from another human, or having to feed from a human myself.

Fortunately, Ambrose has assured me that mated vampires can feed from one another and it's even more powerful than when feeding from a human. Vampires can feed from any living being, but not every creature offers the power that a vampire needs to maintain their strength.

From tonight on, Ambrose and I will only directly feed from one another.

He slows the kiss and eventually pulls back,

bringing his hand to cup my jaw. "Are you ready, my love?"

I lean into his hand, meeting his gaze. I can see the hope in his eyes, the love he holds for me. I can feel it down our bond. Still, I know that if I have any doubts, that if I say no tonight, he will not question me. For as much as I submit to my mate, I always have a choice when it comes to Ambrose.

"More than, mate," I promise him.

I let him sweep me into his arms, knowing how much he needs to control this process even if it means not letting me climb onto the platform myself. It doesn't come any higher than his waist, and he lays me out in the center of it, my head resting on the thin pillow that is hidden under the black cotton cover. Goosebumps cover my skin as he straightens and runs a hand appreciatively from my neck, down between my breasts, to splay possessively over my stomach.

"You are the most gorgeous creature I've ever seen in my life," Ambrose says, his deep voice soft and full of awe. "Words alone cannot capture the beauty you possess, Eloise. And that I get to worship you for centuries to come, that you have allowed your golden light to bond with my black soul, is a treasure I will never be worthy of."

Tears lining my eyes, I capture his hand with both of mine and bring it up to my lips. Pressing a kiss to each knuckle, I speak between each kiss. "You are more than worthy of my love."

Ambrose dips his head, his eyes closing for a moment, and when he opens them again, he tugs his hand free. I let him go, watching him as he moves to cup the back of my head and bring the inside of my wrist to his lips with his other hand. He gives me one more questioning look, and I smile in response, pushing my wrist towards his mouth.

My mate has never gone more than two days from feeding from me once we claimed one another, but when he sinks his fangs into my wrist, he feeds from me with an eager desperation. I gasp as the familiar sting of pain blends into the sensual pleasure I always feel when Ambrose feeds from me. Over the last two years, Ambrose has drunk deeply from me at times, requiring more of my blood than usual after dealing out violence. He's never taken too much, too cautious and caring to push me to the edge.

Tonight though, he continues to drink from me. His golden eyes burn with his vampiric desire as his mouth presses against my wrist. My core warms with lust as Ambrose continues to feed, and soon I'm panting and pressing my thighs together. Always aware of my needs, Ambrose slides his hand from the back of my head down to my hips. He draws up the fabric of my dress, never breaking eye contact. His eyes flare when he realizes I'm not wearing any panties and his fingers encounter the bare flesh of my sex, slick with need.

I moan as he slides two fingers up between my folds, jerking my hips when he brushes my clit. He taunts me as he circles the sensitive bundle of nerves, building up the pleasure slowly. When I'm writhing under his touch, growing lightheaded between the pleasure and the blood loss, he finally presses two fingers deep into my channel. I bear down against his hand, the heel of his palm pushing against my clit as he curls his fingers inside of me, fluttering them and proving he's mastered my body and my pleasure.

Gripping his wrist with my free hand, I ride his hand and refuse to let my eyes close from the pleasure. I want him to be the last thing I see before I leave my human life behind.

Warm blood slides down my arm as he no longer feeds. We've played this way before, where he bites me and brings my blood into his mouth but doesn't swallow it down. Instead, he lets it coat us until we're slick with it and a horrifying mess as we fuck, blood splattering against both of us.

My heart rate is picking up as it tries to keep my body filled with oxygen as the amount of blood in my veins decreases, and my thoughts are growing sluggish. The primitive part of my brain is warning me, but I've grown used to ignoring that part of my instincts when it comes to Ambrose.

My thrusts grow lethargic but Ambrose moves

his hand faster, forcing my body to feel the pleasure he's offering. I give up control of my body as I focus on the bond between us. A flare of panic strikes me as I realize how faint it is. Reassurance pulses down it and it's mirrored in Ambrose's adamant gaze. He warned me of this, that as I grow closer to death, our bond will weaken but it will not break. Neither of us will allow it.

My eyelids grow heavier as I breathe more shallowly. Pleasure and death create a strange dichotomy in my body, until it breaks under Ambrose's skilled hand. Pleasure ripples through me, my eyes now too heavy to open once more as darkness pulls me down towards death's waiting arms. My last sensations are the feeling of love and safety from Ambrose, his fingers leaving my sex, and then something warm against my lips.

Then I know nothing else.

AMBROSE

I refuse to let fear claw its way into my heart in the moment where Eloise is poised between life and death. I will not let Death take my mate from me, even as I feel our bond stretch to nearly breaking. As soon as I dare, I bite into my own wrist and bring it to her pale lips, filling her mouth with the lifeforce of my blood.

With gentle care, I lay her still bleeding wrist off

the table, letting it continue to drain her human life from her veins. Stroking her throat to encourage her body to swallow my offering, I keep my wrist against her mouth. I don't dwell on how translucent her skin has become or how limp she is under me. I only focus on my love and adoration for Eloise, sending it down through our faint mating bond.

I hadn't expected the pain I experienced as I drained the life from her. I only endured the pain of our bond fading by knowing that soon it will be stronger than ever before. That she will never be at risk for human disease or illness, or any mortal death again. That after this, she will be eternally mine.

And I will be eternally hers.

An eternity passes before Eloise whimpers, her eyes still closed.

"That's it, little lioness," I murmur, stroking her hair as she begins to swallow on her own. "Drink from me, my love. Such a good girl."

I continue to praise her, both for her and myself, as my blood overflows from her mouth and down her pale face. I don't stop stroking her hair, silken and dark as a moonless night. I don't look away from her face save for furtive glances at her still dripping wrist. Her bleeding has turned sluggish, a good sign.

I hiss as she begins to suck harder at my wound, not having expected it so soon. The others I turned took hours before they would take my blood eagerly, and each minute of those hours had me fraught with concern that I'd killed another person I had offered life to. I tried to prepare myself as best I could to wait for Eloise's body to transition.

A burst of base desire and hunger hits me from our bond, which is now growing stronger once again. Elation fills my heart as another look at her wrist shows the bite mark healing on its own. Eloise's brow furrows and I cup the back of her head to help her drink more deeply from me.

When her budding fangs scrape against my skin, I groan, my cock going hard. I've never been aroused when turning a human before, but as with everything else, Eloise is different. My breath turns ragged as each suck of her mouth goes right to my cock. Fuck, it's all I can do to stop myself from climbing on top of her and burying myself deep inside her wet pussy.

Her eyes burst open, the whiskey brown melting into gold, her pupils dilating until there's only a slim ring of amber before contracting smaller again. The foggy glaze of a newly turned vampire clouds her eyes and while our bond is returning to its previous strength, she's still lost in the haze.

"Good girl," I murmur, pride filling my voice as I guide her to sit upright. She protests when my wrist barely retreats from her lips, her hands flying to my arm with impressive strength, her nails digging into my flesh. It hurts, but oh, does it feel good. I haven't allowed another to feed from me outside of emergencies or when first turning my children. But to feel Eloise's new strength biting into me... gods, it's fucking divine and my cock strains against my jeans. "Take as much as you want, little lioness. You can have whatever you want. Now and always."

She holds my wrist to her mouth, her eyes half-lidded with concentration. I've been feeding from her daily, preparing for this, ensuring I have enough power and strength to give her everything if necessary. The power of her blood hums in my veins and I fed from her as much as I could when draining her, knowing I will need it to guide her through the transition.

When I'm certain she can sit on her own, I use my nail to cut across my chest over my heart vein. Her eyes widen and her nostrils flare as she scents the fresh blood.

"That's right, darling," I say, leading her closer to my chest with my wrist at her mouth. Fuck, she's strong already as she holds me back, but I'm stronger. "My mate. Claim me once more. Drink from my heart, my love." I rip my wrist from her grip, making her cry out with anger, her nails raking my skin and leaving bloody gouges behind.

Her eyes latch onto my chest and then she's moving, a wild beast as she shoves me backwards onto the platform. I relent under her, not a single part of me wanting to fight back. She's on top of me now, half straddling me where I'm sprawled, and then I feel it. Her sharp, brand-new fangs piercing my chest.

I moan, low and guttural, as Eloise grips my shoulders and drinks from me, marking me as her mate once again. I'm helpless against her, and defenseless against the world. Which is why I have my inner circle stalking the boundaries of the estate. Any closer, though, and I'll struggle against the drive to protect my mate by killing my own vampires.

Eloise grinds down against me, her sex undulating against the rough denim covering my cock. We both moan against the sensation and I force a hand between us and free myself. Then I grip her plump ass, lifting her up until my cock is against her entrance. She rears up, my skin burning from the violence of her bite, and she slams herself down onto me, sheathing me entirely in her tight sex.

"Fuck," I hiss, bracing one foot on the floor and arching my back up as I fuck up into her. "That's it." Hell, I love fucking this woman.

She drops her chin to her chest, her breasts heaving under the thin satin dress that's already streaked with our blood. Her eyes meet mine, still glassy, but with renewed clarity.

"Ambrose," she moans, rocking her hips against me. I love hearing her moan my name. "I feel so…"

Her emotions barrel down the bond between us and I grip her hips, harder than I've ever dared when she was human. I buck up against her, causing a blank jolt in the emotions as pleasure breaks through everything else. She looks down at me in wonder, and damn, she's gorgeous.

Fucking up into her, I grin sadistically. "You look so fucking sexy with my blood on your lips."

She bares her fangs at me in a wicked look and sweeps her hand across the blood on my chest, smearing it across my skin. Then she brings her hands up to cup her breasts, staining the white with bloodied handprints. "As sexy as I do when it's your cum?"

I growl, and flip her over onto her back. She wraps both of her legs around me, trapping me with her thick thighs, and throws her arms above her head, enjoying displaying herself for me. I brace myself over her, gripping her bloody chin with one hand and kiss her hard. "I bet you'll look even sexier when it's my blood and my cum."

She arches upwards, capturing my lower lip between her teeth and biting hard enough to draw blood. "Fuck me, my king."

Snarling, I wrap her braid around my fist and yank her head back. "Gladly, my queen." I sink my fangs into her throat as I fuck her harder.

We're lost in the haze of each other, as her body craves blood and pleasure as it continues to change. Eloise uses her new strength to rip her dress away from her breasts, and somehow I shed my jeans. When she rolls on top of me again, I shred the rest of her dress from her body and then we're bare to each other.

We fuck. We feed. We chase our pleasure, becoming drunk on each other as we struggle to get enough. I take her from behind, rutting into her as I bite down on her shoulder. She rides my cock, fisting my hair and yanking my head back as she bites my neck. I bite her breasts, her thighs, her arms, her fucking delectable ass. She bites me in even more places.

Hours pass before we finally collapse on the floor beside the platform, smeared with blood and cum, bodies humming with power and change and satisfaction.

I'm sprawled on the floor, Eloise half-lying on top of me, her face tucked against my neck. Staring without focus up at the ceiling, I have no room for thoughts or strength to move. All I know is I could live forever in this moment, my lover and mate in my arms, my blood pumping in her veins and hers pumping in mine.

A long sigh brushes against my neck, and I squeeze her tight, turning my head just enough to press a kiss to the top of her head.

"Please," she says before she gulps down a breath before trying again. "Please tell me you didn't fuck the rest of them like that."

I laugh, raspy and hoarse, and her shoulders shake too, her amusement radiating towards me.

"Hell no, little lioness," I answer, my voice hoarse. "Only you. Only ever you."

She hums with delight and somehow finds the strength to raise her head to look up at me, her golden eyes warmer than mine have ever appeared. "Good," she says, before sticking her tongue out at me. "How long is this going to last again? Before we can try to find a new normal?"

I curl a strand of her hair around my finger. "You don't want this to be our new normal?" I tease. "I could spend the next hundred years fucking you and not get enough of you."

She tilts her head, a devilish grin on her face. "We could make Kasar king?" she muses and an unbidden growl escapes me at another male's name on her lips. She starts laughing as I roll her under me, capturing her hands and lacing our fingers together before I pin them to the floor above her head, my cock beginning to harden once more.

"And deprive the world of a queen like yourself?" I murmur just above her lips. I shake my head. "Absolutely not. As for when the frenzy will end, I'm hoping we'll have at least two weeks."

I kiss her, our tongues pressing against each other slowly and languidly. When I pull back, Eloise is looking at me with a love I still feel unworthy of. But now I get to spend eternity worshiping her.

My very own vampire queen.

If you've enjoyed Vampire King, please consider leaving a review on Amazon.
Continue the series with Vampire Enforcer

To stay up to date with the latest Rowan Hart News, sign up for her newsletter!

ACKNOWLEDGMENTS

This book wouldn't have been possible without my family, friends, and supporters! Thank you to Aegast, for beta'ing; Micki for proofing; and all of the Midnight Poppy Land fan fiction authors who joined me for writing sprints.

ALSO BY ROWAN HART

Nightshade Vampires

Vampire King (Fall 2022)

Vampire Enforcer (Winter 2022)

Vampire Savage (Spring 2023)

As Marie Robinson

Blackfang Barons - Reverse Harem

Fawn

Fury

Fate

ABOUT THE AUTHOR

Rowan Hart is a potty-mouthed romantic who is obsessed with all paranormal monsters. It all started with Goliath and Demona.

Since then, Rowan has fallen in love with all different vampires, werewolves, gargoyles, demons, and well... you get the picture.

She's written over twenty books featuring romances between a woman and multiple heroes, or anti-heroes in some cases.

Now she's dedicating Rowan Hart to her love of gritty romance with dark heroic monsters who have to deal with feisty women who refuse to run from the big bad wolf.